cocoa beach Bakery

SWEENEY HOUSE
BOOK 5

CECELIA
SCOTT

Cecelia Scott

Sweeney House Book 5

Cocoa Beach Bakery

Cover designed by Sarah Brown (http://www.sarahdesigns.co/)

Introduction To Sweeney House

The Sweeney House is a landmark inn on the shores of Cocoa Beach, built and owned by the same family for decades. After the unexpected passing of their beloved patriarch, Jay, this family must come together like never before. They may have lost their leader, but the Sweeneys are made of strong stuff. Together on the island paradise where they grew up, this family meets every challenge with hope, humor, and heart, bathed in sunshine and the unconditional love they learned from their father.

Cocoa Beach Cabana – book 6
Cocoa Beach Bride – book 7

FOR RELEASE DATES, preorder alerts, updates and more, sign up for my newsletter! Or go to www.ceceliascott.com and follow me on Facebook!

Chapter One

Taylor

Was this real? It had to be a dream. There was absolutely no way that Kai Leilani had flown across the world all the way from Hawaii to Cocoa Beach to surprise Taylor.

But the longer she stood there, with the warm November breeze wrapping around her and the faint singing of birds in the distance, the more she realized she wasn't waking up.

She blinked a few times as she stared with her jaw slack, caught off guard by the fact that Kai—the gorgeous, charming surfer who she'd spent the better part of the summer falling in love with—was standing in her driveway.

And did he just say...

"You're staying here?" she asked, still processing what he'd told her.

"Yep." His eyes glimmered.

"I can't..." Taylor laughed in disbelief, taking a few shaky steps back. "I can't believe you're here. And how can you stay? What about your family's farm and everything?"

"Well, believe it, Tay." He flashed that signature

smile and held his arms out, displaying a beautiful bouquet he held in his right hand. "My cousin, Kona, wants to run the farm for my parents and they were really cool about it. Plus, I, uh...got a local sponsorship deal with Ron Jon Surf Shop, so brace yourself for seeing this mug on the I-95 billboards."

"Wow." She drew back. "I've only been in advertising for a few months, but even I know that is quite the lucrative gig."

He lifted a shoulder. "No complaints, especially since they want me in Cocoa Beach full-time to be a spokesperson."

She just stared up at him, trying to unpack everything. Was he here for *her*? Or for a career opportunity? Or because his cousin took the job he didn't really love or want long-term?

"You look dazed and confused, Tay," he said on a laugh. "I hope you're just speechless with happiness."

"Oh, I am...happy!" she insisted, maybe a little too enthusiastically. "For you and...for us."

But she'd ended things with him and started something really wonderful with Andre Everett, who right this minute was behind her in the cottage enjoying a family dinner with every person who was dear in her life.

Taylor's heart felt like it was doing gymnastics in her chest as her mind spun in circles.

She had let go of the long-distance romance that wasn't working for her, and let herself get close to a new guy. But now Kai, who she'd dreamed about and cried over and missed desperately, was here in Cocoa Beach and that long distance just got really, *really* short.

Whoa. That changed everything.

Feeling like her knees might buckle, Taylor motioned toward the white wooden bench on the front porch of the cottage. "Let's sit down."

Kai followed her onto the porch and sat down next to her, those familiar brown eyes dancing with excitement.

Why didn't she feel the same? This was Kai. Wanting her. Chasing her. *Flying across the world for her.*

And for a primo position with one of the world's largest surf brands.

Taylor's mind flashed back to Andre waiting for her inside, but she had to have this conversation with Kai.

"So..." He grinned, elbowing her, obviously waiting for an outburst of joy or a leaping hug or some sort of huge, romantic response. "Did you miss me?"

Taylor's heart slammed in her chest. "Of course I missed you."

"You don't seem as..." His expression grew serious. "Thrilled to see me as I expected."

She swallowed, shifting on the bench, glancing over her shoulder to make sure no one could see them. "I just...don't really like surprises."

Kai narrowed his gaze and gave her a playful smile. "Okay, now I know for a fact that's a lie."

Taylor laughed softly. "No, it's just that...I'm processing this, I guess. I was a little caught off guard. Especially after our last phone call."

You know, the one where I told you I need you to let me move on, Taylor thought to herself.

"I know, I get that." He pushed back some long, straight hair out of his face and deepened their eye contact. "It's a shock. But a good shock, right?" He winked, a gesture that would have made her heart flip upside down and her stomach flood with butterflies a few months ago.

But things were different now.

She turned to look at Kai, taking a moment to truly let it hit her that he was on her front porch, for real. She studied his handsome, defined features, that familiar twinkle in his gaze, and the way he looked at her with that deep infatuation they'd both been so tangled up in last summer.

"Yes, it's a good shock." She relaxed a little, letting out a breath.

"And about that last conversation," he said slowly, looking off to the side. "It just opened my eyes, I guess. You told me you wanted to let go, and move on, and that you and I can't go anywhere because of—"

"The distance," Taylor whispered. "I know."

"So, I eliminated the distance." His mouth slid into another smile.

Well, his cousin Kona and a fat sponsorship with Ron Jon eliminated the distance.

"Because I don't want you to let go or move on, Tay."

"I...I just...are you..." Taylor stammered. "This is all so insane, I can't even wrap my head around it. Your cousin is really taking over the sugarcane farm? Hasn't it been in your family for generations?"

He laughed softly. "She's my cousin, so she *is* family. And way better at the whole thing than I am, to be honest. I think everyone's relieved. She's super passionate about it."

"And the Ron Jon endorsement deal? How...when..."

"You did that, oh great marketing queen." He laughed and tapped her nose.

"I did?"

"Well, you put the event together in August and put me in front of all those advertising people for the brand. I stayed in touch and one thing led to another." Once again, his smile faded. "Are you not happy about all this?"

"Oh, I am, I'm just...putting it all together."

"Not much to put together, Tay. I'm here, you're here, and..." He took her hand and brought it to his lips. "We can be together now."

Except for that small problem of the guy she'd been seeing. No, she hadn't been with Andre for very long, but they had been friends—good, real friends—since Kai left. And that friendship was authentic and moving to "more than friends" had been so natural and felt so right.

But now what?

"It's..." She smiled again, her heart twisting with confusion. "It's amazing. I can't believe you're here."

He gripped her hand a little tighter. "Want to take a walk? I've missed this beach almost as much as I've missed you."

"I can't just..." She glanced back at the cottage, which

echoed with the faint laughter and conversation of a Sweeney party. Where Andre was no doubt wondering what was taking her so long. "I can't leave. My family's having this big party."

"What's the occasion?" He glanced at the house, no doubt expecting an invitation to join them.

"Well, it's kind of a bizarre Sweeney thing. Turns out my Grandpa Jay actually had another daughter, before he met Grandma, and my mom and aunt went and found her. Lori, my new aunt, is here now with her daughter, who's pregnant and..."

He smiled. "And dragging your former boyfriend into that mix would just be one complication too many for the Sweeney clan?"

"Exactly," she said on a soft laugh. "I need to...think."

"What's there to think about, Taylor?"

For a long moment, she just looked at him, silent, because she honestly didn't know what to say.

He took a deep breath, searching her face. "In that last conversation, when you told me you wanted me to let you move on, you asked me a question."

She nodded, waiting to hear where this was going.

"You asked me, what's the point of this. We're not technically dating, we're not anything. And yet I missed you like crazy, you're on my mind constantly, and I can't stop thinking about the way things were with us over the summer. I want to feel that all the time."

Taylor felt her eyes shutter as weight pressed down hard on her chest.

Yes, she'd crushed on him madly, a new level of

crushing she didn't even know she was capable of. He'd been her fantasy, her infatuation, her dream guy.

But recently, Taylor had started to understand that there might be a heck of a lot more to love than just wicked attraction and a massive crush.

"And I realized that you were right," he continued. "There *was* no point. It wasn't going anywhere, and we couldn't keep missing each other and not doing anything about it."

Taylor drew back, listening as he echoed the exact words and feelings she'd expressed when she tried—unsuccessfully, evidently—to cut it off. "Right, well..."

"Well, here I am."

"Because your cousin took your responsibilities and you got an amazing endorsement deal."

He looked a little miffed by that. "Yes and yes, but those two things got me here and now I'm..." He shook his head. "Is it not enough that I'm here? Isn't that what you wanted, or...did you change your mind?"

"Kai, this is just a bad time to have this conversation." She chewed her lip, glancing out at the golden tones of the setting sun.

"Right. The party that you are most definitely not inviting me into."

"It's not the right time." She let her voice drift away as she whispered the last word, deciding now was most definitely not the right time to mention that she was seeing someone else.

She would tell him, and she'd tell Andre that Kai was back. But right now? Not now. Not like this.

Kai held up both hands. "It's cool, Tay. I have to get my stuff moved into my trainer's house. He's letting me stay there until I find a place, and, well...I thought you'd want come with me, but I didn't know there was a family thing."

"I would, but..."

He angled his head, a smile pulling at his handsome features. "I'll be here waiting when you're ready."

Taylor swallowed, squeezing her eyes shut as she leaned against the wooden back of the bench. "And I will be...soon. We'll talk. I just need some time."

"Of course. And you have it." Kai gave her hand one more squeeze. "Sorry for the shocking surprise."

"Don't be. I'm happy to see you, I really am." She stood up slowly, a bit wobbly on her feet.

"Of course." He got up and held his arms out for a hug. "You know where to find me."

"I certainly do." Taylor accepted his embrace, but something in the tight hug felt cooler than she would have expected.

He shot her another wink before walking back to what she assumed was a rental car, a black Jeep Wrangler with zip-up canvas instead of doors.

As he hopped in and drove off, Taylor took a slow, deep breath and tried to calm her racing mind and heart.

"How goes it, darling?" Grandma walked out of the front door of the cottage, a warm and curious peace in her eyes. "You all right?"

Taylor sighed noisily as she slumped down and leaned her head on the always supportive shoulder of

Dottie Sweeney. "Could things ever, for five seconds, just be *normal?*"

Dottie laughed heartily, the sound so sweet and joyful it was contagious. "Not in this family, my girl."

"Grandma, what do I do?" Taylor asked, her voice cracking with a whine. "Andre is in there waiting for me, meeting my family, being awesome. I have to tell him that Kai showed up. I don't want to keep secrets. I have to—"

"Shh." Dottie pressed her hand against Taylor's flushed cheek and smiled warmly at her. "What you need to do right now is go hole up in your room with your kitties, rest, think, and calm down. Gather yourself and your emotions before telling Andre—or anyone—a thing."

As lovely as that sounded, Taylor hated the idea of keeping this a secret. She truly cared about Andre, deeply, and she really saw something good with him. "It wouldn't be fair not to tell him."

"Of course it wouldn't." Dottie widened her eyes. "And you will tell him. You can tell him tomorrow, even. But this has been a lot for you, so I think right now, all you should do is say you aren't feeling well and you want to call it quits early tonight. Fill him in tomorrow after you've had a chance to sleep on everything."

Taylor took a deep breath and slumped even deeper into her beloved Grandma's embrace, which somehow had a way of making everything seem okay.

Overwhelmed, dumbstruck, and wildly confused, Taylor decided she would follow Grandma's advice and take some time to figure out how she felt.

Chapter Two

Lori

L ori Caparelli was an only child, in every imaginable sense of the word. Her wonderful angels of adoptive parents, Gene and Amy Caparelli, wouldn't even bring a pet into the house, for fear that it might take some of the attention off of their beloved girl, who they'd spent years praying and wishing and hoping for.

It had always just been the three of them—the older parents who couldn't conceive a child of their own and the miracle daughter who was dropped in their lap by a teenage girl who lived down the street.

She'd spent her life as the sole focus of their abundant love and attention, showered with everything she could ever want—an Ivy League education, a breathtaking wedding, undying support, and the world's greatest grandparents to Amber.

But now, they were both gone. And her husband, despite the six-figure black-tie wedding, had walked out on her after thirty-one years of marriage, leaving her alone with Amber, her twenty-nine-year-old daughter who, at the moment, was as lost as Lori. Lost *and* pregnant.

In fact, it was her daughter's stunning news that encouraged Lori to do the craziest, most impulsive, out-of-character and frankly bizarre thing she'd ever done.

Together, Lori and Amber got in the car and drove down to a quaint, sleepy town in Florida called Cocoa Beach, where she knew no one except the two women who showed up at her office in Raleigh a few weeks ago, boldly announcing that they were her half-sisters.

And, evidently, she had a whole "half family" from her biological father's side that was more colorful, eccentric, diverse, and fascinating than she could have ever imagined.

Lori was a "lonely only" no more.

"Need a refill?" Samantha, the high-spirited woman who'd led the charge to find Lori and connect with her, came closer with an open bottle of rosé. "The party's just about over but this is when the good stuff happens."

"Oh, yeah?"

"The talking. The secrets. The connections." Sam grinned, a spark in eyes that were nearly the same blue-grey as Lori's. "The wine." She poured a healthy amount into Lori's empty glass, giving her a great big smile that, yeah, looked a little familiar, too.

This forty-three-year-old divorced mother of two was her sister, and Lori couldn't help but search for common ground and common features.

"How are you holding up?" Sam asked, easing her toward an empty Adirondack chair on the beach-facing deck. "This family can be overwhelming."

"Well..." Lori swirled the wine and took a deep drink,

her eyes locked on the ocean in front of her as night fell over the idyllic beach scene. "Two days ago, the only family I had on the planet was my daughter and my ex-husband. No cousins, sisters, brothers, aunts, uncles, nieces, nephews, or parents to speak of. And now?" She lifted her glass. "I've got Sweeneys and no small amount of them, either."

Sam laughed, brushing a strand of dark hair behind her ear. "There aren't that many of us! Just four kids, our families, and Dottie. You'll get used to everyone."

"Eventually." Lori shook her head and leaned back in the wooden chair, watching as the moon rose on the distant horizon. "I'm someone who's planned every part of my life, you know?"

Sam snorted. "I don't relate, really, but Erica could certainly understand."

"I got that vibe. It seems to have worked out for her, though," Lori said, remembering the sweet, sharp, and clearly successful youngest Sweeney sibling, who seemed to have her life all together.

"It did." Sam nodded. "But she's had her own trials, just like everyone else."

"And you've all come back here...to your childhood home." Lori glanced over her shoulder at the quaint and charming cottage, with flower boxes in every window and adorable blue shutters.

"Julie and I did," Sam said. "Erica and John never left Cocoa Beach, aside from college. But Julie and I both went off on our own, only to realize not that long ago that we were lost without this family."

"Is that why you and Julie are the ones who came to find me?" Lori asked, her mind flashing back to that day in Raleigh when she met her stranger-sisters and her whole world shifted.

Sam nodded. "I think so. And then when we talked and you shared your struggle with your divorce, I just felt like you needed a family."

"Evidently, you were correct." Lori lifted her glass to her lips. "Although, I have to admit, everyone here really still seems like a stranger."

"Of course." Sam gave an understanding nod. "You and Amber just got here. You need time to settle in, figure things out, get a fresh start."

Lori took a slow, deep breath, smelling the salt of the ocean and marveling at how wildly different this beach scene was from anything she'd ever known. She liked it, though. Maybe she could grow to love it.

"Can I ask you a question?" Sam raised her brows, speaking gently.

"Of course."

"What changed your mind?" She angled her head. "I mean, when Julie and I met you a few weeks ago in Raleigh, it kind of seemed like you wanted absolutely nothing to do with us." She gave a dry laugh. "It's okay. I didn't take it *too* personally."

But Lori wasn't laughing at all. Her heart tugged and she gave Sam an apologetic frown. "I'm so sorry."

"No, no. Please." Sam held up a hand. "Coming from someone who battled her way through a brutal divorce and tried to keep it all together? You get a free pass on irritability. No judgment from me."

Relief lifted a weight off of Lori's shoulders as she turned to face the other woman, feeling some walls break down with Sam. "Honestly, it was just too much in that moment. I was practicing full-time as a marriage and family therapist. And when I say full-time, it's a twenty-four-seven gig."

"Really?"

"Oh my gosh, you wouldn't believe it." Lori sighed. "I have patients calling and texting me at all hours, middle of the night, weekends, all the time. It's constant. And I have to be there for them. I have to be...on it, you know? Sharp, prepared, calm, smart. They depend on me, and I took an oath that I would always put my patients first and do absolutely everything I could to help them."

"Wow." Sam shook her head, holding a hand to her chest as she listened. "But when you have such personal problems and struggles of your own, that must have been impossible."

"I *was* cracking," Lori admitted, thinking of how sad she had been—and still was— about her husband asking for a separation a few months earlier. "Totally cracking. I started to wonder how I could take care of my patients and help their relationships—which is my specialty, if you can believe it—if I can't even help myself and my own marriage."

"I completely get that."

"So, long story short, you and Julie caught me at a

pretty bad moment, and you didn't get the best version of me. So, forgive me." She smiled.

Sam laughed and waved a dismissive hand. "All is forgiven. Besides, you probably thought we were slightly nuts for asking you to pick up and come to a different state to start a new life with a family you've never met."

"And you probably think I'm *extremely* nuts for actually taking you up on that offer."

Sam cracked up. "I'll admit, I was pretty astonished when I saw you and Amber standing in Sweeney House yesterday. But selfishly? I'm so happy you're here. I know from what you said that you are struggling with the divorce, but Julie and I weren't exaggerating when we said this place can heal. It really can."

Lori nodded, looking back at the ocean and thinking about what it would be like to just jump into the water right now.

Reckless, impulsive, and silly. All things Lori Caparelli was not.

Then again, these days? She didn't even know who she was anymore.

"So, to answer your question..." She turned back to Sam. "It was when Amber came to me with the news that she was pregnant. A switch flipped, and everything changed in that moment. We couldn't stay in Raleigh for...many reasons. I took a leave from my practice and we got in the car and Google-searched Sweeney House and...showed up." She sipped her wine. "Craziest thing I've ever done."

"Well, I, for one, am glad you're here."

Lori looked at her, an unexpected wave of emotion rising in her throat. "Thank you, Sam."

Sam leaned in. "If you don't mind me asking, what's the situation with Amber's baby's father? Is that...why you felt you both needed to leave?"

Lori pressed her lips together, shuddering a little as she thought of the look of absolute brokenness on her daughter's face when she revealed what had really happened. But they were both ready for this question. Armed with an answer they were determined to stick to, no matter what, to protect Amber.

"It was a one-night stand," she said. "And she has no way of getting in touch with him because she...she didn't know his name."

Sam grimaced. "Ouch. Poor kid."

"Right? And as the mother of a young woman, I'm sure you feel my pain and her shame. So, we just aren't talking about it, if that's okay with you."

"Of course," Sam agreed. "And that had to have been difficult. I applaud her for keeping the baby and making a go of it."

"Thanks." Lori searched Sam's face, mentally plucking through the litany of questions she asked freshly divorce patients. She opted for simple and honest, since Sam wasn't looking for therapy and Lori was truly curious. "So what happened with your marriage?"

Sam wrinkled her nose. "It's so cliché, it hurts. My husband, a doctor, had an affair with a cute nurse, which was discovered when Taylor walked in on them while she was on winter break in her first year of med school."

"She found them together?" Lori asked, glancing around for Taylor.

"Not, you know, in the act. But it was obvious what was going on."

"Oh, wow. I bet that changed her a lot."

"More than a lot," Sam said. "She dropped out of med school, knowing that's what would hurt her father the most, and started bartending. Then we found out the new girlfriend is expecting and they wanted to move into our house. Our *family* house. The one I decorated to within an inch of its life," she added with a sharp laugh.

"Yikes," Lori said, laughing because everything Sam said was raw, honest, and amusing.

"Yeah, but then Taylor suggested we all pile into our cars and come here, with Ben, my sixteen-year-old son. My mother—an absolute angel—gave us this cottage to live in and showered us with everything we needed to heal."

"Good for her. And for you, for dealing with your emotional trauma in such a healthy way. Very strong, very commendable."

Sam tucked her feet up on her chair, hugging her knees to her chest as she faced Lori. "I'm actually not sorry it happened to me, but it took a lot of time and healing to realize that. Believe me, if you met the version of me who showed up at this cottage with a duffle bag, two kids, and her tail between her legs, 'strong' would not have been the first word that came to mind. But I've grown and it has helped to be surrounded by my sisters, brother, and to take on the project of renovating the family inn with my mother. It's been amazing."

"This family is the kind my clients dream about." Lori brushed her hair behind her ears, a soft breeze tickling her nose.

"What about you?" Sam asked. "Is it the kind of family you dream about?"

She pondered the question as she sipped her wine.

"I never dreamed of another family, honestly," she said. "I loved being an only child. My adoptive parents were godsends. Growing up, it was always just the three of us, and I always felt like that was all I needed. And then, in adulthood, I had Rick, my husband—er, soon to be *ex*-husband, I guess."

"It takes some getting used to," Sam commiserated.

"It does. Anyway, I had Amber, and she was a rock. And I had work, which I needed." She took another sip, this one deeper. "I needed work a little too much, I think. At least that's what Rick said when he packed his bags."

Sam softened, sympathy knitting her brows together. "Oh, Lori."

"I worked too much, I was on the phone too much, I gave all of myself to my patients and not enough of myself to him and...Sheesh." She laughed heartily, shaking her head with disbelief. "I am seriously trauma-dumping on you right now."

"Hey, dump away." Sam raised her hands. "That's what sisters are for. Free therapy."

Lori smiled as warmth filled her chest, accented by the tiniest little shred of hope in her heart. "I have to admit, I kind of like being on the other side of this scenario. Just rambling on and on about all the tragic messiness in my life. And you just have to listen."

Sam arched a brow and nudged her. "Believe me, if you stick around for some of our famous girls nights, you'll be on all sides of the equation. Listening, laughing, loving, trauma-dumping...We do it all."

A sudden sense of peace fell over Lori as this newfound connection with Sam seemed to be the first truly good thing she'd felt in a long, long time.

"This is the first time in my entire fifty-five years that I don't have a plan. I planned college, grad school, my marriage, opening my practice...Heck, we even planned down to the month when we wanted to have Amber. I planned everything, Sam. But then he left me. And I left my job. And my girl is in crisis. And now, I don't have a plan." Lori shut her eyes. "It's scary."

"I know the feeling, I really do. When Max and I split up, I had never even had a job. I didn't finish college. My whole world and life and existence was hinged on him. Or so I thought."

Lori nodded, having heard that story from women so many times. "It's a terrifying realization," she said.

"It was. But I found myself again. Actually, not again. I found myself for the first time ever, once I came here. And you will, too."

"Will I? I don't even have a job. Amber and I found a little three-bedroom townhouse not far from here, and I'm okay financially, but I'm not sure what I can do."

"You can help us renovate," Sam said.

Lori grimaced. "Not my thing, sorry. I like fixing people, not rooms."

"Could you open up a practice here?"

She eased back and sighed. "Not without a state license, which I could get relatively easily, but..." She looked at Sam. "I am mired in self-doubt, to be honest. I don't feel qualified to give advice when I...I...I failed in my own marriage. And Amber?"

Sam held up a finger. "First of all, Amber made a mistake—or you can call it a decision—that a million woman have over the history of time. Second, does your own marriage have a bearing on what you tell clients?"

"Maybe not for them, but it does for me. I feel like a fraud, at least now. I don't think I can help people." The admission hurt, on one hand, but it also felt good to say it out loud. Wouldn't she tell a patient that was step one to healing?

"Well, there are lots of job opportunities around. What do you like to do? What are your hobbies and interests?"

"Let's see..." Lori sighed and stared ahead. "Interests? I love the ocean and have been living inland my whole life. Can I get a job working on the sand? Lifeguard? Shell picker-upper? Can I sell snow cones or something?"

Sam laughed. "Yes, but you actually need a license for that, too. What do you do for fun?"

"What is this fun you speak of?" Lori joked. "Actually, I did do something super fun last year. I got so into yoga, I earned a teaching certificate."

Sam jerked backwards. "You can teach yoga?"

"Well, I am officially qualified, but I don't have a studio, routine, playlist, or...whatever else I'd need. It was a huge outlet for stress relief for me, but I never considered actually using the certification to teach."

Sam clapped her hands, her eyes wide and bright. "You could teach yoga on the beach!"

"What?"

"People do it all the time—like pop-up courses. They advertise on local Facebook groups or with flyers in the restaurants and on the pier, and they set up and teach. Students pay as they arrive and they do yoga sessions."

"I...guess I could do that," she said, suddenly imaging herself on the beach at sunrise, in a relaxing child's pose with a few happy students. "In fact, I'd love it."

"And you can do it as part of Sweeney House!" Sam said, nearly jumping out of her chair with excitement. "You can take that part of the beach right there in front of the inn, and when we have the grand reopening, we'll send you students. You can give our guests a discount and we'll pass you new business."

"Sam." She breathed the name, looking at this woman who was, for all intents and purposes, a complete stranger and feeling the most unexpected wave of sibling affection. "How sweet of you to...well, to do all of this. To find me and bring me into the fold and..." Her voice cracked, which was out of character and embarrassing. "I'm grateful," she managed to finish.

Sam reached over and took her hand. "I'm grateful you gave us a chance. So, yoga? You ready for this new job? Taylor can make flyers and we'll get them up at local businesses and restaurants. Yes?"

"Yes!" Lori exclaimed. It was a start. A joyful one. "I love the idea, I really do."

"Awesome!" Sam popped up. "I'm going to tell my mom. It's such a cool perk to offer our guests!"

She blew Lori a kiss and disappeared inside.

Lori sat for a few minutes, waiting for the self-doubt that had strangled her for so long to get hold of her throat. Teach yoga?! Who was she kidding? Yes, she'd taken that online class and the studio at home let her sub exactly three times when there were no more than four people in a class.

But it was a start, and a new direction. And isn't that why Lori had come to this place? That...and the family she didn't know she had or think she needed.

She sipped the wine, looked at the moon inching up over the water, and smiled from her heart for the first time in what felt like forever.

Chapter Three

Annie

"Yup, okay, right through here. Right—watch the corners! That baby isn't cheap," Annie knew her voice had gone pitchy as three burly men hauled a Blodgett Zephaire double-decker ten-rack commercial baking oven through the back doors of the shop.

The huge stainless steel appliance with four sleek glass windows, the signature red logo, and shiny black handles, set perfectly in the little kitchen nook, completed the last major puzzle piece before The Cupcake Queen could seriously launch into business.

"Right here, ma'am?" one of the men asked as they inched it into place.

"Yes." Annie clasped her hands together, taking a deep breath and soaking in the moment as her dreams started to unfold before her very eyes. "It's perfect."

It had only been a week since Annie locked in her lease at this location, but she'd been on an absolute passion-fueled tear to get her new bakery up and running as fast as humanly possible.

She'd already ordered fabulous pink and white tables with blue chairs, painted the walls, organized and set up the prep area, and ordered the last touches of décor.

It was happening. It was really, truly happening, and Annie often had to pinch herself just to make sure she didn't wake up from this daydream and find herself sitting at her cubicle in Coastal Marketing with a spreadsheet staring her in the face.

No, the accountant life was behind her. So was the steady paycheck, she reminded herself, but this risk was more than worth the reward.

Even John Sweeney, world's greatest boss, had agreed heartily when she told him she'd decided to rent a space and open her own bakery after a lifetime of thinking that was an out-of-reach dream.

John had been so excited for her, he didn't even make her finish out her two weeks, but paid her and promoted Jill, a newer accountant Annie had trained herself, to manage the finances of the small beachside ad agency. In fact, all of the Coastal Marketing crew was thrilled to see Annie follow her dreams. They'd sent her off with a party and a promise that her cupcakes would be featured for every birthday party the company ever celebrated.

She was thrilled, too. Nervous, terrified, overwhelmed, but thrilled.

"Ms. Hawthorne?" One of the delivery men startled her out of her thoughts.

She turned, perking up. "Yes?"

"I have two large cooling racks on the truck, and that should be the last of your shipment."

"Wonderful! They can go back here, next to the oven." Annie stepped away from the kitchen to make room, admiring the soft, buttery yellow of the tiles on the floor. She even loved the floor of this place, she thought with a smile. This was her new home, her fresh start, her beautiful, sweet, comfy bakery.

"Great. Me and the guys will bring 'em in now."

"Thank you!"

She snapped a picture of the new oven to send to Sam, who'd been so encouraging through this whole process. Yes, her closest friend was wrapped up in the arrival of her half-sister, but surely she'd still want to see the oven.

The loud slamming of the back door once again caught her attention, and she waved her hand, directing the men through the back of the shop with her industrial-grade twenty-shelf cooling racks.

They set up the racks, accepted Annie's generous tip, and after a thousand more thank you's, headed out the back door.

Which left Annie alone in her nearly completed bakery.

"This is it, Annie," she said to herself, walking around as she admired every detail and continued forming ideas of how to really make the vibe and décor of the place come together. "This is what you've been missing. All those lonely nights, those long days, that emptiness in your heart...It's all over now." She patted the cool, hard countertop of the frosting station. "You did it."

"Um, who are you talking to?"

The high-pitched, squeaky voice startled Annie, and she whipped around in complete confusion.

What the...

She inched back at the sight of a tiny girl with wispy, wheat-colored hair and giant blue eyes, who stood at the open back door, clutching a stuffed animal in one hand as she stared at Annie.

"Um, hello." Annie stepped forward slowly, glancing around for a parent or guardian for this little urchin with mismatched socks and crooked bangs across her forehead. And an explanation for why she was in the bakery.

"What's your name?" Annie asked, crouching down.

"I'm Wiley."

"Wiley?" She smiled. "Well, you certainly are if you figured out how to get in that door that I'm sure I heard the delivery guys close."

"*Wiley*," she insisted.

"Like coyote?" Annie guessed on a laugh.

Her cheeks turned pink. "Wiley," she repeated, emphasizing the W.

"Ohhh." Annie finally understood, holding up one finger. "My mistake. Riley. Is that right?"

The girl nodded and tightened her grip on the animal.

"And who's your pal, Riley?"

"Funny Bunny," she said, inching up a well-loved and slightly torn stuffed rabbit.

Annie grinned. "Good name. Did you come up with that by yourself?"

She nodded. "I name all my animals."

"A good skill to have, Riley." She straightened and looked out the open door. "So, I'm Annie. And...how did you get in here again?"

The little girl turned and pointed her arm straight out, right at the back door. "Thwough there. The men were bwinging stuff inside, so I came in to see."

"Oh, okay." Annie smiled, taking in the full scope of this wee creature in a pink dress with a unicorn in sequins on the front. "Are your mommy and daddy around? Are you lost, honey?"

"My daddy's next door," she said.

Annie frowned. "Oh, he's at the gym and you... escaped from boring daycare?" she guessed.

"It's gwoss and stinky and noisy."

"Exactly how I feel about gyms," Annie said playfully. "Well, you've come to the cupcake place, where nothing is gross, stinky, or noisy."

The sweet little thing smiled. "And pink walls!" Riley exclaimed, sashaying around the empty floor of the bakery, her sparkly skirt fluttering around her tiny frame.

"And the floors are yellow," Annie added, taking in the bizarre waif. "But your daddy is going to worry if he can't find you when he's done working out."

"He's working, not out," she said.

Mystified, Annie frowned. "Your daddy is at the gym next door, is that right? Lifting weights or bars or whatever?"

"He's in the office until a man comes in for...twaining."

"Oh, he owns the gym," Annie said. She recalled Sam making a comment about tempting all the dieting gym rats with the aromas of her cupcakes every day.

"He's always there, every single day. It's his gym, and I

hate hate hate it! It's so smelly. I like it here. It's pink and it smells good." She giggled and danced around some more.

"You think it smells good now? Wait until my first batch of cupcakes comes out of that snazzy new oven." Annie walked to the Blodgett, pulling open the door just for the fun of it

"Cupcakes?" Riley's eyes grew wide. "I love cupcakes!"

"Who doesn't?"

"My mommy used to make cupcakes."

Something in the child's tone snagged her attention and Annie turned from the oven to find her looking down at her rabbit.

"Does she...not make them anymore?" Annie asked gently, hoping the answer was just because Mommy was on a diet or something.

"She's in heaven," the girl said softly.

Or something like that.

"Aw, that's a shame, honey." She closed the oven door and gazed at the little girl, a swell of sympathy in her heart. "Well, you are welcome here anytime to bake cupcakes with me, but now? I better get you back to your daddy, don't you think?"

She curled a lip. "There are no other kids and it smells and it's—"

"Gross, I remember. But your father is probably worried sick about you, so I think we'd better get you back to the gym."

A lower lip came out slowly, taking over her whole

precious face. "Can I please stay with you, Annie?" She added some puppy dog eyes that probably secured her every demand. "Pwetty please?"

Annie had to smile in the face of the painful cuteness. "You're welcome here anytime I'm open, Miss Wiley Coyote." She bopped her nose playfully. "But I need to go meet your dad at least so he knows who you're with. My guess is he doesn't let you take off on your own."

"He just gives me a coloring book and puts me in the back that he calls a *playwoom* but there's no toys." She wrinkled her nose. "I hate coloring."

Annie bit back a laugh and ushered the little one toward the door. "I get it, but you have to go home. C'mon. Skedaddle, kiddo."

"He doesn't care, I pwomise!"

Annie doubted that, unless... Maybe he was just a terrible father who let his daughter wander off. Or maybe he was in the throes of grief over his lost wife.

Annie reached for the little girl's hand and clutched it in hers. "Come on, let's get you back next door before he calls the police."

Riley's eyes widened. "Am I going to jail?"

Annie stifled a laugh, glancing down at the girl who gripped Annie's thumb hard with her entire little hand as they headed out the back door.

"You might be," she teased. "Running away can have some serious consequences."

As she stepped into the parking lot, she glanced to

the back door of the gym, which was firmly closed. Hadn't he even—

"Riley!" A tall, muscular man in a tank top jogged over from the other side of the parking lot, his face flushed, his long hair damp with sweat. "Holy...cow. Where the heck did you go?"

"Hi, Daddy." Riley dropped her head down, clearly already aware she was in big trouble.

As he got closer, Annie searched the man's face, wondering if she'd have to protect her new little friend from a furious father. What would she do if he yelled or—

"Oh my God," he murmured, dropping down to scoop up Riley, lifting her like she weighed no more than a feather. He squeezed her into him, burying his face near hers. "You scared the daylights out of me, kid!"

"Sowwy. I met the cupcake lady." She arched her back and looked over her shoulder at Annie.

Very slowly, he lowered her to the ground, her tiny hand disappearing in his much larger one.

"The cupcake lady?" he asked with a half-smile that only made him...Yeah. Whoa. Better-looking than she'd first thought. Also jacked and tanned and basically a living, breathing cliché of a gym owner. "Who is that?"

"That's me," Annie said, holding up her hands and meeting a green-gold gaze. "She escaped the playroom that has no toys and found my, uh, new bakery. I'm sorry for not bringing her right back, but I was...enchanted."

He laughed, which took him to a solid eleven, and nodded. "She has that effect on people. I'm sorry."

"No, no. Don't be. She's always welcome."

"Thanks." He glanced behind her at the shop. "So you're the one who scored that prime corner unit." He wiped his hand on his shorts before extending it out. "I'm Trevor Patterson, owner of Ace Fitness and father to the refugee you were fostering."

Annie gave a hearty laugh and shook his large, calloused hand. "Annie Hawthorne, new owner of The Cupcake Queen when I open it in a week, and home to unicorn-wearing refugees anytime."

He chuckled at that and gave Riley's hair a tousle, making it even messier...and making Annie wonder if those big hands held the scissors that produced that poor girl's dreadful bangs.

"A bakery, huh?" He drew back, raising his brows as he admired the property behind Annie. "I wondered what was going to take that spot when the ice cream shop closed. Should have figured, more desserts."

"I'd guess that's good for your business." Annie lifted a playful shoulder, giving a quick scan of a man with under ten percent body fat who had probably never so much as sniffed a cupcake.

"But not my abs." He patted his T-shirt, tight enough for her to suspect it hid a six-pack. Maybe eight. "I've got the biggest sweet tooth on the planet."

"Daddy loves candy," Riley announced. "He stole half of my Halloween candy last week."

"Busted."

"Thanks, Riles." He rubbed her head again. "Hey, I left you the Dots."

"You ate all the Reese's Pieces, Daddy."

"So guilty."

Annie laughed, taking in the exchange, which was clearly grounded in love. She thought of the mother in heaven, and her heart just about folded in half.

"Well, thanks for taking her in, Annie," he said, holding her gaze and then letting his eyes slip down over her for a split second.

Suddenly, Annie was painfully aware that she wore ratty jeans, a purple tank top, and not a molecule of makeup. But who knew she'd be bumping into a fitness god today?

"Daddy, please please please *please* can I stay with Annie for just a little bit?" Riley begged, yanking on his arm as she swung around.

"I think she's very busy getting her shop ready for its big opening and can't have a munchkin running around."

"You're welcome anytime, Wiley Riley," Annie said playfully, crouching down to get face to face with her. "I'll teach you how to make red velvet cupcakes and pink icing."

"Really?" Riley's eyes popped. "I *love* pink icing."

"I love making new friends." Annie gave Riley a teasing wink. "And I might be in the market for a taste-tester for some of my new cupcake flavors before we open the shop. Could I count on you to be up to the task?"

Trevor looked at Annie and raised his brows, a smirk pulling at his lips. "Be careful what you wish for," he warned, a playful glimmer in his eyes. "We're still working on the concept of boundaries."

"Eh...they're overrated." Annie joked as she straightened and looked up at Trevor, who was easily six-one. "Do you always have her at the gym with you?"

"Every day after school." He huffed out a sigh. "Which, unfortunately, are also my busiest hours for personal training. Hence, the playroom I put in, which, clearly, was an epic failure."

Riley wrinkled her nose. "We need toys, Daddy."

"I just have to get some for you." He shrugged a broad shoulder. "Single-dad life," he added under his breath.

Yep, single. Widowed, gorgeous, nice, and...so far out of her league, she'd need a passport to get into his.

"Well, I'm serious, send her over anytime. She's a doll, and I think the cupcake shop with pink walls and thirty different kinds of sprinkles might be a better place to spend the after-school hours. Wouldn't you say, Wiley Coyote?"

"Yes!" she hollered, dancing around in her sparkly dress, but Trevor was looking at her with a strange expression.

"Oh, I know it's Riley," Annie said quickly. "I just... gave her a nickname."

"Yeah, yeah. My, um, late wife called her that, too."

Annie's chest tightened. "Oh, I'm so sorry. I'm...I won't call her that anymore."

"It's fine. It's sweet. I...like it," he added with a slow, blinding smile. "I better get back to training in my smelly, gross gym."

"So smelly," Riley whispered.

Annie tilted her head back with laughter. "I just don't think little girls and gyms mesh too well."

"Little girls and cupcakes, on the other hand..." He nudged his daughter, tickling her side until she shrieked with laughter.

"It was wonderful meeting you both," Annie called as they walked to the door of the gym.

Annie watched them disappear, warmed by the sight of the father and daughter walking hand in hand. She ignored the quick, familiar pang of sadness that came with the frequent reminder that she'd never experience motherhood herself.

She tamped it down, reminding herself that the building in front of her was the truest and most exciting representation of her dreams coming to life, and it was more than she could ever ask for.

The adorable duo next door was just the icing on the...cupcake.

Chapter Four

Sam

A few days after Lori arrived, Sam was already certain that the Secret Sister Search had been a smashing success. She and Lori had an instant connection, spending a day shopping for yoga mats, blocks, and a small battery-operated sound system that could be used for Lori's classes.

In addition, they were making some serious progress on the renovation of Sweeney House, and a few of the suites were nearly finished. She and Dottie were as close as they'd ever been, and for the first time in a long time, Sam felt like she could just...float along on this blissful Wednesday afternoon.

For one thing, she was alone at the inn, immersed in her job and loving every minute of it. Her sister, Julie, was off teaching a guitar lesson, Bliss was at the library prepping to start public school in January, Ben was at baseball practice after school, and Dottie was at her book club.

All around her, workers finished flooring, grouted tiles, and painted some of the upstairs rooms as the place hummed with excitement and newness.

"How's it going, guys?" Sam walked through the

lobby, pushing aside an oversized plastic protective sheet to see the brand-new kitchen being put in for her very favorite part of the reno—the restaurant.

"Making progress, that's for sure." Jim McKinnon, the on-site construction manager, gave Sam a big thumbs-up as he lifted his protective goggles onto his head. "Dust everywhere, but you've darn near got yourself a kitchen, Ms. Sweeney."

Excitement zipped through her as she clasped her hands together and looked over his shoulder at the gray cabinets being drilled into place over a big, sleek counter-top. "It looks fantastic."

"Wait until you see it all cleaned up, it'll be awesome." He grinned and slid his goggles back on.

"Thank you, Jim! Keep up the great work!"

Humming, Sam headed back into the lobby and down the hall that led to all of the first-floor suites. Sunshine streamed in through the sliding glass doors on the back wall and the smell of fresh paint filled the air.

As she peeked into The Erica, the largest downstairs suite, which was being given a coat of soft lilac, she felt her phone vibrate in her pocket.

"I almost forgot!" Sam said to herself with a little gasp as she read the text on the screen.

Ethan was delivering the finished clock today.

She quickly texted him back, saying that she was at the inn and he could swing by anytime.

As she returned to the lobby to figure out the perfect place for her father's special and valuable family heir-loom, her chest brimmed with joy and anticipation.

To see the clock, of course, after Ethan refurbished, restored, and redesigned the horrendously outdated relic that sat as an eyesore in the lobby of this inn for decades.

And, okay, there was maybe a smidge of excitement to see Ethan. Just a teeny-tiny zing of expectation, even though they'd put their budding romance on the back burner.

Her phone dinged again.

Ethan Price: *On my way!*

Yeah, that was more than a teeny-tiny zing. Maybe a small lightning bolt?

What a shame they had to ignore their undeniable attraction and chemistry, and would continue to do so as long as the skilled carpenter and antique restoration specialist also happened to be Ben's eleventh grade calculus teacher.

Small-town problems, Sam thought to herself as she took a passing glance in the mirror on the wall and smoothed some rogue hairs.

After a few minutes of going through paint samples for the nineteenth time and studying the new layout of the beachside dining area, she glanced out the glass front doors and saw Ethan's truck pulling in the driveway.

Shielding her eyes from the blinding afternoon sun, bright even in November, Sam stepped out through the front door of the inn and smiled widely. "Hey, there."

"Samantha." Ethan hopped out of the car, looking all too good in a slightly dirty white T-shirt and faded jeans he surely hadn't worn to teach math today. "How are you?"

"Excited to see what you did with that old, hideous beast of a clock," she said on a laugh, reaching out to give him a casual hug.

"Might I remind you..." He arched a brow. "That that 'hideous beast' was the very thing that brought you your long-lost half-sister."

"I know." Sam took a deep breath, her mind flashing to the day Ethan called her to show her the birth certificate he'd found hidden in the paneling of the clock. "I'm forever indebted to that clock. And to you, for finding it."

He ran a hand through his sandy blond hair and squinted at her in the sunlight. "I've found some pretty bizarre things over the years, but in all my time working on antiques, I've never come across proof of life, so that was a first."

"Jay Sweeney is one of a kind," Sam mused.

"She's here now, right? Lori?"

She nodded, resting her hands on her hips. "She sure is, with her twenty-nine-year-old daughter, Amber."

"Who's pregnant," Ethan added with a playful smile. "I stopped by yesterday to take a peek at the drying progress on that wardrobe, and Dottie filled me in on the latest."

"Of course she did," Sam said on a soft laugh. "Yes, she's here and we're all ready to rally around her and Amber and bring them into the family."

"You must have worked your Sam Sweeney magic from the first, then, if you convinced her to up and move down here from...where was she? North Carolina?"

"Yes, Raleigh. And, well..." Sam waved a hand, fighting a smile. He thought she had magic? "There's a lot more to it than just me. Although we do seem to get along pretty well. I'm hoping I can be a good support system for them."

"You will be," Ethan said softly. "Everyone around you is lucky, Samantha."

Sam held his gaze for a few extra beats, the sunlight bouncing off his ocean blue eyes, lost for a moment in memories of their one and only kiss. As much as she longed for another, she'd promised herself—and had sworn to him—that nothing could happen while Ben was still his student.

But, dang, it was tough.

"So, let's see this bad boy!" She clapped her hands, breaking the tension as they walked around to the bed of his truck, where a paint-splattered white sheet covered the monstrosity of the clock.

"In all its glory." Ethan patted the sheet. "I don't trust myself to carry it in alone and not ding a freshly painted wall or something, though. You got a guy that can help me?"

"Oh, I got guys." Sam backed away. "I'll be right back."

She rushed in, grabbed Jim McKinnon for the favor, and directed him out to help Ethan.

"I'm dying to see it." Sam nearly danced as the two men carried the massive clock on its side, moving gingerly through the entryway and into the lobby.

"I think we should put it back in its spot." Sam

gestured to the blank wall across from the check-in desk where the old clock had always stood.

"Couldn't agree more," Ethan said on a soft grunt as they rotated the clock to an upright position and guided it into place.

The old sheet still hung over it, building up the excitement for Sam to see the finished design.

"Anything else?" Jim stepped back, wiping his hands on his cargo pants.

"Nope, we're all good." Sam smiled. "Thanks for your help, Jim."

"Anytime." He turned and headed back through the lobby to the new kitchen and dining area, pushing aside sheets of plastic and tarp to get there.

"Okay, let's see it." She waved a hand at the covered clock. "Take off the sheet."

"Whoa, whoa." Ethan held up his hands and stifled a smile. "Easy there, tiger. This is a big moment. You can't rush it."

Sam laughed. "I just can't wait to see what you did with this thing. God, the amount of times I've walked past it and thought it was the ugliest piece in the entire inn. Who ever knew I'd be so excited to look at it now?"

"First of all, if you call this limited edition 1912 Howard Miller 'ugly' one more time, I'm assigning you twelve chapters of calculus homework."

Sam gasped dramatically. "You wouldn't dare."

He jutted his chin, winking just teasingly enough to send a shiver of attraction racing down her spine. "Try me."

She inched closer, losing her train of thought in those blue eyes.

"Are you ready?" Ethan nodded at the clock, taking the edge of the sheet in his fingertips.

"I'm ready."

"Behold, the fully restored, totally functional, completely updated Sweeney House Grandfather Clock." Ethan swept the sheet off and it billowed to the ground, revealing a sight that made her melt.

Jay's father's clock would certainly no longer be called the Sweeney House Eyesore.

The stained and faded cherrywood had been refurbished to a gleaming blond shade with a rich finish.

"Holy cow." Sam lifted her hand to her mouth as her jaw loosened. She couldn't even form words. "Ethan, this is...It's magnificent."

"Better with movement and accurate time," he said, opening the glass door in the front to give the bronze pendulum a push and adjust the hands to the right time. "There you go."

Mesmerized, Sam tried to take in the changes and stunning improvements Ethan had made. He kept all the original cabinetry, but the twisted spindles on top that once looked gaudy were now full of character and heart. The details and inlays were delicate and intricate and beautifully integrated into the design.

The original face with Roman numerals somehow looked brand new and a hundred years old at the same time.

"I took a risk with the lighter finish, I know. It was a

bold move, but I felt like in this inn, on the beach, with the vibe you've got going on here, I could really preserve the original beauty and integrity of this clock while also bringing it up to date."

"Yes, yes, a thousand times yes."

"I gotta say." He grinned at her. "I crushed it."

Normally, Sam would have shot back a snarky remark about his lack of humility, but she was far too breathless and speechless and amazed to be witty. Plus, he *wasn't* wrong.

"It's beautiful. I mean, what an understatement. It's amazing, truly. How did you do this?" She turned to him, laughing softly with disbelief. "How did you make it so gorgeous and fitting and elegant while also keeping it the same old clock my Grandpa had?"

Ethan shrugged, beaming at her. "That was my whole goal with this project. I knew it was a special one."

"You have no idea," she whispered.

Sam stepped back to get a full view of the antique that had such deep meaning to her family and her mom and now her, too, considering it was the hiding place for Lori's birth certificate all these years.

This clock led her to her secret sister. Maybe, in some strange, inexplicable way, *Dad* had led her to her sister.

The very thought made Sam tear up unexpectedly. "It's a piece of him," she said under her breath, sniffling a little. "This is a piece of him, and you brought it back to life."

The low ticks of the swinging pendulum accented her words and matched her thumping heartbeat.

"I'm so happy you love it so much." Ethan smiled, leaning his head back and sighing with relief. "This is exactly how I wanted it to make you feel."

She took in a shaky breath and wiped away a tear, running her fingers along the detailed outlining of the wooden side panel. "I had no idea this was how it would make me feel."

Without another word, Ethan just stood next to her, side by side as they stared at the beautiful antique. He wrapped an arm around her shoulders.

A platonic gesture, sure. A gesture shared between friends who were experiencing a memorable and emotional moment together.

But the second she felt his touch, Sam ached for it to be more than friendship. She wished desperately that she could feel both his arms wrap around her tightly, kiss him and hug him and laugh with him as...not friends.

"Thank you." She turned, keeping herself tucked into his embrace, lifting her chin to meet his eyes and bring her lips just inches from his. "It doesn't even begin to be enough, but...thank you for this."

A soft, sincere smile pulled at Ethan's cheeks as he angled his head and deepened his gaze. "It makes me happy to see you happy, Samantha."

She glanced at the clock then back at him. "You did this for me."

"I'd do anything for you," he said bluntly, punctuating his words with a dry laugh. "When the heck are you going to realize that?"

In a moment of weakness, attraction, and possibly just pure insanity, she kissed him.

Again.

When she knew she shouldn't.

Again.

It was stupid and a bad idea. Sam knew that. But the fireworks that lit up in her head and her heart the very second her lips touched his truly said otherwise.

Ethan, clearly surprised, kissed her back, held her closer and made everything seem even more wrong and right and confusing.

After a few seconds, Sam reluctantly pulled back. "I'm sorry."

"For what?" He reached out and tucked a strand of her hair behind her ear, searching her eyes. "I just thought that, you know, you didn't want anything romantic because of—"

"Ben." She nodded, disappointment weighing down on her. "I know. And we can't. We shouldn't. I can't mess with Ben's life when this is the first time I've seen him genuinely happy and thriving in years. How can I be so selfish?"

"Hey." Ethan placed his hands on her shoulders, steadying her. "You're not selfish. You're actually the farthest thing from it."

Sam arched a brow and slid him a look. "I'm kissing his teacher. Again. Do you know how horrifyingly embarrassing that would be for him if it ever got out? If the other kids even caught a whiff that something was going on? I can't do that to him. And my divorce, as you know, is not quite final, although it will be by the new year, I hope. Just a few more weeks."

"And in January, Ben moves on to Calc 2, and he is no longer my student." Ethan cocked his head, thinking as he kept both hands on her arms. "Well, what if...no one found out?"

"Please. In this town?"

"C'mon, Samantha." A slow smile pulled at his sharp features, his gaze intense. "It's so obvious we want to be together. You've been on my mind every single day since I met you. You're incredible, and hilarious, and gorgeous in every way. You inspire me."

Chills danced across her skin. It had been so long since a man had made her feel all of those things, and with Ethan, she knew they were true.

"And I know it would be totally unprofessional and uncool and really not fair to Ben for us to date publicly," he added. "But none of that would matter if we dated... not publicly."

Sam drew back, studying the playful expression on Ethan's face. "What exactly are you suggesting, Ethan Price? A secret relationship?"

"I mean..." He lifted a broad shoulder, leaning closer to her. "Why not? We know we want to give it a go once Ben isn't a student of mine anymore, so who are we harming if we're together on, you know, the down-low until then?" He lowered his voice to a whisper, sending a whole new flock of butterflies swarming through her stomach.

"I don't know. Don't you think that's kind of...silly?"

Sam asked, knowing that turning down the offer was the responsible thing to do. The smart thing. The sensible thing. "We're in our forties."

"So? That means we can't have fun anymore?" He furrowed his brow, giving her a teasing grin.

"Well, what if people found out?"

"They wouldn't."

Sam chewed her lip. "I'd have to tell Taylor. And maybe my sisters. We swore no more secrets."

Ethan chuckled at that. "Well, I guess in your case it wouldn't be completely private. But I trust your sisters not to go spreading it around town, right?"

"Oh, yes. They're very trustworthy."

"So?" He lifted her chin, tilting her face to meet his gaze.

"Are we seriously doing this?" Sam laughed, suddenly feeling more like one of his students and not the mother of one. Not a grown woman contemplating...a secret boyfriend.

The idea of it made her head spin, but everything with Ethan felt so right and stable and comfortable that she didn't have it in her to say no.

"Look, Sam. I know you put your kids first. And your family, and your mom, and the inn, and everyone and everything before yourself. I adore that about you. It's what makes you so awesome."

She felt her cheeks warm.

"But remember—you're in a new chapter of your life," he continued. "And you deserve to have some fun, too, you know? To do something for just yourself."

She reached her hand up, running it along the whiskers that shadowed his jawline. With one more glance back at the grandfather clock, a reminder that her father would want her to be happy, she nodded. "Okay. Let's do it."

"Thank God." He wrapped his arms around her waist, planting a kiss on her lips and lifting her slightly off of her feet. "Because I couldn't go another second without knowing you're mine."

His.

She felt like she could float away on Cloud 9, right then and there. This certainly hadn't been in her big plan for independence and not needing a man.

But she didn't *need* Ethan. She wanted him. And now? She had him. Sort of.

As he spun her around and she kissed him and they laughed in hushed voices, everything felt right. Exhilarating and vibrant and a little terrifying, too.

Best of all, she could feel, moment by moment, all the pain and hurt that Max had caused her rapidly fading away...to be replaced by hope.

And a new secret boyfriend.

Chapter Five

Taylor

W hen Taylor sent Andre home from the party, she never expected the next time she'd see him wouldn't be until several days later at an event she and her team had coordinated for Blackhawk Brewery, his company and her client at Coastal Marketing. She'd been trying to get some private time with him to come clean about Kai's sudden arrival, but the next time they met was for a Trivia Night contest at the brewery, a promotional event coordinated by her agency.

It was a huge success and Andre was stoked by how many new customers it brought to the brewery, but he'd been surrounded by way too many people for Taylor to take him aside and talk privately.

But once the game was over and the crowd had left, all but the hard-core patrons had cleared out. Taylor stayed behind, saying she wanted to help gather the materials and projector that Coastal Marketing had supplied.

She knew that meant they'd get some time alone, even though it was one in the morning.

That didn't matter. Preparing for the event had consumed her and not one more day could pass without telling Andre about Kai's arrival...and his intentions.

Taylor gulped down a wave of nerves, stepping to the side as Andre shook back his braids, looking around the brewery, his gaze settling on the eighty-five-inch projection screen mounted on the side wall of the brewery.

"Coastal killed it tonight." He grinned and put an arm around her, blissfully oblivious to the storm that was about to roll in on their brand new baby of a relationship. "Especially my top-tier account executive."

"Oh, no, this was a team effort." Taylor slipped out of his touch and smiled at him, glancing around to see that the main bar had thinned to just a few die-hards. "But I could use a, um, few minutes alone with you."

"Yes, ma'am." Nodding his head toward a high top in the corner, he walked over and pulled one of the stools out for Taylor.

Always a gentleman.

"I'll grab us a couple of brews, because I'd say we deserve them, wouldn't you?"

Taylor laughed, despite the nerves edging in her chest. "Heck, yeah, we do."

The back wall of Blackhawk Brewing had three large garage-style doors, which added to its rustic, gastropub aesthetic. Outside the open doors, palm trees swayed gently in the salty night breeze, and November had cooled the air just enough to make it feel like it wasn't summer.

"So, Tay. Talk to me." Andre sat down, handing Taylor a pint glass of the Citrus Burst IPA, her favorite Blackhawk beer by far. He patted a hand on the table between them, his sweet, endearing smile beaming at her as those tousled braids fell effortlessly around his handsome face. "How's the new aunt? How's work? How's Annie's bakery? I'm all ears."

Taylor smiled, so wishing that she didn't have a bomb to drop right onto their brand new, super early, tiny sapling of a romance. But she had to be honest with him. She had to tell him that Kai was in town, and fully dead-set on getting back together with Taylor.

Nothing about the reality of that made her giddy or excited or joyful. But...it was Kai. And she was lost.

"There's something I need to tell you." She bit her lip and turned her gaze down to her purplish-pink beer, wiping beads of condensation off the glass with her fingertips.

"Sure. What's going on?" Andre drew back, his brows furrowing. "Everything okay?"

She sucked in a breath, truly not knowing how to answer the question.

On the one hand, everything was awesome. Mom was thriving with the inn reno and the newly expanded family. Work was a dream come true, and Taylor loved every day in her new job. In fact, this town was the best thing that had ever happened to her, and she never felt like she belonged anywhere more. Icing on the happy cake? Well, Andre was sitting across from her.

She felt like what had started as a truly deep friendship with Andre had blossomed in a really organic and natural way. She adored spending time with him.

But, no, despite all of that, everything was not okay.

"I'm just going to be completely straight-up with you, because I feel like that's how we are with each other, and that's what you deserve."

Andre's expression grew more worried, and he leaned his elbows on the table and looked at her with anxious concern and confusion. "Okay...What is it? You don't think we should do another trivia night? Too played out?"

"No, no. It's not that." She swiped a hand in the air between them. "I don't need to talk about work."

"Okay." He sat up straight, squaring his broad shoulders. "Like I said, all ears."

She huffed out a sigh, taking a moment to enjoy the last second of her non-complicated, easy, and straightforward relationship with Andre.

Because it was about to get a whole lot messier. "Kai showed up. The other night, at our family party."

"The surfer," Andre said under his breath, instantly drawing back and glancing away. "Who sent you those flowers."

"Yeah. That Kai."

It was no secret to Andre that there had been something between Kai and Taylor over the summer, since she'd worked so closely with both of them at the Ron Jon Invitational. But prior to last night, the RJI had been the last time Taylor had even seen Kai.

And the invitational was also when Kai had asked Taylor to move to Hawaii with him.

"Does he have another surf competition or something he's training for here?" Andre asked.

"Um, no." Taylor swallowed, her fingers circling the glass as her heart rate kicked up. "Not exactly. He got a sponsorship as the local spokesperson for Ron Jon Surf Shop."

Andre sunk on his stool a little and Taylor swore she could see visible disappointment in his eyes. "Oh, wow. That's a huge deal. Congratulations to him."

"Yeah, big deal. And he's here. And he..." She clenched her jaw.

"Wants to be with you, I'm guessing, based on the massive bouquet I saw on your dresser not so long ago." He gave a smile that, despite it coming from an obvious place of hurt, seemed genuine.

"It seems that way, but he just showed up, out of the blue." Taylor swallowed, brushing some hair out of her face as a very welcome breeze billowed through the room. "I'm not gonna just, you know, go jump right into his arms."

"Do you *want* to jump right into his arms?" Andre asked, his tone more friendly and understanding than jealous and annoyed, but the disappointment was palpable.

"No, I don't..." She bit her lip. "I don't think so. I have no idea what I want, but I did know that I needed to tell you."

"I'm really glad you did." He let out a breath and leaned back. "Look, Tay, I really, really like you. I could see this going somewhere for sure. But if you have something with Kai, and he's here to pursue you and that connection, I'm not going to be the guy that stands in your way."

For reasons she couldn't fully understand, that made Taylor's heart drop to the floor.

"I care about you for real, and more than anything, I want you to be happy."

You make me happy, she wanted to say. But she just looked down. Because she knew darn well that there was a time, not very long ago, that Kai had made her really, really happy, too. And now, he was back.

And it was...messy.

"It was a huge shocker, seeing him." She sighed and ran her hand through her hair, heart pounding.

"I bet." Andre raised his brows. "You had no idea he was coming?"

"Not a single clue." She lifted her gaze to meet his, searching it for answers or clues or direction.

But Andre just looked...kind. Genuine. Sincere. Cool as a dang cucumber.

"Well, that's one heck of a romantic gesture, I'll give him that."

"He came here because of the Ron Jon gig, though. Not just for me."

Andre tilted his head. "You sure about that?"

"I honestly don't know," she confessed. "But I do know that I really like you. I really like what we have and I don't want to mess anything up, but..."

"But you feel like you need to give him a chance, Tay. You owe that to yourself." Andre's voice didn't have a single hint of anger, frustration, or jealousy in it.

Their relationship had started as a real, true friendship. And, it seemed, that's what it would always fall back on.

"I guess so," she admitted, although the thought of spending time with Kai didn't bring the zinging thrill she would have expected. "This feels so unfair to you. I'm really sorry."

"Please don't apologize. You two had a thing before I ever even met you, and obviously it was something special if he left Hawaii and came all the way here wanting to pursue it with you."

"We did have a thing, but—"

"He sent you those flowers, what? A couple of weeks ago?"

"Yes, but after you and I kissed, the night Midnight ran away, I called Kai and I told him I wanted to move on. I told him our relationship wasn't going anywhere because of the distance. I didn't mention that there was someone else and..." She squeezed her eyes shut. "Maybe I should have. But I didn't think in a million years he'd get on a plane and show up in my driveway."

She glanced up at him, saw his dark eyes flashing with hurt, which made her heart ache.

"I get it, Tay. I do." He rubbed his forehead and let out a noisy sigh, taking a sip of his beer before deciding what to say next. "Look, I think it's best, for the time being, that I step aside."

She felt her throat tighten. "Andre—"

"It's all good, Taylor. I promise." He smiled and lifted a shoulder. "We're still friends, we're always going to be friends, and colleagues since you are the Blackhawk account exec I want to work with. There won't be any weirdness. Swear."

"What if...I don't want to just be friends?"

"Believe me, I don't, either." He raised his brows and angled his head. "But you need the space to figure out what's going on with Kai. You have to decide what you want, because he's here now, and that does change things. And it's not like you can date both of us at once," he said it like he was joking, but she didn't laugh.

Of course she couldn't date them both at once. Everything about that felt gross and wrong and all too similar to something her pathetic excuse of a father would do. "No. I can't."

"So..." He lifted both his hands and gave her a somewhat reassuring smile. "This is me, stepping back to being just your friend, for now. Until you figure out what you really, definitely want, without a doubt."

Taylor felt her heart sinking, but she did truly appreciate what he was doing. Everything he said and did always seemed to just be...right.

Nothing about his reaction was even the slightest bit jealous or annoyed, which, frankly, Taylor thought he had the right to be. No, not Andre. Of course he'd be the coolest person on the planet about this, because that's who Andre Everett was. Laidback, easygoing, and good-hearted to his core.

"I'm so sorry to spring this on you." She reached across the table and touched his hand.

"It's okay, Tay, really." He gave her fingers a squeeze

that felt a little too platonic, then pulled his hand away. "It's for the best this way. You can figure out what's going on with him, and decide what you really want. I'll be here, as your friend. I care about you, and I do mean it when I say I want you to be happy. If that means we aren't together in a romantic way, then it just wasn't meant to be. I would only want you to be with me because you're a hundred percent sure, not because Kai's in Hawaii." He punctuated the statement with a playful smile, but it still hit Taylor in the gut like a sucker punch.

"Wow." She shook her head, shutting her eyes as anxiety wove through her chest. "Thank you for being so cool about this. Seriously."

"Of course." He tilted his head. "I don't want you bugging out over any of this. You've got enough stress in your life with work and your randomly ever-growing family. The last thing I'd want to do is give you some sort of ultimatum. I'm here, we're friends, plus we work together a lot, so it's not like I'm just gonna ghost you," Andre teased.

She hadn't realized until that moment just how sad and dreary life without Andre looked. What if he did ghost her? The thought made her want to cry. "You promise?"

He held out his hand, pinky finger extended. "Promise."

She smiled and interlocked her pinky with his.

"I'm here for you, and like I said, I really do want you to be happy. As your friend." He leaned his elbow against the table. "So, figure out what you want, don't beat yourself up, try not to stress super hard, and as long as you're honest and real with me, we'll be all good. No matter what. Okay?"

She breathed a sigh of relief, noticing how much tension and weight she'd had pressing on her shoulders. "I will, I promise."

"Also, I think it's important to add that, um..." He scratched the back of his neck and glanced to the side for a second, before turning back to meet her gaze. "For whatever it's worth, I still really want to be with you. I just don't want to convince you that you should pick me."

"And you shouldn't have to," Taylor said quickly. "I'm not the freaking bachelorette."

"You could be, though," he said playfully. "But Kai's a cool dude. I respect him and I respect you. And I don't want drama."

She sucked in a breath. "I don't want drama, either."

"Exactly." He wet his lips. "So, I'm saving us both from the drama. I just don't want you to take it as a sign that I'm not interested, because that is definitely not the case. I've never vibed with anyone the way we do, Tay. We just click."

She smiled, guilt pressing on her heart. "I know we do. I feel the same way."

"But I'm stepping away for now. So you can figure things out with Kai."

She sighed heavily, dropping her head into her hands and letting her hair fall around her face. "Okay. Thank you, Andre. I don't even know how to thank you for being so insanely chill. You're like..." *A dream guy.* "Just the coolest," she said instead.

"Of course." He stood up, extending his arms for a hug. A *friendly* hug. "Come here."

She accepted his embrace and tried not to notice his toned muscles and comforting arms and the way he always smelled like the woods. "Thank you," Taylor mumbled, her voice muffled by his chest.

"No problem."

She drew back and caught a glimpse of his expression before he knew she was looking up at him.

His eyes were low and sad-looking, his mouth turned down. But the second he caught her gaze, he brightened up again. "So relax, okay? It's all good."

She nodded. "Okay."

Was it all good? How could it possibly be all good when she had no clue what her heart wanted, or how to figure it out?

The worst part of all of this was that someone she cared about deeply was going to get badly hurt, one way or the other.

Taylor didn't want to hurt Kai *or* Andre, and suddenly she wished she could go back to the time when she'd sworn off men forever and promised to only ever trust her family and her cats, because men were not to be relied on for anything.

Now here she was, with two men—great ones, she might add—who both liked her and adored her and wanted to be with her.

What was a girl to do besides talk to the one person on Earth she knew would help her through this mess?

⬤

"Wow, HE TOOK THAT WELL." Sam propped her feet on the coffee table on the back deck as she and Taylor watched the early morning ocean waves roll onto shore. "Shockingly well, actually."

After tossing and turning and barely sleeping all night, Taylor had dragged herself out of bed the second she heard a stir from the kitchen. That stir, to Taylor's joyful relief, was her mother making herself a cup of coffee with no clue she was about to get an early morning drama dump from Taylor.

"I know," Taylor agreed, shaking her head with residual disbelief as she sipped her coffee and watched the waves dance, sunlight sparkling off of the soft swells. "He was so cool, so supportive. When he says he just genuinely wants me to be happy, I completely believe him, you know? I never, ever doubt his intentions."

"He's a good guy." Sam nodded, the early morning sun casting a glow on her skin. "I've really enjoyed getting to know Andre, and you two are awesome together."

Taylor let out a soft groan. "I know. That's what sucks."

"Honey," Sam said on a laugh, reaching her hand out to touch her daughter's arm. "You have what we call a 'good problem.' Two sweet, gorgeous, successful, fun guys both vying for your heart? Isn't that, like, every girl's dream?"

Taylor twisted her mouth, frowning as she hugged her knees to her chest and rested her chin on top of them. It sure didn't feel like a dream. Dreams weren't this stressful.

"I don't know. That's the thing, Mom. Andre isn't 'vying' for my heart," she said with some dramatic air quotes. "Anymore. He kind of...took himself out of the running."

"Do you think that's what he did?" Her brows lifted with concern.

"He said he wants to step aside and go back to just being friends. For now, until I can decide what I really want. He's trying to give me the space and opportunity to figure things out with Kai before I make any rash decisions or have to come up with an ultimatum."

"Wow." Her mother drew back, sipping her coffee again and shaking her head. "He said all of that?"

Taylor shrugged, pulling her fuzzy robe tighter around her shoulders. "Pretty much word for word. Why? Do you think that's a bad sign?"

"No, not at all." Mom turned, brushing a strand of her hair out of her face. "I think it's really admirable, actually. Shockingly mature."

The messy confusion in Taylor's head grew louder every second. "I know, that's exactly what I thought. He was so respectful about it, so kind, so supportive. Here I am, his brand-new, sort-of-almost girlfriend, saying, 'Hey, by the way, my ex just flew here from the middle of the Pacific and declared he wants me back. I kinda need to figure that out.' I mean, most guys would say, take your pick. He's giving me a chance to really think it through."

Sam turned back to the ocean, nodding her head slowly. "He is. And, you know, Tay, nobody wants to feel like a second choice."

Her heart tugged and that dark weight of guilt that came with knowing she had to inevitably hurt someone pressed on her chest. "I know that. And he's not. Neither of them are." She dropped her head down. "That's the problem."

"Well, it sounds like Andre wants you to actually give it some thought, give Kai a chance, consider everything and be completely certain of your decision. He wouldn't want a relationship with someone who might still be thinking about someone else. And I'm sure it didn't help that he saw the bouquet Kai sent you just a few weeks ago."

Taylor flinched at the memory. "No. It didn't."

"So, take the space." Sam gestured out at the ocean. "Talk to Kai, think about it. Follow your heart and your mind and do what makes you happy. You've got two great guys, and from what it sounds like, Andre isn't going anywhere. He just doesn't want to be in the middle of a love triangle, and I don't blame him."

She blew a raspberry, rocking back on the chair and staring up at the clear blue sky.

"I do have to ask you, though," Mom said gently, as if she was a little worried how Taylor might react to whatever she was about to say next. "This is Kai we're talking about."

Taylor nodded. "I know."

"Kai, the obsession. Kai, the fantasy. Kai, the Prince Charming on a surfboard who nearly whisked you away to Hawaii three months ago."

She pressed her lips together. "Yup. That's him."

"And I know you're starting to develop feelings for Andre, and you two have found a great connection, but despite that, you don't seem too terribly thrilled that Kai is here. I mean, Tay, he flew here from Hawaii, gave up his family's business! He did that all for you, and you're not even that eager to see him." She angled her head, arching a brow. "Maybe that in itself is something to consider."

"That's the thing, Mom. I don't think he came here for me. Not *just* for me, anyway."

"What do you mean?"

"The Ron Jon sponsorship. His cousin, Kona..." She squeezed her eyes shut and shook her head, trying desperately to sort out her own thoughts and figure out why her mother was so staggeringly right. She was not thrilled, not even remotely. "He came here because everything worked out for him to come here. Kona wants the farm, and Ron Jon wants a poster boy. Those were the driving factors. I'm...an afterthought."

"You are not an afterthought, Taylor Parker." Sam gave her a stern, motherly look. "And all of that may be true about the Ron Jon thing and the farm cousin, but please. He adores you. They both do."

Taylor laughed softly at the ridiculousness of it all.

"And if you truly, in your heart, feel that way about Kai, then..." She lifted a shoulder and sipped her coffee again. "That's also something to consider."

"It just doesn't feel like much of a sacrifice or a grand gesture when he's getting paid to be here and the family has a better solution for their business."

Mom nodded, knowing she couldn't argue with that. "I hear you, kid. I do. But I think you should see him. Talk to him. See how your heart feels when you two are together."

"Yeah, you're right." Taylor hugged her knees closer and let the cool breeze blow through her hair. "After all, it is Kai."

"That it is."

"Thanks for all the romance help, Mom." Taylor grinned playfully. "You know, for an almost official divorcee, you're pretty darn good at love advice."

Sam snorted at the tease. "Please. I'm probably the last person on Earth who should be doling out relationship guidance right now."

"I was kidding," Taylor said. "We all know Dad was the problem in your marriage."

"I don't mean because of Dad," Mom said softly, glancing off into the distance, a smile playing at her lips like there was most definitely some underlying meaning in her words.

"Um, excuse me, miss?" Taylor nudged her mother's arm and laughed. "What exactly are you hiding from me? I thought we swore no more secrets."

Sam turned, her eyes dancing in a way that Taylor hadn't seen in a long, long time. She recognized the look on her mom's face, though. It was the look she'd had when Ben took his first steps, and the day Taylor got into medical school. It was the same look she'd had when she finally finished redecorating the downstairs of their Winter Park mansion and she was giddy with pride.

It was joy. Excitement. Anticipation. Newness. It was...

"Ethan?" Taylor blurted out, her jaw dropped. "Is something going on with Ethan?"

"Shh." Sam held her hand up, glancing back at the cottage through the sliding glass doors to make sure nobody—likely, Ben—was around.

But it was still and quiet and there wasn't a soul in sight.

"You must spill," Taylor demanded. "Now."

"All right." Sam set her mug down on the coffee table and turned her whole body to face Taylor, that familiar sparkle in her eyes shining bright. "I saw him the other day when he dropped off the clock."

"Oh, yeah," Taylor recalled the newly restored grand-father clock at the inn. "It looks amazing."

"It does. And I was very moved when I saw it. I don't know, it was like he gave a piece of my dad back to me. Back to us, you know? All of us. And it meant so much, and he and I have this intangible...thing. And I kissed him."

"Girl!" Taylor shoved her mother's arm playfully. "I hope no one saw this time."

"No one did." Sam lowered her gaze. "Thankfully. But it got us talking, and Ethan suggested that we date...quietly."

"Quietly?"

"Secretly."

Taylor cracked up, so blown away by the fun and exciting changes in her mom's life that she momentarily forgot about her own. "That is amazing, Mom. He is so into you!"

Sam shrugged, grinning. "Seems that way."

"So, what did you say? Yes, I hope. With no hesitation."

Sam paused, trying to stifle a smile that was so real it simply could not be hidden.

"Mommy!" Taylor reached over, her heart swelling with joy for her mother, who deserved love more than any single human on this planet. She wrapped her in a tight hug. "I'm so happy for you!"

"Don't get too excited. It's not like it's anything serious," Sam said. "We're just...having fun, I guess. I know it sounds so immature and insane, but I'm crazy about him. Fun, huh?"

"Super fun." Taylor laughed. "Does anyone else know?"

"Yeah, a couple people know. We're keeping it really on the down-low, though. I don't want Ben to find out, so please don't joke about it around him."

"Of course." Taylor gestured with her fingers like she was zipping her lips. "Your secret relationship is safe with me."

As the two of them sat side by side, sipping coffee, chatting and laughing, Taylor felt like maybe it was all supposed to happen the way it did.

If Dad had never been awful and cheated on Mom, they wouldn't have split up. Taylor and Ben and Sam would have never moved to Cocoa Beach, repaired their relationships with Dottie and the other Sweeneys, and started a whole new and unexpected chapter of life.

Taylor Parker was still angry at her father and that would never change, or at least it would take a long, long time. But right now, in this one sliver of joy and rightness and peace, she was happy it all happened.

It brought them here. It brought that sparkle back to her mom's eyes, and that silly laugh back to Ben. It brought Taylor to a job she loved and a problem that, well, was a 'good problem,' after all.

Chapter Six

Lori

I t was shockingly hot in Cocoa Beach, even in November. The sun was beating down on Lori's head like it was the middle of summer in Raleigh, but she welcomed the warmth and brightness.

Armed with a hundred fliers designed and printed by Coastal Marketing—thank you, John and Taylor—and a heavy-duty staple gun, Lori and Amber made their way through the most heavily trafficked areas of Cocoa Beach, putting up the papers anywhere they saw fit.

Lori glanced down at the fliers in her hand.

Sunrise Yoga On The Beach with Lori Caparelli
Escape the stress of everyday while you relax your mind
and body with the healing practice of yoga.
Located on the sand behind Sweeney House Inn,
6:30 AM.

"Do you really think anyone is going to come to this?" she asked her daughter, who was stapling a flier onto a tree trunk in the middle of Cocoa Village. "I mean, it's not like my name has any recognition. Plus, if they

Google me, they'll just see I'm a failed therapist. Not a yoga instructor."

"You are not a failed therapist." Amber looked over her shoulder and shot Lori a sassy eyeroll before she drilled another staple into a post. "And I think it's a really good idea, Mom. Yoga has been your favorite thing for the past five years. You should share that with people. It'll keep you busy, if nothing else."

Lori just sighed, searching for more places where her fliers might get noticed by potential clients. "The thing they don't tell you about starting over..." She shoved the staple gun into the top of a flier against a bulletin board outside of a city government building. "Is that there's no roadmap for where your life is supposed to go."

Amber snorted. "Tell me about it."

"You've never had a roadmap, A." She turned to her daughter, watching her deep, auburn-colored hair billow around her face in the warm breeze. Amber was always beautiful, a tiny thing, only a little bit over five feet tall, with high cheekbones, rich, dark auburn hair, and those blueish-grey eyes that matched Lori's.

But as Lori studied her daughter, who glanced off in the distance, she saw the pain in those eyes. The regret. The sadness. Amber looked a bit broken, and Lori's heart cracked as she watched her subtly slide her hand over her lower abdomen, where a little baby bump would inevitably be forming soon.

It was hard to watch Amber go through this alone. Well, not alone—she had Lori, of course—but without the partner who was *supposed* to come with having a baby.

Lori clenched her jaw as the hidden truth behind Amber's pregnancy rang through her head, but she shook it off in the interest of having a good day with her troubled daughter. That's what Amber needed. A good day.

"And you, dear mother, invented the road map. And now you don't have one, either." Amber waved a flier in Lori's face and gave a smile that almost looked real. "So we can figure out this new, weird, unexpected life together."

Lori reached out and wrapped an arm around Amber's waist, holding her tightly as they walked side by side down the quaint brick streets of Cocoa Village. "What do you think of the Sweeneys?"

"They're sweet." Amber sat down on a bench underneath a shady oak tree and motioned for Lori to join her. "A bit overwhelming and plentiful in numbers, but... sweet. I can tell they all mean really well."

"They do," Lori agreed, thinking about her few conversations with Sam that had started to make her feel like she had, well, a sister. That concept was so completely foreign to her she hardly knew what to make of it. "And don't worry about keeping the names straight. I'm still learning."

"I know." Amber laughed. "I'm pretty sure I mixed up all of the kids like four times. One of them is Ellen, and Jada—"

"Jada was adopted, I know her." Lori smiled, her mind tracing back to the sweet eleven-year-old who clung to her mother, Erica, and fit right into the family. Sam had filled her in on the rocky start of the spontaneous adoption, but seeing how they'd grown to really bond and love each other was inspiring.

The thought sent a wave of grief for her wonderful parents rolling over Lori's heart, and she wondered if those waves would ever truly stop.

"What about Taylor?" Lori asked her daughter, turning to the side and shielding her eyes from the sun, which was way too bright for November. But, hey—Florida. "Did you get a chance to talk to her at all? She's only a few years younger than you, and she and Sam are really close, like us."

"Taylor..." Amber frowned. "I think I said hi to her for a second, but, no, we didn't really talk that much. I haven't really talked to anyone that much, to be honest."

"Honey." Lori placed a hand on her daughter's arm. "I know it's weird, throwing you into this family of people we don't know. You've never been around a big family before. I mean, your dad and I were both only children and there's just no extended family to speak of. And now this?" She laughed, gesturing vaguely, as if to emphasize the sheer size of the Sweeney clan. "It's got to be an odd experience for you."

"It is, but...it's not just that." Amber leaned against the arm of the bench and pushed her hair out of her eyes as the breeze blew strands of it around her face. "I'm a little scared to get too close to anyone. Like they might... figure out the truth. About, you know..." She patted her stomach.

"Amber." Lori leveled her gaze and pressed her lips together. "We agreed on the one-night stand story. For all they ever need to know, that is the truth. I will not let that get out, I promise. And the Sweeneys aren't going around trying to sniff out our secrets."

"You sure about that?" Amber raised a dubious brow. "Because they sniffed out their own father's secrets. It brought them to you."

Darn it, Amber. Always with the ironclad logic. She got that from Rick. Just like the dark hair and the cheek-bones. "Well, yeah, but...I'll protect you, A." She squeezed her daughter's hand. "No one will know."

Amber sighed. "Someday, this kid will have to know."

"Cross that bridge, honey."

"It hangs over me, you know? I realize that He Who Shall Not Be Named gave up all rights, but you know truths do have a way of coming out."

Lori put her arm around her daughter and pulled her close, kissing her hair lightly. "Amber, I get that you're ashamed of what happened, but that man lied to you. He told you he was separated and his divorce was imminent."

"He also told me he loved me," she said glumly. "And that was all it took for me to quit my job on his campaign so I wasn't *officially* dating the congressman I worked for."

Lori hadn't agreed with that decision, which gave all the power to Michael Garrison, the thirty-nine-year-old who'd charmed the pants off her daughter—literally. But Amber thought he was The One, walked away from a career she loved, and took a waitressing job.

But when she got pregnant, that smooth-talking

politician suddenly sang a different tune. Not only did he urge Amber not to keep the baby, but he announced he was going back to his wife—"A happy marriage helps win elections," he said. And his high-flying political career could have fallen flat over the scandal of a pregnancy with his junior campaign manager, so he relinquished all rights to the baby.

Proud, broken, and furious, Amber wouldn't even take money from him.

And when he won the election earlier this month, Amber had to leave the town where he was such a prominent citizen. She'd really pushed Lori to make this move to Cocoa Beach...and so far? It wasn't that bad.

Amber sighed, turning back to face the grassy park in front of them, framed with rows of cute brick buildings filled with storefronts, shops, restaurants, and coffee bars. The park bustled with kids playing, dogs chasing toys and frisbees, couples and friends walking around the village.

Even from here, a mile or so inland, Lori could smell the salty air of the ocean and feel the vast openness that the sky only had when you were close to the beach. It was a good change. It was nice.

Change, as much as Lori had spent her life trying to avoid it, could be refreshing.

Suddenly, a buzz in the back pocket of her jeans grabbed her attention, and Lori reached behind her to get out her ringing phone.

"It's a patient, I assume?" Amber asked rhetorically. "Let me guess—you told them that even though you were taking an indefinite leave and you referred them to several different colleagues to continue therapy, they're still calling you at all hours without absolutely zero respect for your boundaries?"

"No," Lori said flatly, as her gaze on the name of the caller at the top of her phone screen. "It's your dad."

"Oh." Amber drew back, her eyes wide with shock. "Take it, Mom. Talk to him. I'll..." She gathered up the pile of fliers and the staple gun, standing up and giving Lori a reassuring nod. "I'll just go hang some more of these around town."

Lori swallowed. "Okay," she whispered, turning her attention back down to the phone.

She and Rick hadn't spoken much since she'd made the wildly impulsive decision to pack up her car, close down her practice, and head to a new state and a new family that she wasn't even entirely sure she belonged in.

She slowly lifted the phone to her ear, and swiped the Answer button with her thumb. "Hey, Rick."

"Lori," he breathed her name, almost with relief, almost with...care. "Where are you?"

"I told you. I'm in Florida."

"The sabbatical to meet this mysterious family, I know." He inhaled sharply. "You're really serious about that? I mean, you're sticking with it?"

"Yeah, I am serious about it." She leaned back against the wooden park bench and crossed her legs. "I'd hit rock bottom, and I needed a new start."

"And Amber's still with you, right? Is she okay? She hasn't been returning my calls and hardly texts me back. Is she mad? I mean...I don't get it. She never ignores me."

Lori felt her eyes shutter.

Of all the people who would someday need to know the truth, Rick was at the top of the list. Despite how close they were, Amber had never told her father she was dating her boss, a bigshot who was ten years older than her. She certainly never told him about her pregnancy or the horrible way the baby's father had acted.

Lori understood why, and had to let Amber decide when and how to tell her father, but it put her in a terrible position. Rick's inevitable disappointment was another reason Amber had wanted to leave town, but they'd all have to face this eventually.

But this was not the time to drop that bomb, nor was it Lori's place.

"She's just been busy getting to know these people we've met."

"The strangers," he said.

"Actually, they're very nice."

Rick paused. "Yeah, I know. I just... I worry about you, Lori. Both of you."

"I'm fine, really. I'm doing okay here."

"Lori." He lowered his voice, saying her name like he didn't even remotely believe anything she said.

"What? I am," she insisted, a hint of defensiveness rising in her tone.

"Lori, what about *work*?"

She sunk down in the bench a bit, watching a flock of birds soar through the sky above the park. "What about it? I told you, I'm taking a break from therapy."

"Why couldn't you have done that sooner? Why did

work have to be your entire life until our marriage fell apart and *now* you want a break? Why couldn't you have taken a break when I was essentially a stay-at-home dad raising our daughter alone?" He wasn't angry or passionate. No, his tone was thick with disappointment and hurt.

She flinched at the words. "You don't need to rehash the litany of reasons why you left me. I know I was a workaholic, I know I was married to my job, I know you always felt like I put my patients before you and this marriage and even myself." Unexpected emotion caught in her throat and Lori felt her voice crack.

"Hey, hey. Please." Rick used that tone, that same sweet, comforting tone he always used with her whenever her uptightness truly got the best of her and she unraveled. "I didn't mean to upset you, I'm sorry. That's not why I called."

She sniffed and got ahold of herself, wiping a tear that had escaped and taking in a deep, centering breath from her diaphragm. "Then why did you call?"

"Exactly why I said I did. I wanted to see how you two were doing. You're so far away and this whole Florida family, no-working thing is very new and...different. I can't picture you not working."

"Well, I'm trying something new. You'd be proud of me." She snorted. "I'm currently putting up fliers around town advertising my sunrise yoga class on the beach. How's that for a new leaf?"

She waited for him to laugh or snort in derision at the prospect of his high-strung, control-freak, Type A soon-to-be ex-wife being a Zen yoga teacher.

But he didn't laugh, not even a little. "I think that's amazing, actually."

The words were genuine, and they ripped at Lori's heart. Hard.

"Really? I know it's pretty out there, but yoga has been such an outlet for me the past few years, and, I don't know. Maybe I can help people in a different way, since I'm clearly woefully unqualified to teach them how to run their marriages and relationships."

"You're not unqualified, Lori. You're a fantastic therapist."

"My own husband walked out on me." She gave a dry laugh. "I don't feel like I'm really the best person to be doling out marriage advice right now."

Rick was quiet, and so was she, as the words hung in the air and the phone call and the hundreds of miles between them.

"I just...I never thought you'd actually stop," he said softly after a long time. "I never thought anything else could hold your attention the way that job did."

"Well, I did stop."

"For good?"

"I don't know." She let out a soft breath, watching Amber stroll through the park, plastering fliers up anywhere she could find the space. "Right now, I don't see how I could ever feel right about being a marriage counselor and family therapist again. Divorced? I'd feel like a fraud."

Rick sucked in a breath like he had something to say, but didn't give a response.

"Anyway, I don't need mean to bring you in on my pity party." She swallowed, her throat tight. "You're not my husband anymore, so—"

"I still care about you, Lori. I'll always—"

"Rick, don't." She felt tears stinging behind her eyes, and squeezed them shut to hold back the emotion. "Please, don't go there right now. You made the choice to leave."

"Lori," his voice was soft and low, barely more than a whisper over the phone. "You'd been gone emotionally for years. You gave everything to work and nothing to me."

"And now I've lost both," she replied, her throat tight. "I've lost you, and I've lost work. Now I have nothing except Amber, and this crazy new family. I have no plan, no direction, no idea what has come of me or where my life is going to go."

"Well, if you ever want to just...talk." He said the last word on a sigh. "If you miss me."

Of course she wanted to talk. Of course she missed Richard Kittle, the only man she'd ever loved, the one who was by her side through college and grad school and adulthood. The one she celebrated with when she finally opened her own practice. The one who held her hand when Amber was born. On her exact due date, naturally.

Because that was Lori's life. Planned. Logical. Outlined to a T. But now? The calendar was empty and the blueprint was nonexistent and the one person she thought would always be a constant was...not.

"I do miss you. But you left me."

"I didn't think you'd ever step away from your practice," he shot back. "I didn't even think there was a remote chance of that happening. You wouldn't even slow down."

"My life fell apart when you said you wanted a divorce." She held her hand to her quivering lips, trying to steady herself with all of the breathing techniques she'd taught clients to use when they felt anxiety coming on in an uncomfortable conversation with their spouse. "Everything shifted and everything changed."

"I'm sorry, Lori." The words came so suddenly and so powerfully and she realized that...it was the first time he'd said it since the day he left. "I'm sorry. I just...I wanted you back. I wanted *us* back. And you wouldn't give that to me, not with that job at the forefront of your mind and heart every second of every day."

Guilt rocked her to her core. "I'm sorry, too. I wish it hadn't gotten to the point that it did."

He sighed, pausing for a long while. "Me, too."

Lori cleared her throat, sat up straight, and decided that had been enough wallowing and probably enough talking to Rick. It was only making her sadder, and clinging to the past and the what-if's certainly wasn't aiding in the fresh start and new life that she was trying to achieve. Like Sam had done.

"Well, I'll tell Amber to give you a call. I promise."

"That would be great, thank you."

"Yeah, she's just been...you know. Busy." Lori shut her eyes, tasting the bitterness of omitting the truth. Not advice she'd give her patients, but hey. What did she know anymore?

"Thanks, Lori. And...like I said, I'm always here. I've got a few jobs lined up—two weddings this weekend and a bunch of walk-ins, but I can make time for you."

A pang hit her gut. He always made time. A talented photographer with a small shop in town, Rick had frequently put his work on the back burner for their family. "I know. Bye, Rick."

"Take care."

Lori dropped her head into her hands, letting the waves of emotion crash over her like the swells at the beach.

She thought for a moment about Sam's divorce—the cheating, the mistress, the pain and agony and betrayal of it all. Thank heavens her split wasn't so messy. She was thankful that she and Rick could be amicable and kind to each other and still care about one another. It was a good thing that there was no trauma or damage or betrayal with some other woman. Rick would never. He only ever had eyes for Lori, and that made this all hurt even more.

It wasn't a younger, hotter woman that dragged him away. No, it was his own decision, influenced by nothing other than feeling so pushed away and disregarded by his wife he was left lonely and miserable.

Hating him sure would make things a little bit easier, and definitely more black and white, but the reality of what happened only made Lori feel like she should hate herself.

"Hey." Amber came over with a considerably smaller

pile of fliers in her hand, waving he staple gun as she approached the bench. "How did that go?"

"It went..." Lori shrugged with defeat, throwing her hands up in the air. "Fine. Well. Great, actually. He's wondering why you haven't returned his calls."

She made a face, dropping her head back. "Because lying to my dad is the worst feeling in the world."

"So is lying to my soon-to-be ex-husband." She pressed a palm to her forehead. "It's just tough, Amber. I wish I'd listened sooner. I wish I'd heard him. I wish I'd been able to fix it before our marriage was so far gone he was packing a bag. How could I, someone who has made a career out of the psychology of marriage and love, have been so completely blind?"

"Oh, Mom." Amber sat down and wrapped an arm around Lori's shoulders, resting her head on one of them. "It's the things we love the most that destroy us."

Lori laughed at the melodramatic statement, cocking her head and studying her endlessly hilarious and surprising daughter. "Did you just come up with that?"

"No. I binge-watched all the Hunger Games movies last night because I couldn't sleep. Suzanne Collins came up with it, I just stole it."

Lori laughed, holding her daughter and giving her a tight hug as they sat side by side on the park bench, watching this new, confusing, completely uncertain life roll out in front of them.

Chapter Seven

Annie

Annie popped a full tray of cupcakes into the oven, smiling like a giddy little kid as she turned the fancy red knob to start the timer, running her fingers over the sleek, stainless-steel handles. This was only the third batch she'd made in the new oven, and even though she was still getting used to its quirks, it was a thing of beauty.

"Okay, my dear, those are cooking and we can complete our frosting!" Annie held up her whisk playfully while little Riley sat on a stool in the kitchen, completely awed by Annie's cupcake making process. "To finish off our sweet, delicious frosting, I have one final touch."

"Chocolate!" Riley blurted out, clapping her hands with excitement.

Annie had to admit, she'd never encountered anyone who was quite as interested in her baking hobby as Riley. She was attentive, fascinated, and focused. Annie loved it, and having her little pal hanging around took away any shred of loneliness that may have crept up.

"No, this is a vanilla frosting. Remember, we're going to make it all different colors?"

"Oh, yeah!" Riley grinned. "For my wainbow unicorn cupcakes!"

"Exactly. Rainbow unicorn. So, my final touch is... drum roll?"

Riley excitedly patted her hands against her knees, kicking her feet back and forth on the barstool that Annie had set up next to the decorating counter so she could have a good view.

"Egg whites," Annie announced after letting the drama build sufficiently. "Pasteurized, of course."

Riley wrinkled up her nose and made a face of pure horror and disgust. "Eww! Eggs? Gwoss!"

Annie laughed, opening the huge industrial fridge—gosh, she loved that fridge—and pulling out a couple of pasteurized eggs to separate. "I know it sounds kind of yucky, right?"

"Super yucky!"

"But..." Annie walked back over to the counter, cracking the eggs and sliding the yolk back and forth in the shells so that all of the egg white fell into her icing mix. "I promise, it makes the most perfect frosting in the world. You have to trust me on this one, Wiley Coyote."

Riley looked doubtful, but kept her gaze fixed on Annie's every move as she beat in the egg whites, creating smooth, creamy, perfectly textured buttercream frosting. "Looks yummy, huh?"

"Uh-huh!" Riley nodded and leaned closer, clearly having already forgotten about her questionable feelings on Annie's secret ingredient. "Yummy! And it smells sooo good!"

"Oh, that's a good sign!" Annie sang, heading over to the oven to take a peek at the tray she had baking in there. "Smelling the cake means they're almost ready."

"I like it in your bakewy, Miss Annie," Riley announced. "It smells so much better than Daddy's gym."

Annie snorted, whipping the frosting a few more times. "I'll bet. Between you and me, Wiley, I'm not a huge fan of gyms myself. Shh. Don't tell your daddy." Annie gave her an exaggerated wink.

Riley giggled and her blue eyes danced underneath those painfully crooked bangs. "I won't—"

Suddenly, the whole bakery was filled with a deafening, shrieking, beeping alarm that scared Riley—and Annie—half to death.

Riley screamed and pressed her hands over her ears, shaking her head rapidly.

Shocked and out of sorts, Annie darted around the room trying to figure out how to make it stop. The fire alarm, she quickly realized. It was the fire alarm blaring at full volume.

"I'm sorry, Riley!" Annie shouted over the screeching noise. "I'll fix it. Just...just hang on!"

Across the kitchen, Annie spotted the alarm on the wall, which was flashing red and yellow lights and had a speaker attached to the front of it—the source of the deafening noise.

Had the oven set off the alarm? The cupcakes weren't burning, but there wasn't any smoke in the room.

Annie could hardly think straight over the blasting sound, but she rushed over the fire alarm box and toyed with it until she finally found a shutoff switch on the side. Grabbing the switch with her thumb and index finger, she yanked it down, and, blessedly, the alarm shut off.

Only problem was...everything else shut off, too.

Riley slowly pulled her hands away from her ears as she looked around in confusion.

The lights were off, the oven was off, the power was completely down in the entire bakery.

Annie let out a sigh of frustration and defeat, leaning against the wall and draping a flour-covered rag over her shoulder. "Great. Well. that's just perfect."

"Miss Annie...wha-what happened?" Riley's eyes, wide and worried, gazed at Annie.

"I think the power somehow got turned off when I shut off the fire alarm," Annie surmised, not knowing literally a single thing about what she was talking about.

"Was there a fiwe?" Riley shrieked with fear.

"No, no, honey." Annie walked over to her, thankful it was the middle of the day, so the sunlight coming in through the windows of the storefront kept the place bright enough even without lights on. "There's no fire. It just...got triggered by the oven somehow. I'm not sure why."

Annie walked over to the oven, which was still plugged in, and tried to turn it back on. Nothing.

Not a single button worked, on anything. Switches were useless. There was no power whatsoever, and something super screwy had happened.

But this was Annie's project. Her bakery, her business, her dream. She was an independent woman, and she could fix it herself.

She hoped.

"Stay right here, Riley. I'm going to go out back to see if I can find the circuit breaker to reset the power." Which was the only thing she knew to do, because it was what her dad did when she was a kid and there was a problem with the power.

He'd shown it to her once, a series of switches on a panel in the wall, and you could flip them back and forth to turn the power on or off for a certain circuit in the house or building.

How hard could it be?

"Okay." Riley nodded, occupying herself with Funny Bunny, the stuffed rabbit she never went anywhere without.

Annie walked to the back door of her bakery, behind the kitchen. She opened it and left it propped, in case Riley needed anything, and stepped outside to search for the breaker box. The landlord she was renting from had given her a key to open it, and she'd absentmindedly stuck it on her keychain, never thinking she'd have to use it.

Well, it was par for the course, Annie supposed.

Sure enough, a few feet down there was a long, flat metal panel with a rusty lock, and her key fit right in. She turned it, pulled off the lock, and opened the metal door to about a hundred switches—*way* more than the one in her dad's closet.

"Okay," Annie whispered to herself, surveying the

switches, all various colors. "I can do this. I can figure this out."

The labels had faded and were impossible to read, but Annie noticed one switch that was facing the other way from all the ones above and below it. That could be it, right? Maybe she just needed to flip it back so it matched the rest.

Okay, she was a baker, not an electrician, but the logic was there, and Annie was willing to try anything to get her precious Cupcake Queen back on track for its grand opening.

Annie closed her eyes and cringed as she put her finger on the switch and shoved it to the other side, holding her breath.

Abruptly, she heard the ominous signs of power shutting down all around her. Air conditioning machines shut off, buzzing motors went silent, everything in the whole strip just...died.

"Oh no." Panic set in as Annie realized what she'd done, glancing down the row of stores and restaurants and business, all now likely without power. She didn't know they were all connected! "Oh, boy. That was not good."

Frantically, she looked over all the switches again, but was far too afraid to attempt flipping another one, lest she power off all of Cocoa Beach.

"Crap!" she blurted out, deciding she was just going to have to give up on the whole independence thing and call in a professional. And fast.

"Hey!" The deep, familiar voice of Trevor Patterson

echoed through the air, and Annie turned over her shoulder to see him jogging toward her.

Great. Perfect. Just amazing. Now the handsome, kind, completely awesome single dad next door would know that Annie was, in fact, solely responsible for the Outage of the Year.

"Everything okay?" Trevor asked, running a hand through his hair, which was damp with sweat. Was he ever *not* working out? "You lose power, too? Where's Riley?"

"She's inside," Annie said quickly, gesturing through the open door at Riley, who was still sitting on the stool, kicking her feet as she talked to her bunny. "And, yeah, I lost power."

"That's bizarre." Trevor shielded his eyes with his hand and glanced up at the clear blue sky. "There's certainly no storm or anything. I don't know what could have caused—"

"It was me," Annie confessed, blood rushing to her cheeks. "Something is wrong with my oven, it set off the fire alarm—"

"That's what all that noise was." A smile pulled at Trevor's face as he leaned against the brick wall.

Annie rolled her eyes. "It wasn't my fault, it's a weird oven."

He held up his hands, giving her a teasing look. "Hey, I'm not one to judge. I've set off more than a few fire alarms with my cooking in my days as a single dad. Just ask Riley."

For some reason, the image that created made

Annie's heart tug a bit. "Anyway, when I turned off the fire alarm, all the power in my bakery shut down. So I went out to the circuit breaker to fix it, and...well..." her voice trailed off.

Trevor laughed, his smile as wide as his daughter's. "And, let me guess. You flipped a randomly selected switch, likely with your eyes closed, in the hope that everything would turn back on and go back to normal."

"No. Well, I mean..." Annie folded her arms over her chest, stifling a laugh. "Sort of."

"Here." He jutted his chin toward the panel and walked over. "Let me take a look at it. You said the alarm shut-off turned off all the power in your unit?"

"Yes." Annie nodded. "It was so weird."

"That is weird." Trevor leaned close to study the switches and breakers, running his fingers over the worn metal pieces. "There's no reason they should be connected like that."

"It *was* odd. I thought so, too." Annie glanced back into the bakery. "Poor Riley. I don't think she was a huge fan of that loud alarm."

"Well..." Trevor glanced over his shoulder and arched a brow. "She's more than a little prone to drama, so don't pity her too much."

"It was pretty deafening." Annie cringed. "Anyway, what do you think I should do?" She craned her neck to study the circuit breaker, as if some answer was going magically appear and make any sense to her.

"My client and I just finished up and I've got a free half hour." Trevor scratched the back of his neck, jutting his chin toward the bakery. "Want me to take a look at the wiring behind the alarm system?"

"I mean, sure." Annie laughed awkwardly, gesturing for him to head inside through the back door. "That would be great."

"No promises. I'm certainly not a professional. But maybe I can figure out where things have gone so wrong."

She sighed as they stepped into her kitchen, and hoped this wasn't going to turn into some sort of massive roadblock, financial or otherwise.

Annie glanced away, trying not to notice Trevor's ridiculous build and muscles in his signature tank top as he walked in front of her and stretched his arms out wide.

"Riley girl!"

"Daddy!" Riley leapt off the stool and sprinted to her father, who scooped her up and spun her around as she shrieked with laughter. "There was a really loud beeping! It was so loud the whole Earth was shaking!"

"The whole Earth?" Trevor drew back and gave an exaggerated gasp, and Annie couldn't help but laugh at the endearing and adorable pair. "That is quite the alarm."

"It was like *beep beep beeeeep!*" Riley shouted, flailing her arms around as Trevor gently lowered her to the ground. "But Miss Annie twied to fix it."

"Tried...and failed," Annie added, giving Trevor another apologetic look. "I just hope we can get the power back on in the gym before your next client arrives."

"No worries." He waved a dismissive hand as he

walked into the kitchen and located the fire alarm box, starting to unscrew the corners. "Jasmine always runs late anyway."

Jasmine. For some reason, Annie had only ever pictured Trevor training men. It was such a masculine gym—so intimidatingly manly, it never even occurred to her that some badass, strong, super-fit women would go there to work out and train.

If Trevor Patterson were to date anyone, it would probably be a woman like that, Annie decided. Not that it mattered. It didn't.

"Oh, man." Trevor glanced over his shoulder, cringing.

"What?" Annie rushed over. "What is it?"

"Well, I took your alarm box off and it looks like your wiring is completely screwed up. All the electrical in here is going to need to be entirely redone, or you're never baking a batch of cupcakes in that oven."

Annie's heart fell and she sank against the counter-top, groaning audibly. "That sounds time-consuming and expensive."

Trevor angled his head, his dark eyes shadowed with genuine sympathy. "I'm sorry. But if it helps, I know an electrician who handled all the wiring at the gym, and he's great. I can give you his number and he should be able to come and at least get the ball rolling on this."

"Oh, yeah. That would be awesome." Annie walked over, taking her phone out to type in the guy's number. "Worst-case, I'm sure my friend, Sam, knows someone.

She's remodeling an entire inn, so I assume they need electrical work."

"Oh, Sweeney House, right?"

Annie brightened. "Yeah, that's right. How did you know?"

"Small town." Trevor shrugged. "Plus, everyone knows the Sweeneys. I went to high school with Erica. Smart cookie, that one."

"Whew, she sure is."

He was Erica's peer, so that made Trevor Patterson forty, or close to it. Not that Annie cared.

"Shoot," Trevor said, scrolling on his phone. "I don't have his number saved, but his card is on my desk at work. Here." He handed her his phone with a blank contact form on the screen. "Give me your number and I'll text it to you later, as soon as I find the card."

"Okay, sure." Annie typed in her phone number, trying her absolute hardest to ignore the fact that she felt like a schoolgirl who just got asked for her digits by the hot, popular quarterback who shouldn't even know her name. "Here you go."

"Awesome, I'll send it your way. Riley!" He gestured to his daughter, who was meandering around the kitchen, showing her stuffed rabbit all the different sprinkles. "Let's head back to the gym, okay? Miss Annie has stuff to do."

"Okay," Riley said with disappointment, dragging herself over to her dad and reluctantly taking his hand.

"I'll see you soon, Wiley." Annie winked at her new, tiny friend.

"Tomowow?" Riley asked with wide eyes.

"Absolutely." Annie grinned. "I'll be here, and I can show you how to decorate. Assuming we have power."

Trevor smiled and gave her one more wave before swinging open the back door. "I'll text you, Annie."

"Sounds good!" She said goodbye and gave him a thumbs-up before the back door clicked shut.

Why was she smiling? She had no power, she'd accidentally shut off the entire building, her oven nearly caught fire, and her whole grand opening might be horribly delayed.

But here she was. Smiling like a darn schoolgirl.

Chapter Eight

Sam

I t was just after six a.m. when Sam woke with the earliest light of sunrise, pulling herself out of bed to open the curtains and look out at the view she loved more every day.

The tiniest slivers of orange beams were starting to peek over the horizon as birds sang, fluttering through the sky, their reflections dancing on the ocean that was calm and peaceful.

Sam's heart soared with them as she pulled on a thin sweatshirt and slid her feet into her slippers. She felt almost like a kid again, having stayed up exchanging texts —yes, *texts*—with Ethan, her secret boyfriend.

The whole thing was just insane enough to be thrilling and fun, and every day she got closer to him, got to know him a little better, and continued to see how good his heart was and how he was, well, kind of perfect.

She wanted to go deeper, past the surface, but right now things between them were just flirty and fun and new, and that was a good place to start.

She yawned and stretched and tiptoed down the hall-way, trying not to wake Tay or Ben. Julie and Bliss were still sharing the Cottage's master bedroom, although Julie had found a furnished townhouse not far from here that they planned to move into by the end of the year.

Sam started the coffee maker, grabbed her mug, and pulled apart the sheer white curtains that draped the sliding glass doors, exposing the sunrise in its full glory and letting the soft light fill the living room.

As she poured her coffee and pulled open the doors to head out onto the back deck, Sam remembered that it was Saturday—the day of Lori's first sunrise yoga class.

Eager to see how it was going, she quickly peered over to the beach behind Sweeney House, expecting to see a decent-size gathering of women standing around wearing leggings and rolling out mats.

But that was not the case.

Sam walked to the edge of the deck and scanned the whole beach next door, and saw no one but Lori, sitting on a mat, alone.

"Oh, no."

She put down her mug, hopped off the wooden deck and headed over to the beach behind the inn, still in sleep pants and a sweatshirt. As she got closer, she could see that Lori had her head in her hands as she sat slumped on the yoga mat.

"Morning, sunshine," Sam called.

"Hey." Lori looked up at Sam with sad, darkened eyes. She was wearing a fitted tank top and long leggings, the classic yoga clothes showing just how in shape she was.

No surprise, though. Lori was the type of woman who took care of herself, who had it all together. Except right now...she didn't. And that broke Sam's heart.

"No one came." Lori sniffed, hugging her knees to her chest. "Who am I trying to kid, Sam? I'm not a yoga teacher. I'm a fifty-five-year-old failed therapist. No one wants to go to a yoga class with me."

"I don't know about that, it's still early." Sam dropped on the sand next to her. "I'm sure people will show up."

Lori shot her a "get real" look. "The sunrise is already almost over, Sam. And I should be halfway through our sun salutations and into standing poses by now. No one's coming."

"Well..." Sam stood up, giving a bright grin and planting her feet in the cool, damp sand. "I showed up."

"I know." Lori smiled weakly. "And it was nice of you to come and check on me, but I think I'm just gonna pack it in and head back home. This was a stupid idea."

"You can't leave." Sam frowned. "I was promised a sunrise yoga class."

"Sam." Lori laughed softly and arched a brow. "You're in pajamas."

"And you're in no place to be picky about dress code," she shot back playfully. "Now, let's get started."

Lori smiled, a hint of a spark returning to her eyes. "Okay. I brought a spare mat."

"Of course you did," Sam teased, jogging to grab the purple yoga mat that was rolled up and leaning against the railing of Sweeney House's back deck.

Sam whipped the mat open a few feet away from Lori, took off her sweatshirt and stretched her arms. "This is awesome. It's like a private lesson."

Lori angled her head, clicking a button on a small Bluetooth speaker she had set up next to her, which started playing soft, classical music. "Have you ever practiced yoga before?"

"I went once with some of the other PTA moms when Taylor was young and I was really trying to embrace the whole doctor's wife life, but I felt out of place. I'm about as flexible as a steel rod."

"You," Lori said, pointing at her. "Are definitely made of steel, but we can work on your flexibility."

"Just keep it at beginner level."

"Sure thing." Lori stood and situated herself on her own mat, taking in a huge breath as she faced the sun as it rose above the horizon behind her. "Match my moves, and think about one thing and one thing only: your breath. Everything in yoga is about breathing, and it's life-changing."

"I'm here to change." Sam lifted her hands over her head like Lori did. "Also, to have your abs."

Lori laughed at that, then talked Sam through a variety of warmup poses, stretches and movements that felt both foreign and weirdly comforting at the same time. Instead of a strict lesson, she kept it easy and light, talking and joking through many of the positions. Before long, they were laughing *and* breathing together.

"Okay, now down to a child's pose," Lori instructed in a voice that was soft and warm.

"Oh, now that one I know." Sam kneeled, then rolled over, curling her arms around her body and folding up into a little ball. "That feels good."

"Doesn't it?" Lori agreed, her voice muffled as she faced down.

The quiet splash of the ocean wrapped her in a sense of calm and peace, and Lori's soothing tone and gentle instructions brought Sam even more tranquility.

"And now is the time..." Lori added softly, "...to truly look inside yourself..." She drew in a slow breath, and Sam did the same. "To think about the things that are weighing heavy on your mind and heart."

Sam stretched and breathed and leaned into the calming effect of the yoga poses and Lori's voice.

"What's making you feel happy and light?" Lori asked as she sat up and swung her legs in front of her. "What's making you feel heavy and sad? How can we find harmony between those things?"

Sam thought hard as she stretched out her legs like Lori did, closing her eyes and letting the soothing sound of the ocean waves wrap her in peace.

"Sam," Lori leaned over a little. "What's on your mind?"

Sam opened one eye. "I didn't know I was actually supposed to answer."

Lori laughed and crossed her legs with her ankles on top of her thighs. How did she do that?

"Lotus pose," she said. "Just do your best. And typically, you're not supposed to answer out loud in yoga class, but given that it's just you and me, we can talk.

Ever since we did hips, I can feel your emotions wafting out. Something is troubling you."

Sam worked into the lotus pose. Something *was* troubling her, but why? She had such happiness and peace in this chapter of her life, coupled with the excitement and thrill of her new romance. Taylor was happy. Mom was happy. What was eating at her?

"I don't know," Sam replied, meaning it.

"Yoga..." Lori sat cross-legged on her mat, facing Sam and slowly raising her arms and stretching them up over her head. Sam copied the movement. "Is about opening up. Your mind, your heart..." She let out a deep breath. "All in alignment with your body."

Sam breathed the same way Lori was, long, slow inhales and soft, controlled exhales as she sat on the beach and followed the stretches. "I want to open up."

"Then talk to me." Lori smiled, so kind and warm and non-judgmental, it was no secret why she'd been a successful therapist. And, as Sam was learning, one heck of a great yoga teacher.

"Okay, I'll talk."

"And stretch. And breathe," Lori instructed. "Stand, and let's work on balance. That will help bring your honest thoughts forward and let your guard fall down. Simple tree pose."

"I have a secret boyfriend," Sam blurted out, punctuating the sentence with a soft laugh as she fell out of the pose before she even stood straight.

Lori turned to stare at Sam with wide eyes and a slack jaw. "Well, your guard came down quick."

Sam shrugged. "I don't have much of a guard these days. Although it's supposed to be a secret, but you have me being all open and the breathing and the calm and..."

Lori laughed and dropped to the mat, gesturing for Sam to do the same. "Let's skip tree and tell me more about Mr. Mystery."

Sam sat and hugged her knees to her chest and leveled her gaze with that of her sister, who, in this moment, felt like exactly that. She filled Lori in on the Ethan Price saga—how he was Ben's teacher and the restoration specialist for the inn; how he saved her butt with the city council; how Ben walked in on them kissing after he saved her butt with the city council; and how they had decided to embark on a secret relationship like a couple of grounded teenagers.

It felt good to get it all out there with Lori, who listened like the pro she was, asking a few pointed but quite relevant questions.

"Wow." Lori raised her eyebrows when Sam finally finished everything that had happened between her and Ethan up to that point. "It sounds like you two really have an undeniable connection."

"We do," she replied, looking out at the gentle ocean waves. "We're really attracted to each other. Not just physically, either. He makes me feel like I'm witty and interesting and smart. He makes me feel...adored."

"And, I imagine," Lori tilted her head, "the feeling of desirability is so refreshing and even intoxicating after what your ex-husband put you through."

"Yes! Completely."

"When he cheated on you with somebody younger, he sent you the message that you were the furthest thing from desirable, and that had to seriously hurt."

"It did." Sam sighed, pulling her knees closer against her chest and resting her chin on them. "It hurt so much."

"I can't even imagine," Lori said softly. "And now, you have this great guy, Ethan. He's attractive, smart, talented, and he is starting to heal that wound left by Max, by making you feel young and gorgeous and wanted."

"You got it." Sam pointed a finger at Lori, laughing. "Hit the nail on the head."

"But deep down, in your subconscious, you may be worrying if it has the potential to ever be more than just a fling. Dare I use the word...rebound?"

Sam drew back, processing the question, suddenly very overwhelmed by how accurate that description of her feelings was.

"Yeah," she said slowly. "Yeah, exactly. We have this chemistry, this connection, and it's really fun. He definitely makes me feel young again, pretty, even. But I think, in my heart, I am worried it's just filling the void that Max left, a little bit. I'm concerned Ethan is just the natural rebound because of how shattered I was, how broken."

"Of course," Lori agreed. "And you deserve to feel young and beautiful and desired. And Max ripped those feelings away from you in the worst imaginable way."

"And Ethan brings them back," Sam said. "Full force. Like a kid. Like a...crush."

Lori narrowed her gaze, a slight smile pulling at her cheeks, almost as if to say, "Now we're getting somewhere."

"What?" Sam asked, picking at a thread on her pajama pants. "What is it?"

"You didn't like saying that word. Crush. It looked like it tasted bitter to you. Why is that?"

"Because I'm scared that's all it is." The words flew off of Sam's shockingly honest tongue as if she'd been injected with truth serum.

"Uh-huh." Lori nodded, almost like she knew that's what Sam was going to say.

"I'm scared it's just a crush. I'm scared it's just a fling-y, rebound-y thing. It's fun, it's exciting, it's new. But is it real? Is it deeper than just flirty attraction and making me feel better after my divorce?" The questions poured from Sam's mouth like they had a will of their own.

"Does it feel real to you?"

"It could, I think. It really could." Sam let out a breath, the sun warming the air around them. "I just want to go deeper with him. I want to talk about things that matter and learn about him and get to know him below the surface."

"So, why don't you?"

"Because I'm..." Sam looked at Lori, meeting her gaze and suddenly realizing that she was no longer at a yoga class—she was in therapy. "I'm scared."

"I know." Lori nodded understandingly. "And that's completely expected and natural. Who wouldn't be scared after what you went through?"

Sam swallowed. "So what should I do? Next time I see him, just whip out a list of personal questions and start begging for answers?"

Lori laughed, shaking her head. "Why don't you start with a question that is at the forefront of your mind? Something about him or his life that you'd really like to know, that might bring you some more clarity about the trajectory of the relationship."

"I want to know about his divorce." Sam clenched her jaw, brushing some hair out of her eyes as the ocean breeze blew it around her face. "He's hardly mentioned it, and I want to know what happened. He seems closed off about it. He seems closed off about a lot of things, and that's what scares me. That's what's troubling me and, *wow,* you are good at this."

Lori tilted her head back, laughing heartily. "I'm sorry, I didn't mean to go full therapist on you. I just sensed the turmoil in your heart and I thought I could help you talk through it."

"Are you kidding? You knew what was wrong before I did. I feel so clear-headed and calm and ready to tackle this issue with confidence. I didn't even know I *had* an issue twenty minutes ago. You're a genius, Lori Caparelli."

The other woman's face fell and her eyes flashed with darkness. "I don't know, Sam. I'm good at listening and asking questions that bring people to realize their own truths, but I can't spend my days saving marriages anymore. I couldn't save my own."

Sam reached out and placed a hand on Lori's leg, giving her a loving look of sympathy. "I refuse to believe it was entirely your fault."

"Rick would probably say otherwise, but...who knows? Anyway, I'm just glad you feel better."

"I do. I really do. I know you don't want to hear it right now, but you seriously have a gift. Although, I have to say, the environment helped a lot."

Lori looked intrigued. "How so?"

"All of it. The yoga, the posing, the breathing. The way you talk through the yoga class and encourage all sorts of deep thought and clarity and peacefulness. Plus, being out here." She gestured at the beach. "It's so relaxing. I'm not sure if I had walked into a therapist's office and sat down if I would have felt as comfortable and calm."

Lori sat back, leaning on her palms as she cocked her head and thought about Sam's words. "Huh. That's really interesting."

"Yoga therapy," Sam teased, giving a little shimmy with her shoulders.

"Yoga therapy," Lori repeated slowly. "Wow."

"Now, prepare yourself—I'm going to hug you."

Lori cracked up, reaching her arms out wide and accepting Sam's embrace. "I'm glad I'm here," she whispered quietly, her voice thick with emotion.

"Lori." Sam hugged her tighter for an extra second. "I am so glad you're here."

She smiled, nodding her head and sitting up straight.

"Oh, and the whole Ethan thing—if you could just... you know, keep it on the down-low?"

"My lips are sealed." Lori winked. "Believe me, I can keep a secret."

Chapter Nine

Taylor

Although Taylor's heart felt a bit heavy ever since Andre said he wanted to go back to being "just friends" while this whole situation got sorted out, she knew it was for the best.

She also knew that she had to face it, head on, with maturity and respect and confidence. More than anything, she didn't want to hurt anyone, but did want to do what was best for her and made her happy.

Piece of cake, she thought as she pedaled her bike down the long wooden boardwalk that connected almost all of the main areas of coastal Cocoa Beach. She'd opted for a bike ride to go and see Kai as opposed to driving, because she hoped the fresh November air would clear her head and calm her down.

So far, though, the ride only seemed to be raising her heart rate and heightening her anxiety as she made her way to the Ron Jon Surf Shop, where Kai had told her to meet him for a walk on the beach.

Still not entirely sure why they couldn't have just grabbed a coffee or ice cream or something, Taylor figured he must have been finishing up a photo shoot or signing autographs or kissing babies or doing whatever celebrity surfers did for their endorsement money.

"No bitterness, Tay," she muttered to herself as each plank of wood bounced the tires of Mom's old beach cruiser.

But she couldn't help but feel like an afterthought, since Kai had come there for a job that every surfer dreams about.

He'd come here for her, too, she reminded herself. The first place he went was the cottage, the first thing he did was surprise her. That was something that shouldn't be ignored.

With a deep sigh and a failed attempt to gather herself, Taylor biked up to the back side of the bright yellow landmark that had helped put Cocoa Beach on the map.

Ron Jon Surf Shop was a colorful, tourist-filled, three-story maze, sporting every well-known surf and skate brand imaginable. Beachy clothes, gifts, gear, and rows of surfboards as far as the eye could see filled the floors, and people from all over the world shopped and took pictures.

Lingering near the back of the shop, she leaned against a rack of bright green and yellow skim boards and texted Kai to let him know where she was.

Waiting for him to respond, she ran her fingers over a huge display of wildly overpriced bikinis—cute, though, she had to admit—and slowly wandered along the back of the first floor.

Near the swimsuit display, she noticed a section of wall that was covered top to bottom in shiny, framed photos of professional surfers who had competed in Cocoa Beach, all autographed in black marker.

Of course, she found Kai's right away, running her thumb along the side of the black frame. She held her gaze on the photo for a long time, taking in the deep blue wave, his effortless glide through the tunnel practically moving in front of her in the picture. She could see the water spraying out around the front of his surfboard, and she remembered the way droplets always fell from his hair and down his cheeks when he got out of the water.

And she remembered how he'd grin or wink, shaking out that hair when he saw her, making her toes curl in the sand.

Was that magic still there? That intangible, inexplicable, wild attraction and connection and chemistry? Could it be something more? Could he be her...forever?

"You found me."

Startled, Taylor whipped around to meet the dazzling gaze of Kai Leilani, which somehow always made her feel like he was seeing her for the first time. "Oh! Hi."

"That's an old picture." He jutted his chin toward the framed photo. "I was maybe, like, seventeen there."

"Well, you made the, uh, *wall of fame* as a teenager, so that's pretty cool."

He gave his signature shrug. The halfway lift of one shoulder that somehow said, "I know I'm awesome, but I'll always be humble enough to make me even more awesome."

"You want to take a walk?" He nodded toward the back door of the store. "I'm dying to get out of here."

"Yeah, yeah." Taylor gestured for him to lead the way. "Let's go."

Tension, nerves, and a hint of awkwardness danced in the space between them as they stepped out into the back lot of Ron Jon's, and then eventually across the boardwalk and onto the sand.

This area of Cocoa Beach was always crowded. With the famous pier, a collection of bars and restaurants, huge hotels, and, of course, Ron Jon's, tourists flocked here by the thousands, especially in winter.

The crowds on the sand made Taylor wish they could have done this at the relatively private beach behind the Cottage and Sweeney House, but Kai had invited her here.

"How's the whole sponsorship thing going?" She gestured back toward the gargantuan surf shop as they began striding along the sand near the water. "You having fun being Mr. Ron Jon?"

Kai chuckled and shook his head, running a hand through that silky brown hair—a gesture that, admittedly, sent a shiver of attraction down Taylor's spine.

"It's cool. I've been having a lot of fun with it. I've had lots of sponsorships in the past, but this is different. It's very consuming."

"You're their spokesperson now, right?"

"The face of Ron Jon's." He held his hands out in front of them, spreading them apart dramatically.

"That's incredible, Kai." Taylor smiled and shook her

head. "I'm happy for you. That's got to be a dream come true."

Kai angled his head and raised a shoulder. "The dream come true is that I got to move here and be with you. The job is...a perk."

Was it? Or was *she* the perk?

Taylor's heart fluttered in her chest, propelled by something that felt like a weird mixture of butterflies and anxiety.

"Right," she whispered.

The waves crashed next to them and Taylor glanced down at the sand, watching their feet leave side-by-side footprints pressed onto the beach.

"Okay, Taylor." He turned to her, his gaze level and his expression stone-cold serious. "What is really going on here? I mean, I know you tried to end things with us on that last phone call, but it was because of the distance. Now, there's no distance. I'm here. You're here. Why are you not...happy about that?"

She swallowed, her throat tightening as her palms started to prickle with sweat. She hated confrontation like this. She hated everything about it.

Kai was amazing, her dream guy. She should be happy. She didn't have a real answer for him except...

"I met someone else." The words slipped out before she could stop them, and suddenly everything shifted.

Kai's pace slowed, practically to a stop, and she could feel the shock and hurt and disappointment radiating off of him in waves.

"You...what are...you have a boyfriend?" He looked at her, those dark brown eyes wide with astonishment.

"No, no," Taylor answered quickly, her head spinning. "It was never really official, or anything like that. And I explained to him that you had come back to town and we have a history and he's sort of...stepped aside. He's giving me space to figure out what I want to do, because it's...complicated." She chewed her lip, her heart thumping in her ears as she waited for him to say something. "I was honest with him, and—"

"Why weren't you honest with me?"

"I was!" Emotion bubbled up in her chest. "I never lied to you about anything, Kai. I told you I wanted to move on, because you talking about how much you missed me and sending me flowers was keeping me completely stuck on you. I wanted to be able to let go."

"But I'm here now, Tay." He stopped, turning to face her, the breeze blowing his hair around his face.

"I didn't know," she squeaked, tears threatening. "I had no idea you were going to just show up here. Just move here for a job and, and—"

"And for you." His voice was low. Soft and calm and...hurt. "If you had told me on the phone that there was another guy, I wouldn't have surprised you like I did. I wouldn't have assumed that the second we were together again, it was going to be some sort of magical reunion. I didn't know you were...dating."

"Nothing happened until I ended it with you. He was just a friend," she assured him. "And that's all he is now. I swear."

"Who is it?"

She glanced off. "Do you remember Andre, one of the guys who owned the brewery that we had the event for at the Invitational?"

Kai nodded slowly. "Yeah, he was a cool dude."

Taylor didn't need to say anything else.

"You like him, then."

She swallowed, clenching her jaw as they resumed walking along the water, their gazes both fixed downward onto the sand. "I mean, I started to like him."

He just nodded, the silence killing her.

"What was I supposed to do, Kai? Just spend the rest of my life hung up on you? Pining over the one that got away? I never dreamed in a million years that you'd be able to leave Hawaii for any real length of time."

"But I did. And I'm here. And you like someone else."

"I still like you, too, though."

He huffed out a breath, locking his hands behind his head as they walked. "Look, Taylor, I don't want to get into some sort of competition with Andre."

"I know," she said quickly. "I don't want that at all. And, like I said, as of right now, Andre and I are just friends. Nothing more. I wouldn't date two guys at once."

He lifted a brow.

"I wouldn't!" Taylor insisted, irritation slamming through her as she realized Kai might not necessarily trust that statement to be true. "I'm not dating either of you. I just...need to figure things out."

"What's there to figure out, Tay? We always said that

if we could be in the same city—or even in the same state —we would be together. Did a few weeks with this Andre guy really change that?"

Did it? Taylor honestly didn't know. What she and Andre shared was so drastically different from the fiery crush she'd always had on Kai, it was almost impossible to compare the two feelings.

"No. I mean...I don't know. I don't think so, but..." She could feel tears stinging behind her eyes, emotion constricting her throat like a snake.

She should have stuck to her rule of never getting attached to a man.

As Taylor felt her lip start to quiver and tears start to fall, she sat down in the sand, right in the middle of the beach, and cried.

"Hey, hey. Whoa." Kai crouched down, instantly reaching for her cheek to wipe a tear and brush some hair out of her eyes. "Taylor, don't cry. I don't want you to be upset."

"No, I know." She sniffed. "It's not your fault. It's mine. I should have told you about him on the phone. I just...I wanted to let go of you, Kai." She looked up at him, wiping her eyes. "I wanted to be free of the... obsession. I didn't think it could ever go anywhere, but..."

"But now it can." He sat down next to her, close enough for her to smell the salty, beachy cologne the Ron Jon reps had him wearing.

He was right. Now this relationship *could* go somewhere. A few months ago, this would have been like a fantasy to her. But now everything felt so muddy and confusing and she truly cared about Andre.

"Did you really come here for me?" Taylor asked, hugging her knees to her chest and pinning her gaze on Kai's.

"Of course."

"But...the sponsorship. The Ron Jon stuff. That's why you're here. I mean, that's what got you here."

Kai ran a hand through his hair and lifted a shoulder. "Okay, yes. If it weren't for the sponsorship, I probably wouldn't have necessarily been able to come here right now, but that doesn't mean I'm not here for you."

Taylor's heart sank and she dug her toes into the cool, damp sand, watching the waves splash one after another onto the shore.

It wasn't a sacrifice. It wasn't a grand gesture. It was just...good timing.

Was that real? Was that long term?

"I just think we should talk more." Taylor gathered herself, inhaling slowly. "I want to figure everything out."

"I want to figure it out with you." He placed a hand on hers and gave it a squeeze. "I'm here to be with you, Taylor."

"You're also here for—"

"Kai, Kai!" The female voice startled both of them, and they stood up and turned to see a man and a woman jogging toward them in Ron Jon's T-shirts and black pants, carrying iPads. "There you are."

"Hey, Christy." Kai stepped away from Taylor. "Sorry, I was just taking a break with—"

"Okay, that's fine, but we need you to get to wardrobe." The woman looked right through Taylor, as if she wasn't even there. She tapped the iPad. "We're shooting the Spring Break spread for the new Quicksilver collection this afternoon, and you're the face of it, remember?"

"Right." He sighed. "I'm sorry, Tay. Duty calls," he added with a playful grin, but Taylor didn't smile back. "I'll text you later, I promise," he added.

"'Kay."

Kai turned around and left with the Ron Jon's people, leaving Taylor stunned, alone, and more confused than ever.

He glanced over his shoulder and mouthed, "I'm sorry," but somehow it didn't make her feel any better.

Chapter Ten

Lori

"How's it going, hon?" Lori strolled into her new living room, which had a surprisingly good amount of natural light for a townhouse. Although right now, it wasn't bright at all, since Amber had closed the blinds on the picture windows.

The three-bedroom two-story unit wasn't exactly furnished with the same style as her red brick beauty in Raleigh, but it was new, in a quiet neighborhood near the beach, and had a bright white kitchen and a modern feel.

She pulled the blinds open and got a quick whimper of objection from Amber, currently lying on the couch, mindlessly scrolling through job openings in the area, headphones in, no doubt some hip-hop blasting in her ears.

"Hey. Too bright." That was all Amber could muster as she swiped her fingers over her iPad screen.

It hurt Lori's heart to see her girl like this, to know the reality about what happened, and, worst of all, not to be able to do anything to help her.

"Hey. Too depressing." Lori sat down on the edge of the sofa, placing a hand on Amber's leg, which was buried underneath a fuzzy blanket.

She pulled her earbuds out, rubbing her eyes as she looked up at her mom. "What's up?"

"How are you holding up, really? Is there anything I can do for you?" Helplessness strangled Lori as she squeezed her eyes shut.

"I'm okay, Mom."

Lori reached down and moved a piece of silky, auburn-colored hair out of her daughter's beautiful, tragically depressed face. "Really? This doesn't look okay."

"I'm hanging in there. I'm scared. Okay, okay, that's the understatement of the century." She gave a dry laugh. "I'm downright terrified. I never thought I wanted kids, I never in a million years was supposed to be a mother. I'm not cut out for it, I'm—"

"Shh." Lori took Amber's hand in hers and gave it a squeeze. "I know this isn't what you planned. And, believe me, I hate plans changing more than anyone else. Life threw a massive monkey wrench at you—at both of us—but we will handle it, okay?"

"Mom." Amber looked up at Lori, her blue eyes filling with tears. "I can't even take care of myself. I can't make good decisions, as proven by the fact that I'm carrying a baby fathered by a married man and—"

"He told you he was divorced, Amber. Or about to be. You didn't have an *affair* with a married man. Don't talk to yourself like that."

"I might as well have, because I'm that stupid. And I can't even get a job doing what I love because...hello, recommendation. Will Representative Garrison write one for me? Doubtful. Plus, whose campaign can I work on? Election season is over. Now what? Oh, now...this." She tapped her lower belly. "This? *Alone*? I just...I don't know if I can do it."

"You're not alone." Lori leaned down and pressed her forehead against Amber's hair, smelling that fruity, sweet shampoo she always used. "I know this sounds absolutely insane, but you are going to do it. And you are going to be amazing at it. I promise."

"Everyone keeps saying..." Amber bit her lip as her eyelids fluttered. "That the moment I hold the baby, the moment he or she comes into the world and I hold it in my arms...that everything changes."

Lori just nodded.

"But...what if it doesn't?" Her daughter's voice cracked with a whisper. "What if I don't look into the face of my newborn and have some kind of life-altering, earth-shattering, instant love and connection? What if I'm not a natural mother? What if I can't love the baby, because every time I look at my own child I see Michael Garrison's face and remember that he lied to me, used me, then cost me my career?"

"Amber, you've got me." She offered a smile, holding her daughter's gaze, wishing so badly she had answers or a plan or a solution. "I'm not going anywhere, and I will always be here for you."

"You can't raise this baby for me."

"I can help," Lori said. "I can guide you, support you, and love you. Also, there's a pretty hefty village called the Sweeneys who would probably swoop in with major-league assistance, too."

"Yes, I've heard it takes a village. But I'm not so sure that village is going to be there for the midnight feedings and first day of school and college and...oh."

"College? You're seriously getting ahead of yourself. Let's just make it through the second trimester."

Amber finally smiled, letting out a sigh of possibly a smidge of relief. "You're right, as always. They're a good village, those Sweeneys."

"Very much. I'm growing closer with Sam, and I've never had a sister, but I think I'm beginning to get the hang of it. I really like her."

"That's amazing." Amber smiled again, and this time it reached her eyes. "It's so nice that you're finding a place in the family."

"You can, too, you know." Lori raised her eyebrows. "They're wonderful people, and everyone wants to get to know you."

Amber just nodded, her expression falling as she glanced into the distance. "I know. It's a bit over-whelming and I've been through a lot."

"Taylor is only a few years younger than you. Maybe you two could be buds? I mean, you are technically cousins. Half-cousins?" Lori cocked her head and frowned. "I don't know. But she's there, and I'm sure she'd love to hang with you."

Amber shrugged, twisting her mouth. "Taylor seems nice, I'm just...not really feeling it lately. I just want to crawl into a hole for a while."

Lori let out a slow breath, the mother in her knowing that she had to respect that and be understanding, even though the therapist in her screamed that hours of purposeless solitude was the *last* thing a nearly depressed pregnant woman needed.

But she didn't push. Amber didn't need a therapist right now, she needed a mom, and Lori had learned long ago that it wasn't her place to use her techniques to try and help her own loved ones.

"Okay, well, I'll leave you to it." She patted Amber's leg and stood up.

"Where are you off to?"

"Sam asked me to go over to the inn and give my opinion about upholstery options for the new dining room. She insisted that I have an eye for design, and that they desperately need my input, but..." She lifted a shoulder. "I think she just wants me to feel included."

Unemployed, almost divorced, and totally lost, Lori welcomed the escape to the inn and the distraction of Sam and Dottie from her massive mountain of personal issues.

"That sounds like fun."

"You're more than welcome..." Lori suggested, a hint of hope in her heart.

"Nah, I'm late for my daily self-pity nap," Amber quipped, yanking the fuzzy blanket up to her neck and turning over onto her side. "I'll be here."

Lori reluctantly kissed her goodbye and went out to the car to drive up A1A to Sweeney House, a route that was already growing on her. She'd never thought of herself as beach girl, and always assumed she'd be miserable without four changing seasons, but there was a certain charm to this endless summer.

Sunlight seemed to fill the air with optimism, and the palm fronds swayed gently in the breeze as she cruised down the road, the sky behind them as blue as ever.

There was a feeling here, Lori decided. A very specific, unique sensation that surrounded this place, and she realized she was truly starting to understand why Sam and Julie kept saying it was "magic."

Maybe there was something to that. Maybe this town, this weather, this family...maybe it all really could heal her and Amber.

"Speaking of Amber," Lori whispered to herself as she pulled into the driveway of the Sweeney House inn, noticing Taylor's little red Honda parked in front of the quaint yellow house.

Lori whipped her car to the left to go to the cottage instead.

She parked right next to Taylor's car and stepped out, instantly blinded by the sun. Lori shielded her eyes as she walked up to the front door and gave it a knock.

Was she supposed to knock? Surely she wasn't family enough yet that she could just walk in and out as she pleased, the way John and Erica did, but...she was sort of family, right?

Before she had any more time to ponder, the door swung open to reveal Taylor in a sweatshirt that said "Cat Mama" and black leggings.

"Oh! Hey, Lori." She smiled, but there was a wariness in her expression. Her eyes were rimmed with pink, and her cheeks looked flushed.

Had she been crying?

"Hi, Taylor." She had to hold back the immediate urge to ask Taylor why she looked sad and if she wanted to talk about it. She settled for, "Everything okay?"

Taylor let out a sigh and stepped aside, gesturing for Lori to come in. "Oh, everything's fine. Just dealing with some extremely silly and yet somehow still stressful problems."

That was her cue. "Do you want to talk about it?"

Taylor blinked at Lori, visibly surprised by the question. "Oh, I mean..." She glanced around, and Lori could tell she was probably home alone. And probably crying, or at least she had been earlier. "It's no big deal, just...like I said. Silly stuff."

"Gotcha." Lori nodded, not sure how to segue into the real reason why she stopped into the cottage before heading over to the inn.

"I was just making a pot of half-caf, if you're interested." Taylor walked over to the kitchen and Lori followed.

"Sure, I'd love a cup."

Taylor pulled two mugs out of the cabinet and set them onto the countertop next to the freshly brewed pot of coffee. "Sorry, I'm not my normal self. I don't mean to be so standoffish." She poured the two mugs of steaming coffee and handed one to Lori with a smile. "I'm happy you're here. Milk or sugar?"

"Black is perfect." Lori graciously accepted the coffee, as warmed by Taylor's words as the mug in her hand. "Thanks, Taylor. And, please, never apologize to me. I don't even know who my 'normal self' is anymore, so I'm sure I haven't always had my best foot forward since we arrived here."

Taylor sat down next to her on a barstool along the kitchen island and tapped her mug against Lori's. "Cheers to moping."

Lori snorted and sipped her coffee, her mind flashing back to Amber on the couch before she'd left. *Speaking of moping.*

"Let me guess." Lori studied Taylor, raising her brows. "Boy problems?"

"How did you know?" Taylor asked on a playful laugh. "Yes, 'boy problems' seems to be a pretty accurate summation of my issues. But it's not the typical I got my heart broken or I want someone who doesn't want me or whatever. I'm sort of caught between two guys, and being sad or stressed or anxious about it makes me seem like the worst, most ungrateful person ever. I mean, who *complains* about having two great guys like you?"

"Well, that sounds extremely stressful, actually," Lori said.

Taylor glanced over, her brown eyes dancing. "Really?"

"Are you kidding? You obviously care about both of these young men, and from the sound of it, they each care about you quite a bit."

"They do. But shouldn't that make me the luckiest girl ever? I have my pick. I mean, why should I be whining and crying?"

Lori frowned and shook her head. "No way. It's a very tough spot to be in, especially for someone who is an empath. The thought of hurting or rejecting either one of them pains you, I'm sure, and all the while you're supposed to be following your own heart. It might not be in your nature to think about yourself before others, and that could make you very uncomfortable. My guess would be you get that from your mother."

"Selflessness?" Taylor cocked her head. "It certainly didn't come from the Max Parker side of things, that's for sure."

Lori gave a sympathetic laugh.

"But you're right. It's like, what good is following my heart if it just feels selfish and mean and hurtful to someone who doesn't deserve to be hurt? I never asked to be in this position, you know?"

"Does it make you feel guilty?"

"Sometimes," she answered quickly, sipping her coffee. "I think I could have been more upfront and possibly saved a bit of stress and drama, but I had no idea what was going to happen. The whole thing just makes me feel very self-involved, and I don't like that."

"Why do you think that is?" Lori asked, not able to help herself. "Why do you hate thinking about yourself and your own desires?"

"Because I see people like my mom, and my aunts and uncle and you...and you've all gone through such real and serious and major things. Like, problems that matter and shape you and strengthen you. And I just have...boy drama. It feels small and stupid."

"Choosing a partner, long-term or short, is not small or stupid." She couldn't help but think of Amber. "And, from what I'm gathering, you are looking for something more serious with one of these guys, yes?"

"Yeah, I...I think I am." Taylor swallowed. "I'm only twenty-four, but not really one for casual."

"Not to mention, Taylor, you have also gone through very real and serious things. What you experienced with your father and your parents splitting up was a traumatic instance. You and Sam are resilient and tough, and you've both flourished here, but that doesn't mean you've never faced adversity, you just overcame it."

Taylor sighed, leaning back and staring off as she processed this. "Yeah, I guess that's true. And I guess that's why the boy problems seem so petty and invalid. I just don't want to be one of those narcissistic, self-obsessed girls who whines over which boy to date."

Lori laughed, rolling her eyes. "I don't know you that well, but I do know, without a doubt, you are not one of those girls."

"Thanks." Taylor smiled, then nudged Lori playfully with a wink. "*Aunt* Lori."

A little flutter skipped in Lori's chest, and she felt washed with gratitude and even more certainty that she'd made the right decision coming here.

"I know 'follow your heart' is stupid advice and means virtually nothing, so all I'll tell you is to trust your gut instinct. And be honest, always. With men, with your loved ones, and with yourself."

Taylor nodded, inhaling slowly. "That's good advice."

"And for heaven's sake, stop invalidating yourself and your own feelings. Just because other people have worse issues doesn't make yours any less overwhelming and stressful and real."

Taylor brushed some dark hair out of her face, taking a deep drink of coffee. "I really appreciate that. I feel better. I need to see Kai again, when I'm not overcome with emotion and I can actually talk to him. If he can ever make time for me with all the Ron Jon stuff going on and..." She glanced at Lori and laughed. "Anyway, I'm rambling. But thank you for listening."

"Of course." She held up the mug. "Thank you for the coffee."

"Anytime."

"Um, Taylor..." Lori ran her fingertip in circles along the top of the white ceramic mug. "There's something else I wanted to ask you...a favor, of sorts."

Taylor lifted her brows. "Sure. What's up?"

"I know this is going to sound like the lamest, most 'Mom' thing ever to ask, but...would you, maybe, try to hang out with Amber a little bit? You don't have to be her best friend or anything like that, it's just that...she's so lonely, and she's been through a lot. I think she could really use a friend who isn't her mother constantly giving her life advice. Is that too weird to ask?"

Taylor laughed softly, shaking her head. "No, not at all! I'd be happy to get to know Amber and hang with her. I honestly didn't think she really had any interest. She kinda brushed me off at the party when you guys first got here, and I haven't seen her much since."

"I know. Like I said, she's going through a lot."

"I totally get it. No judgment here." Taylor smiled. "I would love to be friends with Amber. Maybe she can help me figure out my love triangle."

Lori laughed, lightness filling her chest. "She'd love that."

Okay, "love" might have been a stretch. But the distraction would be good, wouldn't it? Amber certainly couldn't spend her days holed up in that townhouse with all the blinds closed, reliving her trauma and wallowing in her fears about motherhood.

"Awesome." Taylor stood up and took her empty mug to the sink, rinsing it out. "Tell her to shoot me a text anytime. We can grab dinner or something."

As she glanced over her shoulder and gave Lori a smile, she suddenly looked so much like Sam it was stunning.

"You're the best." Lori stood up. "Well, I'm off to Sweeney House to help your mom and grandmother pick out upholstery."

"Ooh, upholstery fun." Taylor playfully shimmied her shoulders. "I'd join you all, but I've got to catch up on work, since I've spent the better part of the weekend immersed in self-pity."

Lori chuckled at that. Maybe Taylor and Amber really would get along.

Chapter Eleven

Annie

Annie looked up from behind the display counter when Sam breezed into the bakery through the front door, pink toolbox in hand—yes, a *pink* toolbox that Taylor had gotten her when she and Dottie started the renovation.

"Please officially label me as the World's Worst Best Friend," Sam announced.

"Why would I do that?"

"Because I seriously cannot believe I haven't been over here to help you more."

"Oh, would you hush?" Annie waved a dismissive hand and came around the counter to greet her friend. "You've had more than enough going on with the new additions to the family, plus Taylor's turned into the hottest bachelorette in Cocoa Beach."

Sam rolled her eyes. "Don't remind me."

"How do you feel about all of that? What's your take?"

"Honestly? I have no idea. I really just want Tay to be happy, of course. And I don't know Andre that well, but I've adored him the few times I've met him. Kai is a cool kid, famous and rich, so I think he's a little more fairy tale-ish. But sometimes I worry about his intentions, although he's never really given me a reason to. I don't know. It's hard for her."

"I can imagine." Annie took the toolkit from her and set it down on a table, extending her arms and grinning at Sam. "I'm happy you're here now. Pink toolbox and all."

Sam hugged her tightly. "I'm so happy I'm here. I'm ready and equipped to hang artwork and help with any other finishing décor touches you need and...wow." Her eyes popped open wide as she looked around The Cupcake Queen. "It looks amazing in here. Annie, it's..." Sam slowly walked through the store, studying the soft pink walls, the glossy white trim, the yellow tile floor and multicolored tables and chairs. "It's sweet."

"As a cupcake bakery should be. Thank you." Annie could feel herself beaming with pride, still riding the high of opening her own business. Well, nearly opening it. Not quite yet. "I've just been having the best time getting it ready. Because it was an ice cream shop before, it was already in a pretty good state to serve as a bakery. I've obviously added a lot of my own touches, though."

"I see that." Sam ran her fingers along the back of a high-top stool, which was made of swirls of baby blue metal surrounding a soft blush cushion. "Have you hit any snags?"

Annie's mind flashed back to the oven and the alarm and the power and the...neighbor. She cleared her throat and shook her head.

"A small electrical issue with my beast of an oven, but I was able to get an electrician out here the next morning and he seemed to have fixed it right up. Although, he said I'd need a follow up inspection from a supervisor, but I'm not too worried."

"Oh, good. Honestly, I am so, so unbelievably happy for you." Sam spun around the center of the store, taking it all in. "It's, like, the brightest, most cheerful place on Earth. Like the perfect embodiment of a cupcake, in store form."

"That's exactly the vibe I'm going for." Annie laughed.

"Well, you achieved it. And you have the product to keep people coming back over and over again. I think you're going to be quite the success, Annie Hawthorne." Sam poked her arm playfully.

Annie sucked in a breath, nerves and anticipation fluttering through her. "Let's hope. I'm trying to open before the end of the year, hopefully drum up some holiday business to kick things off."

"Good idea." Sam held up a finger. "So that means open in, what, like three weeks?"

"Fingers crossed." Annie shrugged. "Everything is pretty much ready to go, aside from hiring and finalizing some small details."

"Like wall art." Sam picked up her tools, waving the box around.

"Exactly." Annie clasped her hands together. "I've got a bunch of prints in the back."

"Let's do it."

Annie showed Sam the stack of big, framed prints she had leaning against the wall in the kitchen, each of them depicting a fun, almost animated, colorful cupcake, all with different decorations—sprinkles, cherries, frostings, and adorable patterned backgrounds. Polka dots, plaid, stripes, and colorful swirls filled the oversized posters and made the sweet desserts pop with color and life.

"These are beyond cute," Sam cooed, stretching her arms out to look at a poster of a pink and yellow cupcake.

"I know, right? Etsy." Annie lifted a shoulder.

Sam used her recently refined decorating skills to plan out the wall art, mark the nail locations, and get to hanging. As they hammered the picture hook into the wall for the first one, Sam was noticeably smiling to herself.

Annie glanced over at her as she made a pencil mark, raising a curious brow. "You really like hanging art, huh?"

"What do you mean?"

"Sam. You're grinning like a little kid. And humming."

"Was I humming?"

"Yes. Now what on Earth has you all Cloud 9-y? Things going really well with Lori?" Annie jabbed the pencil mark into the wall where they needed to nail in the next hook.

"Well, yes, but..." Sam's voice trailed off as she reached for the level. "Can you hand me the measuring tape?"

Annie grabbed the roll of measuring tape and held it up next to her, out of Sam's reach. "Not until you tell me what is really going on."

"Okay, okay." Sam climbed down off the step stool

and let out a deep breath. "But you have to promise not to tell anyone."

"Ooh! A secret?" Annie gasped with intrigue. "Another long-lost sibling, perhaps?"

Sam snorted. "Not quite. It's..." She lowered her voice to a whisper, even though they were the only people in the bakery. "I'm seeing Ethan. Secretly."

Annie's jaw loosened. "Really? Like, *dating* dating?"

"Yeah, I think so. But it's super-quiet, since Ben is still his student and there's so much weirdness there. I don't want to upset my son, so we're keeping things private until Ben's out of his classroom."

Annie laughed, shaking her head as she marveled at Sam. "Look at you, Sam Sweeney! This is fun. I love it."

"It seemed silly at first, but the more I think about it, the more I think it's actually a good thing. Obviously, it's fun and exciting and new."

"All the good things," Annie joked.

"But I think keeping our relationship on the DL is going to give me a chance to really get to know him on a deeper level before deciding if this is actually something I want to pursue. I talked to Lori about it, and she helped me a lot to figure out where I want it to go."

"Sam." Annie reached over and wrapped an arm around her dear friend. "You do realize that you are unrecognizable from the broken divorcee who showed up here at the beginning of the summer, don't you?"

Sam looked at her with misty eyes. "Thanks, Annie. You, too, you know. Quitting the corporate world to follow your dreams! I'm proud of *us*."

"I'm *so* proud of us," Annie said, stepping back to watch her friend line up a frame between two windows. "So, how are you two sneaking off without getting caught?"

"We're texting a lot," Sam said with a wry laugh. "He certainly can't come to the cottage, and I'm too freaked out to go to his place and be seen by someone coming or leaving. We don't really have anywhere we can hang out alone, since the inn is always overrun with workers and people and my mom. So not much sneaking off."

"You could come here," Annie suggested. "I'm not open yet, so you'd have privacy and somewhere to talk."

Sam drew back and laughed. "Like a secret date spot? I love that idea, Annie."

Annie clasped her hands together, grinning widely. "I would love nothing more than to house you two secret lovebirds. But one condition."

"Anything."

"You and Ethan need to sample cupcake flavors to help me narrow down my opening menu."

Sam laughed. "Lady and the Tramp style? I think we can do that."

Annie hooted. "I'll hide in the back while you kiss like teenagers."

Still chuckling about it, they finished hanging the last of the prints and were admiring their work, when the sound of the back door opening and slamming shut caught their attention.

Sam whipped around and glanced at Annie with concern. "Is someone here?"

"It's okay," Annie said, fully aware of the tiny little human who frequently let herself into the bakery with no warning. "It's my new best friend."

"Excuse me? You have a new—"

"Miss Annie!" The high-pitched joy cry of Riley Patterson echoed through the bakery, and Annie couldn't help but laugh at Sam's complete and utter confusion.

"Sam..." Annie gestured to her friend. "This is Riley. Her dad owns the gym next door, and she's been hanging out here with me a lot."

"Hi!" Riley gave an exaggerated wave to Sam.

"Well, hello there." Sam smiled, crouching down to meet Riley's gaze, likely noticing the crooked bangs, botched haircut, and totally mismatched outfit that couldn't scream "single-dad alert" any louder if they tried. "It's wonderful to meet you, Riley."

"I love Miss Annie's cupcakes. She even lets me help with stuff. Do you make cupcakes, too?"

Sam laughed softly. "Only the ones that come from a mix in a box."

Annie gasped dramatically and covered Riley's ears. "Don't poison her little mind with thoughts of store-bought baking mix."

Sam chuckled and stood back up. "So, Riley, you've gotten to know my best friend Annie, huh? Isn't she pretty great?"

"She's the gweatest!" Riley held her arms out wide. "The gym is gwoss."

"Gross and stinky." Sam wrinkled her nose and shook her head. "The worst."

"So I started coming here, and then she gave me cupcakes and Daddy said I can come as much as I want." Riley skipped around the tile floor, admiring the framed cupcake prints on the walls. "I like these pictures! I want one for my room. Can I have a cupcake?"

"Hmm." Annie narrowed her eyes, pretending to be deep in thought as she pondered the question.

"Please, please, Miss Annie. I haven't had any sweets today and if I don't have one I might die! I *need* a cupcake."

"Well!" Annie gasped, exchanging a look with Sam, who was cracking up. "We certainly don't want that, do we? I bet you can find one in the back fridge, if you look really, really hard."

Riley perked up. "Buttercweam?"

"Only the best." Annie winked.

Riley scurried off to the kitchen and Annie turned to Sam. "Cute, isn't she?"

"Beyond. I'm worried I've been replaced in the role as your best friend."

"Hah!" Annie tilted her head back. "She definitely gives you a run for your money, I'll say that."

"Hello, Riley? You here?" The unexpected sound of a man's voice floated into the empty store, and Annie turned to see Trevor coming through the front door.

"Oh, hey, Trevor," Annie greeted him. "She's in the kitchen scavenging for buttercream."

"Why am I not surprised?" Trevor laughed and shook his head, running a hand through those waves of chestnut hair that always looked just the perfect amount of sweaty.

"This is my friend, Sam. The one who's renovating the inn." Annie stepped aside and introduced them. "Sam, this is Trevor Patterson."

"Nice to meet you." He shook Sam's hand, but his eyes flicked back to Annie.

"Gym-next-door guy." Sam nodded and smiled kindly. "And father of the world's cutest little girl. I've heard tell."

"Have you now?" Trevor's lips pulled into a playful smile as his eyes slid up and down Annie.

She felt her cheeks warm. "Not that much tell," she added quickly. "Minimal tell."

Trevor smiled at her, his gaze glistening like the little beads of sweat on his collarbones. His shoulders, of course, were ever-exposed in a black tank top with the Ace Fitness logo in the center.

"So, what have you two been up to?" Trevor looked around, admiring the finished walls and framed prints. "Place looks awesome."

"Thanks." Annie grinned. "Sam helped me hang up all the artwork, and I'm looking to open in a few weeks."

"Dang, that was quick." He smiled enthusiastically, his eyes dancing with sincerity. "You whipped this place up in no time. Took me ages to get the gym off the ground."

"Well, Ace involved a lot more heavy equipment, I'm sure. All I needed was an oven and a couple coats of paint."

Trevor crossed his arms over his chest, nodding slowly as he looked all around and took in the details of

The Cupcake Queen. "Well, congratulations, Annie. This place is going to absolutely kill it. Opening day is right around the corner."

"Hopefully not *too* soon," Sam interjected, raising her finger playfully. "I need the bakery to stay closed for at least a bit longer."

Trevor glanced between them in confusion.

"So I can test all her recipes," Sam said quickly. "She's the best in the world, you know."

Trevor smiled, his gaze locked on Annie. "I've heard tell," he joked. "From Riley."

"My number one fan." A soft blush warmed her cheeks, something she realized happened every time she held eye contact with Trevor for too long, or noticed any features of his Greek god-like body.

"And I better go..." Trevor jutted his chin toward the kitchen, where Riley had been a little too quiet for a little too long. "I've actually got a hot date to get to myself."

Annie drew back, surprised by how much her stomach fell at the words.

Darn this stupid, silly, ridiculous crush.

But...she didn't know Trevor dated. She'd thought he was a grieving widower and probably wasn't interested in women and if he was interested, it certainly wouldn't be in her.

"You do?" Sam asked, breaking the painful tension and Annie's shocked silence.

"Oh, yeah. Me, Riles, and the brand new Barbie movie in IMAX."

Laughter—and, admittedly, a bit of completely unjustified relief—bubbled up in Annie's chest. "They're showing Barbie in IMAX?"

"Evidently." Trevor shrugged. "The life of a single girl dad."

Annie snuck a glance at Sam, who was holding her hand to her chest and smiling at Trevor in the way that any living, breathing woman would smile at the endearing, heartwarming spectacle of Trevor and his love for Riley.

"I better go grab the munchkin or I'm gonna be watching Barbie by myself."

"That would be creepy," Annie said on a laugh.

"Very much so. Riley!" he called, walking back to the kitchen. "Where you at?"

"Hi, Daddy!" Riley leapt out of the back room with a smudge of blue frosting on the tip of her nose.

"Oh, boy," Annie whispered, chuckling softly.

"Ready for the movie, Daddy?" She jumped into her father's arms and he swung her around, slinging her onto his back as they waved goodbye and headed out the door.

"Nice to meet you both!" Sam called.

"You as well," Trevor said as they walked out.

The back door latched shut, and Annie could literally feel the flaming pierce of Sam's gaze burning a hole into her skin.

"What?" Annie shrugged nonchalantly, busying herself by fiddling with a screwdriver.

"Um, *excuse* me?"

Annie shot her a look over her shoulder. "Excuse you for what?"

"Your new business is next to a total HSD whose painfully cute daughter worships you and you weren't going to *tell* me?"

"First of all..." Annie shut her eyes. "What in the world is an HSD?"

"Hot Single Dad," Sam explained, matter-of-fact. "Taylor and I coined it when she was a teenager and we'd see Robert West jogging in our neighborhood in Winter Park all the time."

Annie laughed, sitting down at a table as Sam sat across from her. "Who is Robert West?"

"Guy in our old neighborhood, mid- to late-thirties, had a cute kid and got full custody after a super-messy divorce. Apparently, Taylor and I weren't the only ones with an eye for the HSD. He didn't stay single very long."

Annie raised her brows and leaned her elbows on the table. "Well, as charming and handsome—"

"And totally ripped."

"And totally ripped as Trevor might be, his story is a little different than your old pal, Rob."

Sam frowned. "He's not divorced? He called himself a single—"

"He's widowed."

Sam's face fell and her smile instantly faded. "Oh. That's so sad. That poor little girl."

"I think she was a little too young to remember much of her mother other than some small bits and pieces, but... yeah. I feel for him."

"How long has it been?"

Annie shrugged. "A few years, I think. He seems

okay, but I hardly know him. I can't even imagine how tough it's been."

"He's got great energy, and he's clearly an awesome dad. Plus, wow, gorgeous. I mean, like—"

"I know." Annie held up a hand. "I have eyes."

Sam fanned herself dramatically.

"Would you stop?" Annie said through laughter. "Yes, okay, he's cute. And built, and nice, and all of that. But he lost his wife, and even if he wasn't a widower, there is no way he would ever even notice me like that, so please wipe that all-knowing smirk off your face."

But the smirk stayed, Sam's eyebrows rising up and down to make things worse. "Let me tell you this, Annie Bananie. He noticed you."

"Please." She rolled her eyes.

"He *noticed* you. Anyone could see the way he was checking you out. All playful and cute."

"Sam, he's a personal trainer who looks like Zeus's son. I'm a...not-slender accountant who makes cupcakes."

"You..." Sam raised her voice, her gaze stern. "Are perfect from head to toe. And, my dear friend..." She gestured around the room. "You are not an accountant anymore."

Annie smiled, leaning back and taking a deep breath, savoring the fantasy of the dreamy bakery around her. "Well, that you're correct about."

"Anything can happen." Sam smiled. "Just remember that."

And, Annie supposed, anything could.

Chapter Twelve

Sam

"Sam, honey, something came for you in the mail." Dottie strolled into the cottage with a pile of envelopes, her flowing maxi dress billowing around her. "I hope you're ready for girls night, because I may have gone a bit overboard with the appetizers."

With Ben staying over at a friend's house for the night, it was just the women at the Cottage, and Dottie prepared in full force for all the Sweeney ladies to gather.

Sam chuckled and took the envelope from her—a legal-size manila folder—and tore the top of it open. "Please. Are there ever really too many appetizers for a Sweeney girls night?"

"And it'll be our first proper one all together since the arrival of Lori and Amber," Dottie added, sounding pretty happy.

Sam lowered the envelope to focus on her mother for a second. "How are you feeling about all of that, Mom? Is it weird getting to know Jay's daughter, who isn't yours?"

"You know, Sam..." Dottie opened the fridge and pulled out a beautifully assembled platter of tomato mozzarella salad, decorated with fresh basil and red onions. "For fifty years, I filed Lori away under things Jay didn't want to talk about or think about, and therefore I wouldn't talk or think about her, either. We knew she had a wonderful adopted family and a good life, and that was all there was to it. I admit, at first I was a bit closed off to the idea of getting to know her or having her in our lives at all. It felt somehow like a betrayal to Jay, who wanted these things separate."

Sam nodded. "I get that, Mom. I do."

"But on another note, I think Jay led us right to her. I like to believe he's sitting up there right now, on some recliner in the clouds, smiling down at the sight of all his beloved babies in one place. Lori needed us, Sam, and he led you right to her."

Sam felt her eyes fill and she held her hand to her heart, an ache of missing her Dad rocking her for a moment. "Wow. I love that."

"So, I welcome her and her daughter here with open arms." Dottie reached down into the little wine cooler and pulled out a sparkling rose. "And open bottles."

Sam laughed, smiling and shaking her head as she returned her attention to the folder that arrived in the mail, tearing open the top of it and sliding out a thick stack of papers.

A sudden gut punch nearly knocked her off her feet when Sam realized what exactly she was holding in her hands. "Oh my gosh," she whispered through shaky breaths as she slowly flipped through the pile. "They're my divorce papers. He...he signed them."

"Sam." Dottie rushed over, abandoning her stuffed mushrooms to place her hands on Sam's shoulders, always immediately ready to offer love and support. "Honey. How do you feel?"

She drew in a slow, deep breath, her eyes locked on Max Parker's black ink signature on the line at the bottom of every page.

Max Parker. Those words, that name. Her mind flashed through more than twenty years of memories in half a second—laughter, vacations, fights, tears, two kids, long nights, distance, sadness, apologies, pain, love, betrayal...

How could so much good and bad be wrapped up in one person? So much joy and pain all tangled up in the same confusing mess of a man?

Sam had given him her life for a long, long time. Now, she'd taken it back. And as she held those papers and stared at the words, she felt nothing but relief.

"I feel good, Mom." She set the stack down and smiled at Dottie. "It's finally over, and I can finally let go. I don't hate him anymore. I'm just done with him. The chapter is officially closed."

Dottie leaned close and gave Sam a kiss on the cheek. "I am unbelievably proud of you."

They hugged tight and shared a moment of true closeness and sentiment, and Sam realized that Max Parker, while he did a lot to wreck her life and break her heart, pushed her right here to Cocoa Beach. Right where she needed to be.

It happened the way it happened, and despite all of the hurt, Sam wouldn't change anything.

"Hello, beautiful family!" Erica's voice floated

through the cottage, and Dottie and Sam pulled away from their hug to greet the youngest Sweeney sister.

Shortly after Erica's arrival, Imani came in. Then Annie with cupcakes, and Julie and Bliss, who had a guitar slung over her shoulder. A bit later, Taylor came back from work, and finally, Lori and Amber arrived.

Usual positions were assumed on the back deck, with the new additions claiming a small loveseat next to the sofa, sharing a blanket to shield them from a dip in the November temperatures.

Dottie brought out platters of snacks and refilled everyone's drinks, and the women—all in various stages in their own personal journeys—came together as sisters, cousins, aunts, mothers and daughters in a way that no one else could.

"I've been so out of the loop." Imani shook her head and took a sip of rose. "Please, everyone, fill me in on your entire life. And accept my sweeping apology for the millionth time for running off to California like that. I missed you all so much."

"Honey, please." Erica placed her arm on Imani's shoulder. "You don't owe us an apology for doing something for yourself. It's okay."

"Turns out doing something for myself meant nothing but loneliness and regret." She gave a mirthless laugh. "I missed the heck out of being a mom and wife."

"I'm sure John's so glad to have you back." Dottie gave her daughter-in-law a loving smile. "And no one, I mean no one, holds anything against you, Imani. Know that."

Imani's expression filled with gratitude. "Thank you. And he's definitely happy. We all are. It's been wonderful just going back to normal life with him and the kids. I'll never take it for granted again." She turned to Erica. "Speaking of kids, how's Jada? On a fast track to winning a Nobel prize, I assume?"

Erica laughed and waved a hand. "Not yet, but she is totally crushing it in sixth grade. Her tutor has been such a blessing, and I can tell her confidence in school and in social circles has just skyrocketed. She's thinking about trying out for soccer next year."

Coos of, "That's amazing!" and, "Good for her!" echoed around the group, and conversation dove into Julie's blossoming career as a guitar teacher and Bliss's excitement to be at a real public high school starting in January. Annie invited everyone to the big grand opening of The Cupcake Queen, but stayed silent about her dashing new neighbor.

Sam told everyone about their idea for Lori's "yoga therapy" and it was a huge hit.

"Once the inn is back open, you can do regular classes for guests and students. We could offer our guests a discounted rate," Dottie suggested.

Lori's eyes lit up, almost as if Dottie's approval and generosity truly meant a lot to her. "That would be amazing."

"I'll do it," Taylor raised her glass. "Lord knows I could use a little guidance."

"Oh, Tay," Sam said sympathetically.

As the women chatted, snacked, listened, advised,

and laughed a lot, Lori seemed to relax and loosen up, and Amber even shared a few stories from her waitressing job in Raleigh, though Sam couldn't help but notice a quiet darkness that seemed to linger over Lori's daughter.

Also, not that she was judging, waitressing didn't seem to be a good fit for Amber. A casual mention of college gave away her education, and though she was quiet, she was articulate and clearly well-read.

Once the conversation lulled, Sam decided it was time to finally drop in the lead she'd been burying since her sisters got here.

With a deep breath, she lifted up her glass. "I have one more thing to share. It actually just happened before you all got here, and..." She grinned. "It's kind of a biggie."

Taylor was the first to blurt out, "What?" as everyone turned all their focus on Sam.

She shut her eyes, so ready to say the words she'd been waiting to say for months now. She smiled, taking in the moment. "My divorce is final."

"Oh my gosh."

"Sam!"

"Heck, yeah, girl."

As Sam accepted the chorus of love, support, and relief from her family, she instantly looked over at Taylor, who was quiet and still.

"You okay?" she whispered to her daughter.

Sam couldn't help but watch Taylor's eyes flash with sadness as she no doubt remembered what had been a darn good childhood. The Christmas mornings when she and Ben were little. The vacations filled with laughter and fun. The way Max would throw her onto his shoulders and run around the backyard while she shrieked with laughter.

There were good times. They were a family, long ago. And, with the divorce final, that family that Taylor and Ben had grown up in was officially gone.

"Yeah." Taylor nodded after a long pause, then smiled at Sam, pressing her lips together. "I'm good. I'm glad it's done. You're free."

Selfless girl that she was.

Sam lifted her glass. "To freedom."

"Independence," Erica chimed in, raising hers.

"In all its forms," Imani added.

"To family," Dottie said.

"To..." Taylor spoke softly, taking a wistful breath as she clinked her glass to everyone else's. "Moving on."

"Cheers to that." Lori smiled, shooting Sam a wink.

Sam felt lighter the rest of the night, the weight of the divorce finally released from her shoulders. She quietly filled Imani, Julie, and Erica in on her secret relationship with Ethan, because, at this point, it wasn't fair to tell *some* Sweeneys and not others, right?

As the evening went on, things felt more and more peaceful, and the name on the bottom of those papers meant less and less every minute.

Fueled by the high of a finalized divorce, a couple glasses of sparkling rose, and Lori's motivational and inspiring voice in her head, Sam was more than ready for her late-night meetup with Ethan.

And, this time, she was ready to make it more than just flirtation and kissing and surface-level chatting. She was ready to go deeper, to see if this was the real deal.

Ethan's truck pulled into the driveway of the cottage with the headlights low, like it was some sort of secret mission, even though every female member of the family now officially knew what was going on.

Whoops.

"Hey, you." Ethan's voice was husky as Sam swung open the passenger-side door, the dim glow of moonlight reflecting off of his eyes.

"Hi." She smiled, planted a kiss on his lips, and settled into the seat.

"You look particularly gorgeous tonight." His gaze flicked up and down in a way that made her heart skip a beat. "You're glowing."

"Am I?" She laughed. "It's probably the rosé."

"Enough that you needed me to come and pick you up," he teased, backing the truck out of the driveway and heading down A1A to his house, where they'd sit on the dock, dangling their legs over the canal.

"I just wanted to be extra safe," Sam said, deciding to wait until they got to his place to drop the news of her divorce. "How was your day?"

"Slow," he glanced at her. "But good. I wanted to finally get done with the refinishing on that headboard for the Samantha suite, but I had to grade quizzes all evening."

"Snore! The Samantha headboard is so much more important," she joked.

"No kidding. But these kids seriously aren't clicking with integration by parts, so the quiz grading was brutal. I'm going to have to reteach the lesson next week, because something about it didn't get through to them. Or maybe I'm just a terrible teacher," he said playfully.

Sam angled her head. "How did Ben do? Or do I not want to know?"

"Well, he got a C, but—"

"A C?" Sam gasped, all flirtation instantly thrown out the window. "A hook? Ben got a hook? Oh, that is completely unaccept—"

"Samantha." Ethan looked over at her while the car slowed to a stop at a red light. "He got one of the highest scores in the class. The median was a 64."

"Wow." She leaned back, easing up on her instant urge to call Ben and tell him to do nothing but study calc all weekend. "Maybe you *are* a terrible teacher."

"Or maybe..." He pulled the truck into the driveway, shifting it into Park and locking eyes with Sam. "I've been a little distracted lately."

Warmth flooded her as she laughed and kissed him, enjoying how every moment spent together was even more comfortable and fun and relaxed than the one before. "I think that might be my fault."

"I think maybe a little."

"Come on." She shoved her door open. "Let's go inside. There's something I want to talk to you about."

"Nightcap?" Ethan asked when they got inside. "A snack?"

"Just water for me, thanks." Her stomach was too full of butterflies to eat.

This conversation had been looming over her head ever since her sunrise yoga therapy session with Lori, and the signed divorce papers could not have shown up at a better time.

"What a night, huh?" Ethan sighed with contentment as he walked her out to the wooden deck that faced the wide canal behind his old Florida-style ranch house.

The waterway ran east to west, lined with docks and private boats, a mile or so inland from the beach but with access to the Indian River. The canal was dark and still tonight, with the distant sound of sail riggings clanging in the breeze and the heady scent of brackish water hanging in the air.

Sitting next to him on a rocking loveseat that faced the water, Sam opened her bottle and took a tiny sip, then inhaled slowly. "It's a gorgeous night. Who would want to live anywhere else?"

"Sixty-five degrees at the end of November." He raised his bottle to his lips and gave her a look. "Paradise, indeed. So, Samantha Sweeney, what is it you wanted to talk to me about?"

She smiled, joy rising in her heart at the sound of her maiden name. Her real name. Who she always should have been.

"I got my divorce papers." She shut her eyes, feeling a smile pull. "He signed them."

Ethan lit up, his gaze widening with surprise and what Sam hoped was pure happiness. "Really? Are you serious?"

"Completely." She held her hand up earnestly, as if making a vow.

"Sam," he breathed her name, kindness and goodness radiating from his voice as he reached his arms out and hugged her tightly. "How are you feeling? I know it can be a lot...the day you get the papers."

She drew back, realizing that was one of the very, *very* rare times he'd ever even referenced his divorce. It reminded her to steer the conversation toward her questions about his past, just like Lori told her to do.

This couldn't get serious until she knew him better, deeper, for real.

"I'm feeling good." She took a breath, resting her head on Ethan's strong shoulder. "I expected to be a little sad, or melancholy, or even just reflective and wistful about it, but...I don't feel any of that. I'm just relieved. I'm free. Is that completely terrible of me? I mean, this is the man I loved for over twenty years, the man I had two kids with. Shouldn't I be at least moderately somber?"

"There's no should and shouldn't with divorce." He shrugged, stiffening a bit. "You feel how you feel, and, in your case, you don't owe anyone any apologies, least of all yourself."

In your case?

What about in his case? Did he owe someone an

apology? Was he the bad guy in his own broken marriage? Sam couldn't physically dream up a scenario in which Ethan would hurt someone he loved, but...who knows? She'd been wrong about people before.

"Right, thanks." She brushed some hair out of her eyes as the salty breeze swept through the air, bringing the slightest hint of a chill to her skin. "So, yeah. I'm happy. Good day. Weird day, but in a good way. It's like I can finally move on."

"Cheers to that." He lifted his bottle and tapped it to hers.

Sam took a small sip, but her throat was tight with nerves. Why was she so anxious? What if the answer to her questions about Ethan's divorce was...not what she wanted to hear?

She had to ask, though. She had to know. He couldn't keep these walls up and expect this to move forward, right? He had to open up at some point if things were going to get real between them.

She sucked in a breath, held her bottle tight, and turned to him. "Speaking of finalized divorces..." She added an awkward laugh. "What happened in your marriage? I feel like you never really talk about it, and, I don't mean to pry, it's just kind of been on my mind. You know every tragic detail of my split, and it seems like I don't know anything about your past marriage, or your... past in general."

Her words hung in the air between them, and she studied Ethan's expression, watching it grow uncharacteristically stoic. "We just didn't work out."

Seriously?

The lump in Sam's throat rose and her anxiety heightened. What if he was a cheater like Max? Clearly her judgment had been off about men in the past. What could he be hiding?

"Usually, there are reasons for that, you know." She attempted to lighten her slight pry with a soft laugh and a playful nudge, but Ethan was stone-still.

"Samantha, I really don't want to talk about my ex-wife or my divorce." He swallowed, turning to her with quite possibly the most dead-serious expression she'd ever seen on his face. "I'm asking you to respect that, okay? I know you're very open about your divorce and the circumstances around it, but it's not like that for me. It's something I'd rather keep to myself, and I just would really appreciate if you would respect that."

Suddenly, the breeze was as cold as ice, and a shiver zipped up Sam's spine. Tension filled the space between them and became shockingly palpable within a matter of seconds.

"Oh...okay. Of course." She cleared her throat awkwardly, feeling more worried and uneasy than ever.

What happened? What did he do?

"I'm sorry, I didn't mean to—"

"You're fine." He smiled, but it was forced and strained and his eyes seemed to be looking a million miles away. "Look, I came to Cocoa Beach for a fresh start, just like you did. So I'm really hoping you can understand that I didn't bring my past here with me. It's not a part of my life anymore, it's not who I am. It's over and done with. I only want to look forward, okay?" He leaned over and kissed the top of her head, wrapping an arm around her shoulders. "With you."

"Okay. Yeah, I get it." She nodded, leaning into his embrace, trying to accept that and shake the fear and worry as millions of questions bounced around in her mind like a pinball machine. "Let's just look forward."

How could she possibly do that when she feared now more than ever that he could be hiding something? Did Sam have it in her to truly let go of the past...both hers and his?

Her mind flashed back to those divorce papers, the black ink signature at the bottom. She'd trusted Max. She'd loved Max desperately, in a way that was hard to describe. She was so blinded by love for him that she didn't see his dark secrets.

Sam looked up at the man next to her, hoping and praying he didn't have dark secrets of his own.

Chapter Thirteen

Taylor

The back conference room at Coastal Marketing was brimming with sunlight and productivity, and Taylor sat ready and waiting at the table, with all of her notes on her laptop, fully prepared for a quarterly check-in meeting with her favorite client.

"Ready for Blackhawk?" John clasped his hands together as he breezed into the room, a tangible lightness and joy surrounding him that Taylor hadn't seen since before Imani had left.

It was so refreshing to see Uncle John be himself again.

"Born ready, boss." Taylor gave a mock salute.

Uncle John may have been vaguely aware that there was a close friendship forming between Taylor and Andre, but he'd been so caught up in his own marriage and work and kids and life that he probably didn't give it much thought.

Taylor, on the other hand, had given it endless thought, some might even say ad nauseum. And while she and Andre were currently firmly locked into a "just friends" status, it was not to be ignored that her heart skipped a beat when he walked into the conference room.

He carried himself with that certain kind of swagger that came with a man who had absolutely nothing to prove. He was just so effortlessly *him*. His style, his hair, his vibe...everything about him was so ridiculously cool.

He never tried too hard. He didn't have to.

"Hey, Tay." Andre walked up to her, notching a brow. "You look like you're ready for business."

Taylor laughed softly and pushed her chair away from the table, standing up to give him a totally platonic friend hug while also not at all noticing how good he smelled or the way his button-down hugged his shoulders.

Shouldn't she be thinking about Kai, anyway?

"I've got extensive notes, as always." She gestured to her laptop. "You guys have been so successful at your Cocoa Beach location, this meeting is going to be fun. Just one big pat on the back for everyone involved."

Andre laughed, low and deep and comforting. "I'm here for all the back pats."

John stepped to the front of the room and started off the meeting by greeting all of the coastal marketing employees who had been working on the Blackhawk project, who'd all assumed seats around the table.

Andre sat at the back head of the long table, facing John, kitty-corner from Taylor.

"Welcome, everyone, to our quarterly marketing meeting with Blackhawk Brewing." John smiled and caught Taylor's gaze. "Let me start off with a congratulations to Andre Everett, and Brock, of course, who's still up in Asheville at the other location. You guys obviously have a special product and something awesome to share with the world, and I'm so happy we could help you do it."

"I'm beyond grateful for all of you." Andre glanced around the room, lingering on Taylor for an extra beat. "I couldn't be happier with everything everyone at Coastal Marketing has done for our brand and visibility this past year. Starting with the amazing Taylor Parker..." He laughed as he gestured at her. "Best account exec in the game."

She felt her cheeks flood with warmth as she waved off the compliment, but kind of loved every second of it. "Please, I couldn't do any of it without all of you. But speaking of growth, Jill and I have final ROI numbers for the year and the projections for next quarter, if you're all ready to dive in."

"Let's dive." John gestured toward the screen at the front of the room where Taylor walked up, plugged her laptop in, and along with Jill—who wasn't Annie but was a warm and very competent accountant—talked numbers, projections, budgets, and ideas.

As the meeting went on, Taylor felt completely in her element, inspired and invigorated by the creative brainstorm, the analysis of their success, and by the man at the end of the table who beamed at her with pride. Like a... friend would.

Everything regarding Blackhawk's plans and strategies for the new year was discussed and after a fun and upbeat meeting, Taylor finally packed up her computer, ready to head back to her desk.

She knew she should be feeling lighthearted, happy, at peace. She loved this job, and she was undeniably excelling in it. Six months ago, the thought of leading a quarterly as an account exec would have had her shaking, and now it was second nature.

So why was she still so darn blue? Why did she want to run up to Andre and hug him and kiss him and not be just friends?

"Crushed it, as always." Andre held up a hand for a high five as Taylor slid her laptop into her tote bag and coiled up the charger.

"Thank you, thank you." She smacked his palm and smiled. "I'm getting used to it."

"Oh, you're way past 'used to it.' Not only are you great with all the organization and plans and numbers, your creative ideas are what made this Blackhawk branch so successful." He pointed to the screen at the front of the conference room, which displayed a detailed line graph of Blackhawk's ROI on advertising and marketing in the past quarter. "That's all because of you."

And Kai...who drummed up a booming start to their business with his appearance at their booth at the Ron Jon Invitational.

"I appreciate it, Andre. Everyone is so great to work with, and I'm having a ton of fun."

"Are you?" He cocked his head, a braid swinging in front of his dark eyes as he studied her. "You don't look too terribly thrilled."

Was it that obvious?

"I am...with work, anyway. I just have a lot going on right now."

His dark eyes flashed, as if the reminder that she was 'choosing' between him and another guy smacked him right in the face.

Taylor glanced around, realizing that the conference room was empty, and she and Andre were alone.

"I'm a little overwhelmed at the moment, that's all," she whispered, meeting his gaze.

The truth was, he was her friend before he'd become anything else. And, wow, she missed that friend. She needed him right about now, but she sure as heck couldn't talk to him about the love triangle when he was one full side of that equation.

"Things going well with Kai?" Andre asked causally, breaking the ice somehow without much awkwardness.

"I don't...I don't know." Taylor let out a soft sigh, pushing some hair behind her ear.

"It's fine, Tay." He held up a hand. "You don't have to get into it. We're cool, I promise."

How was he so great about this?

"Thanks," she said on a breath of relief, feeling physically lighter.

"I have to know, though..." He raised a brow, making her mind instantly race, wondering what he could possibly ask about Kai and how she was going to answer it. "How is Midnight getting along with Mr. Minx?"

Taylor laughed, feeling more relief and comfort as he referenced her cats—one whose life he saved. "Actually, so well. I caught Minx bathing Midnight the other day, and they snuggle constantly."

Andre laughed, shaking his head. "That's too darn cute."

"And no more Houdini escape acts, thankfully."

He glanced at her, his eyes twinkling. "Well, if you ever need someone to crawl underneath the back deck and fish out a kitten, you know I'm your guy."

Unexpected emotion tightened her throat. "What about you? How's life?" Taylor asked, not wanting this catchup to end.

"Life is pretty good. Still getting used to the whole no seasons thing." He chuckled. "But I'm headed out to Colorado with Brock and a couple of our buddies for a ski and boarding trip next weekend, so hopefully that'll scratch my winter itch a little."

"Oh, wow, that's going to be so fun. I know how much you love it out west." Taylor remembered that Andre had said multiple times moving out to Colorado or Utah to snowboard was a big dream of his.

"Yeah, it'll be cool. And how's the fam? Any more secret aunts show up?"

Taylor laughed. "No more random relatives at this point, but they're all good. I'm actually getting dinner tonight with Amber, my new...half-cousin? I guess? She's pretty quiet but Lori thinks she could use a pal, so I texted her to make plans. And Ben is—"

His phone vibrated on the table, catching both of their attention.

"Oh, you can take that," Taylor gestured at it, waving

a hand to dismiss their totally not important but somehow wonderful conversation.

"Nah." Andre grabbed the phone and hit Decline. "It's just one of our suppliers. I'll call him back."

"Andre, really, it's fine." She nodded at the phone. "Work stuff is important. I don't want to keep you—"

"You're important, too, Taylor." He gave a cheesy grin. "I miss my only friend here. I miss..." Their gazes locked for a few breathless seconds. "You."

As more than a friend, she gathered.

Taylor shut her eyes, keeping them closed for a long second as everything in her pulled her to Andre. "I miss you, too. I'm sorry about—"

"Hey," he cut her off with a smile. "Don't apologize, okay? Your man came back for you. It's romantic, it's big. I get it."

"He's not my man," Taylor said, surprising herself and Andre.

"Tay..."

"He's not. I still want..." *You*. "I still don't know what I want. I'm confused, but I miss you, and you're so understanding and supportive, and—ugh." She dropped back down into a chair at the conference table, dropping her face into her palms.

"Whoa, hey." He sat down next to her, placing a solid hand on her back. "Everything's okay, Tay. I'm here. I'm not going anywhere. Even if that means just being your friend. You mean too much to me."

She turned her face up to him and smiled. "Thanks, Andre. You mean a lot to me, too."

His phone buzzed again with another incoming call from the same number.

"Please take the call." She shoved his ringing phone toward him with a laugh. "You not answering your supplier is stressing me out."

"It's fine." He shook his head and chuckled. "Work can wait. I'm talking to you right now."

It was impossible to ignore the jitters in her chest, the peace in her heart, and the absolute disappearance of everything else when she was with Andre.

It was more than what friendship should feel like, that was for sure. But Taylor was still lost and confused and had a date planned with Kai for that weekend, although she couldn't imagine spending an entire night thinking of anyone but the man in front of her.

THE BACK DECK of Sharky's Sea Shack was one of Taylor's favorite spots in town, despite it being the scene of her first breakup with Kai. That seemed like history now, and she'd had so many joyful girls nights, family time, and memories on this beachside deck that any hurt done by Kai was long healed.

The waves splashed in the distance as the sun slipped behind the clouds to set. The sky was streaked with blush-pink clouds and the palm trees rustled in the ocean breeze.

But tonight, she was here with a new face, and Taylor

truly had no idea where to begin this strange and awkward relationship.

"I'm really glad we could get together." Taylor gave a bright, cheerful grin and willed herself to focus on tonight's date—which was, blessedly, not with Kai or Andre.

Amber Kittle, Lori's somewhat distant, twenty-nine-year-old daughter, stared at Taylor from across the table at Sharky's, barely managing a smile.

Why doesn't she like me? Taylor couldn't help but ask herself. Lori was really sweet and pretty outgoing, but Amber seemed to exist behind a fortified brick wall that no one in the Sweeney clan could take down.

But Taylor told Lori she would try, and she intended to hold true to that, even if this budding friendship felt more like pulling teeth. If nothing else, it was a welcome distraction from her current love triangle.

"I know the circumstances are totally bizarre, but it's nice to finally have someone around who's closer to my age." Taylor sipped her drink, her signature pina colada with extra whip.

Pregnant Amber—even though she never talked about it—opted for a mocktail, which she stirred absent-mindedly, a faraway look on her face, which was quite pretty, Taylor thought, if she ever deigned to smile.

"You're right," Amber said after a long pause, her eyes fixated on her swirling straw. "It's definitely bizarre."

Taylor swallowed.

Pulling. Freaking. Teeth. But now she was just kind

of determined to get this young woman to open up, at least a little bit.

"How are you liking Cocoa Beach?" Taylor asked, launching into the small talk. "I'm sure you were probably completely shocked when your mom said you were moving here to be around her birth father's family..." Taylor screwed up her face. "But it's not too bad, right?"

"The beach is nice..." Amber sighed. "And, actually, it was my idea."

"Wait, what?" Now, that was news.

"Coming here," Amber said, matter-of-factly. "My mom told me about Sam and Julie showing up at her office and suggesting she start things over in Cocoa Beach and, at the time, we brushed it off because it seemed totally insane."

Taylor wasn't sure whether she should be offended by that on her mother's behalf, but she just stayed quiet and listened to the most words this girl had spoken since she'd gotten there.

"But then I found out about..." She glanced down at her stomach, her eyes flashing. "This. And everything changed. We needed to get away, to start over. I threw out the crazy idea and my mom jumped on it. So...hooray. Here we are."

"Wow." Taylor drew back, processing the hint of dry sarcasm that had potential to cover a wry sense of humor, if she and Amber could get closer. "That was a huge decision. Why did you want to leave so bad? If you don't mind me asking," she added quickly.

Amber looked directly at Taylor, her dark eyes nearly

glaring. "I just needed to get away. From Raleigh, from my job, from all of it."

Her job? Had she been a waitress all her adult life? It seemed like a slightly rude question, so she asked the more obvious one. "And the father is..." she started gently.

"Not in the picture," Amber replied instantly. "And never will be."

"Oh." Taylor nodded, taking that as her cue to stop asking questions. "Okay. Right."

"It was a one-night stand," Amber added, a bit awkwardly, as if it was really important to make that clear. "So, I don't know him. I didn't even get his name. It's embarrassing, I know. I hate talking about it."

"You don't have anything to be embarrassed about," Taylor assured her. "It's 2023 and you're a grown woman. But don't worry, you don't have to talk about it ever again."

Amber looked at her, a smile pulling at her pretty, delicate face and almost reaching her eyes. "Thanks."

"Of course." Taylor, feeling the first glimmer of hope since this evening began, decided to roll with the momentum. "Hated your job, too, huh? I can relate all too well. I was bartending before we moved here, and oh my gosh, if I never clean up spilled beer or get hit on by a creepy drunk dude again, I will be one happy woman."

Amber gave a half-hearted nod and looked a little pained by the comment. Maybe waitressing was how she had her one-night-stand. Maybe—

"I was in politics before waitressing."

Taylor drew back with surprise number two. "Really? I wouldn't take you for—"

"On the campaign side," she added quickly. "I'm kind of a number-crunching type and I analyzed a lot of polls as a junior-level campaign manager."

"So interesting!" Taylor exclaimed. "Whose campaign did you work on? Anything national?"

"Oh, just, no one you'd know," she said.

"But then you waitressed?" Taylor asked, wondering how a math-oriented number-crunching campaign manager ended up in a service job.

"Yeah, it, um, was better at the time," she said vaguely.

Better than a political campaign? Something in her generic non-answer made Taylor back off and search for some other common ground.

"Well, I have a love-hate relationship with food-service jobs," she said. "The tips can be banging when you really put in effort. I just never put in the effort at good ole O'Leary's pub in Winter Park, Florida."

Amber smiled. "How'd you end up there?" she asked, giving Taylor hope when she finally showed some genuine interest.

"Truth? I dropped out of medical school to be a bartender, and I did it solely to stick it to my dad."

Amber's jaw practically landed on the table. "You've got to be kidding me."

"I mean, it wasn't like I had any real calling to be a surgeon. I just felt pressured into it because of who my father was. And then I caught him cheating on my mom and realized I don't actually care what he thinks of me in the slightest, because he sucks as a person. So I quit and never looked back."

"Wow." Amber nodded slowly, a smile pulling. "I didn't peg you as a badass rebel, Taylor."

She lifted a playful shoulder. "I have my moments."

They both laughed, and the tension started to ease even more.

"I'm shocked, honestly." Amber glanced down.

"Why?"

"Because." She shrugged, sipping her mocktail and leaning against the back of the barstool as she studied Taylor. "You seem so...grounded."

"Really?"

"Uh, yeah." Amber gave a dry laugh. "You have this killer job, you're best friends with your whole family, you've got boys fighting for your heart, apparently."

"They're hardly fighting," Taylor said softly. "But thank you. Things have gotten a lot better for me since we moved here at the beginning of the summer. Like, *a lot* better. And I really think it can be that way for you and your mom, too."

Amber's eyes flashed, seeming to cast a shadow down her face. "Maybe. I'm in a really...unsettled place, as you can imagine."

Taylor wanted to ask about the baby, the pregnancy, the father...Questions burned in her mind, but she could tell Amber needed to go at her own pace with the whole opening-up thing. And her own pace was...slow. But progress was being made, and there was nothing Taylor loved as much as a challenge.

"You know what always makes me feel better, though? Literally no matter what?" Taylor asked, lifting her glass playfully to lighten the mood.

"Uh, no real pina coladas for me."

"No. I meant my cats." Taylor grinned. "I've got two now, and they are seriously like therapy for me. Are you an animal person?"

"Actually..." Amber pushed some hair out of her face, her gaze meeting Taylor's. "I love dogs. We had one when I was growing up, but he passed away when I was eighteen. He was sixteen—almost seventeen—so it was a good, long life."

"Aw." Taylor pressed a hand to her chest. "That is a good, long life."

"He was the best. A sweet, chunky Dachshund named Junior." Amber smiled, sparks of happiness at the fond memory glimmering in her eyes. "He used to burrow in my bed in the winter when it was cold, smushing himself all the way down under the covers by my legs."

"That's beyond cute," Taylor cooed. "It's like, how could anyone possibly be sad with a sweet, happy furball cuddling with them?"

"I know, right?" Amber laughed. "It was the best."

"Maybe you should consider adopting a dog?" Taylor suggested gently. "I know it's not a solution or answer to anything, but an emotional support animal can't exactly do any harm. It could be part of your new chapter in life. Dog mom."

Amber visibly winced at the word "mom," and Taylor instantly regretted using that phrase. "I don't know. Pretty soon I'm gonna have to be a real mom," her voice trailed off and faded at the last word.

"When's your due date?" Taylor asked.

"May 10th," she said on a sigh. "It seems like a long time away, but it's barreling toward me and, holy heck, I have zero clue how to be a mother."

"You have your own," Taylor said. "I'm sure she'll have advice and has been a role model."

"We're close, yes, but a role model? Only if I want to know how to be a workaholic," she said on a dry laugh. "My dad was actually the hands-on parent. He had a much more chill job as a self-employed photographer, so he was the one who picked me up from school and got me to my activities and helped me with English essays, because I was more of a math girl."

"Oh, that's cool. I sure can't say the same thing about my father. So maybe he can give you some advice."

She gave Taylor a look that she couldn't quite interpret. "Yeah, but..."

"But your parents' divorce makes that awkward?" she guessed.

"Not exactly. They haven't really put me in the middle, which I appreciate, but..." She swallowed and gave Taylor a really guilty look. "I haven't told him I'm pregnant yet."

Taylor's eyes widened. "How do you think he'll handle it?"

"I don't know. I'm just way too embarrassed."

"Oh, Amber." She reached across the table. "Don't be. Things happen. Babies get conceived and I'm sure your father loves you and will be a wonderful grandfather."

Her eyes filled and she looked back down at her drink. "I just thought I'd get through the next few weeks or so. I'll tell him eventually. I have to."

Not sure what to say, Taylor just squeezed Amber's hand briefly, giving her a warm smile.

"Look, I know you probably feel lost right now, and I can tell you've been through a lot and this is scary and rough. I won't even pretend to be able to understand, because I seriously don't. But...if you ever want to talk to anyone who I swear is not judging you for anything, I'm here."

Amber shut her eyes tightly for a moment as she drew in a deep breath. "Thanks, Taylor. And I'm sorry if I've come off as kind of a..." She paused, biting her lip. "B-word to you since I got here. I just have a lot going on and you seem so perfect and happy and together and *not* accidentally pregnant. I guess I was a little jealous."

Taylor's heart folded and she angled her head, giving Amber a look of love and sympathy. "Oh my goodness, you were not a B-word."

Amber arched a dubious brow.

"Okay, maybe a little bit of a B-word." She laughed.

"But, please, it's all good. I'm just sorry you feel so alone in all of this."

Amber sighed. "It's weird." She touched her belly. "I feel completely alone and somehow completely not alone at the same time. Like, I'm isolated and scared and about to be a single mom, but I've also got a tiny kidney bean inside me that's going to become a whole entire human."

"It's kind of amazing," Taylor said softly, with a warm smile. "And, for whatever it's worth, I think you're gonna be a killer mom."

"I hope so, but you know? I think I'm going to take your advice and adopt a dog."

"Yay!" Taylor grinned. "That's a wonderful idea."

"I need something to take care of." Amber raised a shoulder, which Taylor noticed had a small tattoo. "For practice, I guess," she joked.

Taylor laughed. "We can have pet playdates."

"I'm so scared of doing it on my own," Amber admitted suddenly on a breath of raw, genuine realness.

"You're a Sweeney now, my friend. We don't do *anything* on our own."

Chapter Fourteen

Lori

This morning's sunrise yoga session had a whopping three people in attendance, and Lori was pretty sure that all of them were other moms from Ben's high school who Sam had referred.

But clients were clients, and Lori was just grateful for the chance to really try her hand at something completely new.

Plus, small class sizes, she guessed, would be much more conducive to openness, growth, and conversation, which Lori was quickly learning were huge pillars of her somewhat nontraditional style of yoga teaching.

Yoga therapy, as Sam had dubbed it.

"Now, feel your spine being pulled straight up to the sky, as if there's a string on the top of your head," Lori instructed her three students, who had assumed tree pose on their mats.

The sun was rising over the horizon behind her, casting a hazy orange glow on the sand and on Sweeney House.

"And relax," Lori said on an exhale, guiding her clients to lay on their mats for *shavasana*, the final section of yoga practice. Since the famous corpse pose mainly involved lying flat on the ground and not moving, it was generally a fan favorite for beginners.

And a favorite for Lori, since it was her chance to really get personal and hopefully share some wisdom and peace through the yoga practice the way she had done with Sam's private lesson.

"As you lay here, feeling the sand under your body, hearing the waves splashing against the shore..." She formed the words slowly, drawing them out the way all her best yoga teachers always had. "I want you to think of a word. A focus, an idea, a person, a concept...It can be anything. Something or someone that's been weighing on your heart, something you're joyful about, a goal you have for yourself, anything at all." She stood up, slowly and quietly tiptoeing between the three mats, leaning down to drop a few drops of lavender essential oil onto the wrists of her students.

Deep exhales echoed between the women as Lori gently dropped the lavender oil onto the last woman, who'd introduced herself as Lena.

"And as you're thinking of your word, and everything it means to you in this moment, I want you to feel the warmth of the sun on your skin as it rises above us. If you're feeling open and comfortable, you may share your word out loud. If you'd like to keep it to yourself, that's completely fine. Whatever brings you peace."

Lori turned and walked back to her mat, assuming all three women would likely stay quiet, considering she'd never been to a yoga class where personal sharing was necessarily encouraged or part of the practice. But Lori wanted to give them the option. She wanted the chance to help and listen.

"I'll share my word," said one woman, Angie, Lori remembered from the beginning of class.

She was a sweet, soft-spoken redhead who looked about Sam's age and had a son in Ben's grade.

"Wonderful." Lori sat cross-legged on her own mat, placing her hands gently on her knees and straightening her spine. "We would love to open up this moment to you, Angie."

"My word is forgiveness," Angie said, lying still in *shavasana*. "I got into an argument with husband last night. He forgot that I'd planned a romantic dinner, since both the kids were spending the weekend at their grandparent's place. He stayed at the office late catching up on work, and by the time he got home, the candles had melted and the food was cold. A total cliché, you know? I know I should have just texted him and reminded him. But...I wanted him to be looking forward to it as much as I was. I couldn't believe he just...forgot. He apologized and I know he feels bad, but I've been carrying it since. I was so hurt that something that mattered so much to me didn't even cross his mind."

Lori nodded understandingly, her brain instantly flooded with a thousand deeply ingrained marriage counseling techniques she'd like to discuss with Angie. But this wasn't a therapy office, this was yoga on the beach.

"It's completely understandable that you were hurt, Angie. But I think the main thing here is that he apologized and communicated that it was truly an honest mistake."

"He did." Angie sighed, raising her arms above her head to stretch. "And I want to forgive him. He's a good man, and I love him. I just hate how much he has to work sometimes. It feels like it always comes first."

That stung, hard. Lori couldn't even begin to count the number of times that Rick had uttered those words to her. She thought about how many romantic dinners she'd skipped out on or cancelled or missed because a client needed her.

"I think forgiveness is a wonderful word for you today," Lori said, sniffing and holding in her own splash of regret. "And I have to commend you for being so self-aware and compassionate toward your partner, even in an instance where you felt wronged. That's not easy to do. Do you feel like you've gained some peace from practice? And you're ready to forgive?"

Angie nodded, smiling with her eyes shut in her *shavasana* pose. "Definitely."

"That's fantastic. Thank you for opening your heart up to us today."

"I'll share my word." Lena, the third woman in the row of yoga mats, opened one eye and smiled at Lori.

Excitement zipped through her chest. This just might be a really good thing.

"Please do," Lori said slowly.

"My word is Patrick. He's my father. He passed away three months ago, and I miss him every single day. Whenever I come to the beach and see the sunrise, it's like I can feel him here with me."

"Oh, Lena." Lori sighed, feeling the weight of grief pressing on her own heart, the way she always did when a patient talked about loss. She felt what they felt, and it was both a blessing and a curse, Rick used to say. "I am so deeply sorry."

"Thank you. He had a wonderful life filled with family and love. It's really all you could ask for. I just miss him, but I feel close to him now. I feel his spirit."

"That's beautiful." Lori walked over, taking Lena's hand. "His spirit lives on powerfully through you and your loved ones sharing his memories and holding him in your hearts."

"He loved the sunrise," she said with a peaceful smile. "He'd come out here fishing at five o'clock in the morning. We all thought he was crazy."

Lori laughed softly. "I just know this man was well-loved."

"Beyond."

"I'm sorry again for your loss, Lena. I hope that during this practice, especially with the sunrise in front of you, you're able to remember all of the wonderful things about your father and continue to feel his energy and spirit."

"I really do." Lena whispered. "Thank you."

"It's my turn now, I guess," the last woman, Keisha, lifted her hand slightly off her mat.

"Only if you're comfortable, Keisha," Lori explained gently as she walked back to her mat and sat down.

Keisha let out a soft exhale, keeping her eyes closed and her pose still. "My word is patience. I'd really like to work on my patience, especially with my daughter."

"I think that's an amazing goal, and something that so many of us can relate to," Lori said, reaching into her warmer box to distribute the best part of yoga practice— the hot towels.

She picked up three hot, rolled-up washcloths from the towel warmer and slowly walked around, placing one on each woman's forehead as they rested, thought, and enjoyed the sunrise practice.

"She just..." Keisha continued. "She's sixteen now."

"Tough age," Lena interjected.

"No kidding," Keisha responded with a laugh. "And it's like she tries to push every single last one of my buttons. I mean, that girl has some sass. Too much sass. Of course, my husband always says he knows where she got it from."

The other women laughed as they positioned the warm washcloths over their eyes and breathed slowly.

Lori gently handed a towel to Keisha, leaning down. "If she's talking back to you a lot, it sounds like she might be testing her boundaries with you."

"She's testing *everything* with me."

Lori chuckled at the tone. "You need to remember she's in a spot in her life where she's feeling more like a woman and less like a girl. She needs you, but she doesn't *want* to need you. She could be trying to see how hard she can push and still have your love and support, but also feel simultaneously like she's got some independence."

"I'm her momma," the woman said. "She could be in jail and she'd still have my love and support."

Lori smiled, standing up again. "I would make sure she knows that, without a doubt. It never hurts to express that unconditional love to her, and make sure she feels safe and secure in your love, even when she makes mistakes."

"I will. I'll do that." Keisha smiled, opening her eyes. "Thank you."

"This was a wonderful class, Lori." Lena sat up and held her knees to her chest, her face visibly more calm and relaxed than when she had first showed up to take Lori's yoga class that morning. "I feel rejuvenated."

"Oh, awesome." Lori clasped her hands together, pride swelling in her heart. "I'm so glad."

"You have a gift," Keisha agreed with a nod as the women began packing up their mats.

"Well, I don't know about that, but I have really been enjoying sharing my practice." Lori closed her eyes and drew in a deep inhale, filled with salt and warmth and...home.

"Coffee?" Sam offered Lori a steaming mug as soon as she wandered into the cottage after her morning yoga class.

"Absolutely. Thank you." Lori wrapped her hands

around the cup and smiled, marveling at how quickly and seamlessly this beachside cottage had become such a place of comfort for her.

Sweeneys were always just *around*. Sometimes more than others, but they were always there in some form of gathering, like honeybees at the hive. There was always food and drinks and good company. The cottage was a home base, a place where they could all go at any hour of any day and find family, laughter, and support.

Lori had never known anything like it, but after this past month, she wasn't sure she could ever live without it.

"So, class was good?" Sam asked brightly, guiding them out to the back deck where Julie and her daughter, Bliss, were strumming guitars and humming a soft, pretty tune. "I peeked over and saw you got some customers."

Lori slid Sam a playful look as they assumed seats on the cushioned sofa out back. "I know they were your friends from Ben's school."

"So?" Sam shrugged. "They were your yoga students. I just helped them find the best instructor in town."

"Thank you," Lori said, genuinely meaning it. "It was a wonderful class. I'm loving every second out here on the water."

Julie looked up from her guitar, her straight black hair falling around her face. "There's really nothing like it, is there?"

"Nothing at all." Lori rocked back, lifting her coffee mug to her nose and inhaling the deep, rich smell as the waves lapped up onto the shore.

"Your yoga class looked like fun," Bliss chimed in,

looking bright and glowing and beautiful, with mountains of shiny blond hair and skin like porcelain. "I'd love to take one sometime."

"Please do," Lori said with a joyful smile. "You're always welcome. Plus, I give a one-hundred-percent-off family discount."

Bliss giggled. "I can't wait."

Lori studied the pair for a moment, Julie and Bliss. The way they nudged each other with laughter as they played all different notes and chords on their guitars. The way they could seemingly read one another's minds as they conjured up the earliest draft of song lyrics.

It was a beautiful relationship between a mother and daughter who were truly bonded and totally inseparable in their hearts. Sam and Taylor were the same way, and it seemed that each Sweeney daughter shared that kind of connection with Dottie as well.

It was beautiful, but sad, as Lori's heart throbbed with grief for her own mother, who had adopted her as an infant and gave her the most incredible life.

Dottie emerged from the kitchen, looking almost ethereal in a long, flowing, light blue cotton dress, with her soft white curls falling around her face. "Look at all these gorgeous girls on my back porch."

"Hey, Mom." Sam scooched over to make room for Dottie on the couch.

She sat down, wrapping her shoulders in a soft green throw blanket. She turned and gave Lori a kind smile. "Yoga class this morning looked lovely."

"Thank you, it was." Lori nodded and took a sip of

her coffee. "I was just telling these guys how much I'm loving it here on the beach."

"I'm thrilled for you. It is truly a magical place."

Dottie's words sounded genuine, and she was as sweet and angelic as anyone could be. But Lori still couldn't help but feel a bit weirder around her than she felt around any of the other Sweeneys.

After all, she was Jay's daughter with another woman. That was an elephant in the room that just couldn't seem to disappear, at least in Lori's mind.

But Dottie was such a force of goodness and love and kindness, it was hard to tell if she was even bothered. Unless she was extremely bothered and just putting on a good face for Lori, because, well, that's who Dottie was.

"So, Lori." Julie set her guitar to the side and leaned back on her deck chair. "I'm happy you're enjoying it here. You know, when Sam and I ambushed you in Raleigh a couple months ago, we never thought this is how things would end up. It's seriously such a gift, although I know the circumstances that led you here were obviously not ideal."

"That seems to be the common pattern," Sam chimed in, laughing softly.

"No kidding." Bliss snorted. "We came here because I needed a kidney. *And now I neeeever want to leave!*" She sang the words like a bird, laughing up at the sky.

Lori's heart warmed. "You know, I have to say, I really do feel like I'm doing it. The whole...starting over, new chapter thing you all talked about."

Sam gave Lori a knowing look, beaming at her. "Once you drink the Cocoa Beach Kool-Aid, you're hooked."

She laughed. "I am hooked! I'm inviting change, embracing spontaneity...This is all very new to me, you know? I'm that person who's planned every detail of her life from the time she was in kindergarten. But I feel like I'm diving into this new beginning, and it feels really good." She placed a hand on Sam's and gave it a squeeze. "I'm so thankful for you all."

As the love and support echoed around the deck, Lori couldn't help but notice that Dottie was a little quiet.

Lori's mind stirred, but she decided that the best way to approach all of this was one step at a time.

But the steps were being taken, and, despite the ache in her heart over her broken marriage, the constant worry about Amber and sadness for the pain her daughter endured...she was moving forward.

Little by little, she was becoming whole again.

Chapter Fifteen

Annie

The newly installed chimes on the front door of the bakery echoed through the store, and Annie looked up from her mixing bowl to see a face that made her very, very happy.

"Well, would you look who the cat dragged in?" Annie brushed the flour on her hands onto her apron, which was already coated it in, and rushed over.

Taylor Parker had walked through the doorway, her mouth gaping with shock and awe as she looked around at the nearly finished bakery. "My Ex-Work Mamma is killing it already! This place looks stunning!"

"Thank you, girlie!" Annie gave Taylor a hug and invited her to sit at the little two-top by the front window, Annie's personal favorite perch in the small bakery dining room. She hurried back to the kitchen and brought out two freshly decorated Key Lime Bliss cupcakes, a new experimental flavor. "You haven't seen it since I first leased the place, right?"

Taylor made a pouting face, peeling the paper off the cupcake. "I'm so sorry I haven't been here more, Annie. Things have been crazy at work and even crazier in my personal life. I'm sure Mom has filled you in."

Annie nodded, folding her hands together on the table between them. "The romance puzzle isn't getting any easier to solve, is it?"

"Not even remotely." Taylor shook her head. "It's just...they're both such great guys. Such different guys. And I never intended for this to happen, you know? It's not like I set out on a quest to find a man and now I've got to choose one. I was supposed to hate men. Isn't that what crappy dads do to their daughters? Make them hate men? Why didn't that work on me?"

Annie laughed sympathetically and gave Taylor's hand a loving pat. "Because you're strong and smart and aware enough to know that not all men are untrustworthy cheats like your father. Sorry."

Taylor held up a hand to say no apologies necessary.

"As I've said a thousand times," Annie continued. "You deserve love. And, clearly, both Kai and Andre think so, too."

She blew out a sigh, taking her first bite of the Key Lime Bliss cupcake. "I guess, and..." Her eyes popped out wide. "Holy cow, Annie, this might be your best ever."

"Really?" Annie gasped excitedly as she nibbled the edge of her own cupcake. It was pretty dang good, if she did say so herself. "Thanks, Tay. I'm trying to come up with a huge variety of new flavors before I open, and I was really trying to drive home that Florida feel with this one."

"Well, you nailed it." Taylor took another bite, closing her eyes with pleasure. "This literally tastes like vacation."

"I'm glad to hear it. Anyway, enough raving—tell me more about your suitors."

Taylor curled her lip, clearly more interested in her dessert than talking about her love life. "I'm just stuck. Kai is my dream guy. You know all too well how much I pined over him when he left."

"There was pining," Annie conceded. "There was a good bit of pining."

"But Andre is...so caring and sweet and has quickly become one of my best friends. And I feel like Kai is here for the Ron Jon thing, even though he says he's here for me. I just can't shake the feeling that I'm, I don't know, a perk. An added benefit of a move he would have probably made regardless."

Annie nodded. "I get that."

"But isn't that, like, super insanely selfish of me to think? Who cares why he's here? The fact is he's *here*, and I should be happy. But Andre is constantly on my mind. I miss him when I'm not with him. Everything makes me think of him. I wonder if what I have with Kai is more of an attraction."

Annie finished her last bite of fruity, cakey deliciousness and gave Taylor an understanding look. "I know this is the last thing in the world you want to hear, but no one can figure this out for you except you."

"You're right." Taylor licked some soft green frosting off the tip of her finger. "That is the last thing I want to hear. But enough about me, please. What's new with you? Besides, you know, opening the world's most fabulous bakery."

Annie laughed, glancing around with beaming pride as she indulged in Taylor's compliment. The Cupcake Queen was, in fact, shaping up nicely. "Not much, really. This has taken up pretty much all of my time and energy."

Taylor raised a brow, not buying it. "I've heard a rumor about a hot single dad who owns the gym next door?"

Annie cracked up. "Who spread that rumor? As if I didn't know."

"A little birdy." Taylor chuckled. "Who requested to remain anonymous."

"Oh, Sam. She's one to talk about love lives. The woman who is having the world's most public 'secret' relationship." She held up air quotes.

"Hah! I know, right?" Taylor shook her head. "Literally the whole town knows. Except Ben, I guess, which is what matters. Now, what's the deal with gym guy, Annie? Please let me meddle in your life to distract me from my own. It seems to be what I do these days."

"There's no deal, really." Annie leaned back in the high-top chair, brushing a couple of crumbs into her napkin as she thought about Trevor Patterson and how there was, in fact, nothing at all going on.

Even though part of her—a big part, growing bigger every day—might have wanted there to be.

Taylor shot her a signature "get real" glare, so Annie continued.

"There isn't," she insisted. "His daughter, Riley, is a sweet and gregarious little thing. She followed her nose to the smell of cupcakes and the color pink and found her way into the bakery when I was first setting up. We bonded, and I told her she could come around anytime, as long as it was okay with her father. Yes, Trevor is, I admit, a rather good-looking man. Early forties, owns a gym."

"So basically rom-com material."

Annie let out a sigh. "Basically, except that he lost his wife, Tay. And this isn't a rom-com. He's still grieving, and probably will be for a long, long time. He's raising that little girl all by himself—believe me, you can tell from the way her bangs are trimmed—so he's not exactly prime dating material. Besides, I was supposed to swear off men after my Click dates went completely awry. The bakery is my destiny, remember?"

Taylor laughed, waving a dismissive hand. "You just haven't met the right person yet, Annie. The bakery *is* your destiny, but that doesn't mean you should do it all alone. And, from what my mom described, this Trevor guy had total eyes for you, and it was not subtle."

The reminder made a zing of hope zip down Annie's spine, but she quickly pushed away the ridiculous notion. "Your mother is prone to hyperbole. Even if he wasn't a widower and I was actually looking to date someone— which I'm *not*..." She emphasized that with a glare. "He would never even look at me that way. Please. He's so out of my league it's laughable."

Taylor arched a dubious brow. "The little birdy says otherwise."

"The little birdy is misinformed and exaggerating," Annie said playfully. "If Trevor dates anyone, he goes after fitness models and gym rats. Not bakers with a few extra pounds on 'em."

"Annie Hawthorne!" Taylor shot back, fire in her brown eyes. "You are gorgeous, inside and out, and a complete and total catch. Any guy would be lucky to have you."

Annie smiled and felt her cheeks warm. "You're sweet, Taylor. But—"

"I'm dead serious." And she looked it. "You have got to see your worth, Annie. That dude likes you. He obviously trusts you with his daughter, and from what it sounds like, he finds any excuse to come over here."

"Well..." Annie twisted a curl. "He did come and help me with the circuit breaker when I was having one of my many electrical issues."

"See?"

"And he's popped in to taste a few flavors here and there when he picks up Riley..."

"Any excuse." Taylor raised her brows. "He's into you, Annie. You should do something about it. Like you did about the bakery. You felt a strong pull, a calling for something, and you went out there and made it happen. And now? Look around." She gestured at the bakery. "You've done it! You can't sit and wait for life to happen to you."

Annie took Taylor's words in and processed them slowly. "Taylor Parker..."

"What?"

"You are so wise beyond your years, it's mesmerizing."

Taylor straightened her back and grinned proudly. "Thank you. I'm also right. Why don't you go over there with a few of these heavenly Key Lime bad boys?"

"Just...because?" Annie could already feel nerves tingling in her chest at the very thought of stepping foot into Ace Fitness and seeing Trevor, who would no doubt be in some sort of muscle tank with the perfect amount of sweat beading along his hairline.

"Because you made this new flavor and you thought he and Riley would love it." Taylor shrugged. "What more reason do you need?"

"Well, I suppose I could..." Annie dug hard for a reason not to do this, a way to talk herself out of it...but she couldn't find one.

She had to admit to herself that Taylor was annoyingly correct. She did feel sparks with Trevor, even more so than she'd admitted to anyone else. Maybe he did notice her. Maybe it wasn't completely in her head.

Maybe it was time she grabbed the bull by the horns —well, the cupcake tray—and made a move.

After all, what did she have to lose?

"Let's go." Taylor popped up out of her chair, grabbing Annie's arm and giving her a solid yank. "You have all those delicious cupcakes just sitting there, waiting to be your ticket to romance."

Annie laughed and glanced at the tray on the counter. She had to admit, they were gorgeous.

Normally, she'd bring the extras over to The Sanctuary, a women's shelter down the street that often reaped the benefits of Annie's overbaking, but something clicked in her mind and heart at Taylor's encouragement, and one question rang through her mind loud and clear:

Why not?

"Now..." Taylor looped her arm through Annie's as she grabbed the tray of six Key Lime Bliss cupcakes. "I'm going to go to my car, because, believe it or not, I do actually have to get to work. And you are gonna take that adorable booty next door and reciprocate some of that interest he's been showing you. 'Kay?"

Annie took a deep breath, feeling light on her feet and a bit giddy. "Okay."

Taylor swung the door open and held it for Annie, giving her a reassuring wink before she flipped her car keys out of her purse. "Go get your man, Annie Bananie."

Annie rolled her eyes and shook her head. "Why is it always you talking me into these ridiculous things?"

"That's what ex-work daughters are for!" Taylor gave an exaggerated hair flip as she flounced through the parking lot to her little red car and opened the driver's-side door.

As she watched Taylor pull her car out and drive away from the shopping center, Annie took a deep breath and shut her eyes, inching closer to the front door of Ace Fitness.

It was just a cupcake delivery. It didn't mean anything. Did she want it to mean something?

Well, kind of. She couldn't deny she liked Trevor. But...who wouldn't?

As thoughts bounced around in her mind, Annie sat

down on a wooden bench outside the front of Ace Fitness to gather herself before making her big move.

She placed the covered cupcake tray next to her on the worn-out wood, and as she was setting it down, something caught her eye—something she'd never seen or noticed before.

On the back of the bench, there was a faded golden plaque. She leaned over to read the words.

"In Loving Memory of Alexandra "Ace" Patterson. My wife, my lover, my best friend. We miss you every day."

EMOTION HITCHED in Annie's throat as her hand rose to her lips and her high came crashing down. Fast.

This bench had been outside of Trevor's gym since Annie moved into her bakery, but she'd never read the plaque before. She'd never known the gym was named after his late wife.

Ace.

Suddenly, reality hit her like a ton of bricks, and she grabbed her tray of cupcakes, stood up, and headed right back into the bakery.

What was she doing? What was she thinking? Trevor Patterson was a broken, grieving widower who lost the mother of his child. She had no place to come in and try to flirt with him—it was wrong on every level.

His heart was taken by someone else—someone he called "Ace," and it always would be. Annie would never compare to the woman he lost, and she would never even think about trying.

Her mind flashed back to the question that got her out the door in the first place: why not.

Well, that was why not. And that was why it never would be.

Chapter Sixteen

Sam

"Oh, yes." Dottie smiled widely, nodding with approval as she and Sam stood next to each other, admiring the newly installed drapes that hung from floor to ceiling in the lobby of Sweeney House. "Those are fantastic."

"Aren't they?" Sam studied the window treatments, sheer white curtains with thin blue stitching running vertically through them. The blue complemented the vast ocean and sky that filled the sliding glass doors between the drapes, and it brought everything together in such a perfect way.

"So..." Dottie turned to Sam. "What's next? Everything seems to be coming along quite well."

"It really is." Sam pulled out her phone to look through one of her many renovation plans and checklists, taking note of their rapid progress. "We're going to have to tackle the decorating of the dining room, which is pure fun."

Dottie grinned, her eyes brimming with excitement. "Can't wait for that one."

"Most of the suites are close to finished. A couple of the downstairs bathrooms need to be retiled still, and of course Ethan is working on several antique restorations at the moment. We'll have to figure out where we want all the furniture to go when he's done." Sam did her best to speak about Ethan Price as if he was nothing more than a colleague, a friend, and Ben's math teacher.

"Mm-hmm." Dottie arched a brow, not buying the coyness but letting it slide. "And what about the kitchen?"

They walked side by side through the lobby to head back and check out the progress in the brand new, state-of-the-art kitchen, which hopefully would bring all of Sam's visions for an in-house restaurant serving "laidback luxury in a beachfront oasis" to life.

"We're just waiting on a stove and a walk-in freezer..." Sam said slowly, tapping through her notes about the orders. "We should be able to open back up for business by, maybe, spring? Assuming all goes according to plan."

"That's a big assumption," Dottie teased, nudging her shoulder. "But that would be wonderful."

As they walked through the lobby, a truck pulling into the circular driveway of the inn caught Sam's attention through the front doors. She immediately recognized the truck as Ethan's.

"What is he doing here?" Sam asked, with a little more excitement in her voice than she'd intended.

"Not sure," Dottie said. "Is he dropping off a finished piece?"

"He didn't mention anything to me." Sam walked toward the front door to greet him.

"Maybe it's a surprise." Dottie added an exaggerated wink. "I'll leave you to it."

Sam smiled at her mother and stepped out onto the front porch of Sweeney House, the sunshine warming her skin. "Hey, you." She waved a hand.

The front door of Ethan's truck swung open, and he hopped out, wearing that cheesy smile that felt more and more like home the more Sam saw it.

A quick jolt of anxiety zipped through her as she thought about their last heavy conversation and his weirdness about his past, but she tamped it down.

She had to respect his wishes. They could still eventually develop a serious relationship even if she didn't know his full story, couldn't they?

"This is a surprise." Sam walked forward, shielding her eyes from the afternoon sun as Ethan opened his arms for a tight embrace.

"How are you?" he asked, holding her close.

"Better now." Sam pulled back and smiled, planting a soft kiss on his lips. "Whoops. Hope no one saw that."

Ethan shook his head and laughed, his blue eyes dancing. "I just wanted to stop by to bring you something."

Sam craned her neck to peer into the truck bed, expecting to see a piece of furniture covered in a sheet, ready to be displayed and adored in one of the Sweeney House suites. "Whatcha got for me, furniture man?"

"Actually, it's not in the truck." His eyes danced in the sunlight as he smiled down at her.

"Oh." She furrowed her brow in confusion. "What is it?"

Ethan reached into a pocket and pulled out something small, cupping it in his hand. "It's silly, but...I made you something."

Anticipation zinged through Sam as she looked into his hand.

He opened it, revealing a small circle of shiny wooden beads. "It's a bracelet!" She gasped, taking it gently from his hand and admiring the perfect spheres of the hand-cut beads. "I love it."

"I carved the beads out of wood scraps from your dad's clock. I knew how important the clock was to you, so when I shaved it down and cut some pieces to reshape the finish, I was really careful and saved the extra wood. I wanted to use it for something special."

Sam ran her fingers over the shiny finishing on the wooden bracelet, sliding her fingers across the beads. Suddenly, she noticed carvings on three of the beads. "You engraved it?" She looked up at him with wide eyes.

"Yeah, look." He leaned in, pointing to three letters etched side by side into the wood. "S, T, and B. For Samantha, Taylor, and Ben. So they're always with you."

Sam felt her eyes fill as she pressed the bracelet against her heart, clutching it tightly. "I love it so much, Ethan. Thank you. I'll never take it off."

He grinned. "I'm so glad. Anyway, I've got a mountain of derivative tests waiting to be graded, so I better head back, but..." Ethan cocked his head, a playful, adoring smile on his lips. "See you tonight?"

Sam slid the bracelet onto her wrist, swallowing the rise of anxiety in her throat.

Could this move forward? Could this become something real? Was Ethan her second chance at lifelong love?

She glanced up at him, wondering how in the world she would ever be able to accept the fact that there were things about him she won't know. She'd never fully understand him or his past, but...

She twisted her wrist around, staring down at the bracelet.

"See you tonight."

As Ethan kissed her again then got in his truck and drove away, Sam was left with a breathless uncertainty, mixed with the heady whirlwind of knowing that she was falling in love, and nothing could be done to stop it.

"What was that all about?" Dottie asked with a raised brow as Sam stepped back into the lobby of Sweeney House. "A little not-so-secret rendezvous?"

Sam rolled her eyes and stifled a laugh. "No one's around. And his visit had a purpose, actually."

"What was that?"

"Look." Sam held out her wrist, showing Dottie the handcrafted bracelet and pointing out the engraved initials of her and her kids. "He made this for me with some wood scraps from when he renovated the clock."

Dottie gasped, her eyes visibly filling at the very mention of Dad's beloved grandfather clock. "Jay's clock?"

"Yes." Sam smiled. "Isn't it beautiful?"

Dottie gently touched the wooden beads, rolling

them around between her fingers. "S, T and B. Wow. He made this for you. It's...it's so lovely, Sam."

Sam took a deep breath, weight pressing on her chest. "It is. I love it. He's so thoughtful, and...he's amazing."

Dottie looked up from the bracelet, her brows furrowed instantly as she detected the flatness in Sam's tone. "He is amazing. But why do I get the feeling you're having second thoughts about all of this?"

"Oh, Mom." Sam huffed out a sigh and shook her head.

Without another word, Dottie guided them both over to the sitting area in the lobby, which, despite the sawdust and plastic sheets hanging up around them, was still a lovely place.

"Talk to me." Dottie took Sam's hand and leveled her gaze. "You have this new, budding, *secret* romance, but something is wrong. I sense it."

"Nothing is wrong, really." Sam toyed with the bracelet. The longer she looked at it, the more her heart folded over how sweet and wonderful it was.

But were there things about Ethan she would never know? Could she live with that? Could she go all-in on this relationship and accept that?

"Then what is it, honey?" Dottie frowned with confusion and concern. "Are you not happy that the relationship has to be secret? Certainly once Ben is out of his classroom, you two will naturally be able to shift to—"

"No, no." Sam shook her head. "It's not that. Besides, I don't really think the whole thing is that much of a secret anymore."

Dottie angled her head. "It's not. But I've kept my lips sealed."

Sam snorted. "It's fine. It's not that."

"Well, if you're questioning his commitment or his feelings for you, you ought to stop right now and look at what's on your wrist." Dottie punctuated her sentence with a firm nod. "I hate to even breathe this name, but Max never did anything so thoughtful and adoring."

"No kidding," Sam said. "I know that. It's just that... he's divorced, Ethan."

"Right. So are you."

"Yes, that's not the issue. When I ask him about his divorce, his ex-wife, his past marriage, any of it...he gets really weird."

"Weird how?" Dottie asked.

"He just sort of shuts down and puts a wall up. He said, in no uncertain terms, that he wants to leave the past in the past and only focus on the future with me. He doesn't want to talk about it or tell me what happened, and I'm not sure he ever will."

"Oh." Her mother leaned back, processing this with surprise. "I can certainly see how that would raise some red flags for you, Sam, but I do also understand that sometimes the past should stay the past."

"Well, yes, it shouldn't be dredged up and rehashed, but...if I'm going to get serious with this guy, shouldn't I at least know why he got divorced? What if he did something bad?"

"Do you think that's a possibility?" Dottie asked, matter-of-fact.

"I don't know," Sam said, toying with the bracelet. "What if he cheated? What if he did what Max did to someone else and he doesn't want me to know, because I won't want to be with him?"

"Oh, Sam." Dottie reached her hand out and touched Sam's arm, giving her a loving look of sympathy and support. "I'm so sorry your experience with marriage was one that became clouded in deceit and betrayal. You never deserved an ounce of it."

Sam swallowed a wave of emotion. "Thanks, Mom."

"With that in mind, maybe your trust issues are working overtime."

Sam eyed her. "You're starting to sound like Lori. Going all therapist on me."

"Well, am I wrong?" Dottie laughed.

"No, I guess not. Obviously, I'm bruised, and it's not fair to him for me to just assume the worst. But isn't it a little odd to you that he won't share anything about it?"

Mom leaned back, considering this. "I suppose it's odd, but he may open up to you in time. He's trying, Sam. That much is clear."

She couldn't argue that Ethan was making a full-court-press-level effort to pursue something real with Sam. And...it felt good.

But that nagging voice of worry in the back of her head wouldn't quiet down, and Sam feared that it would only get louder and louder the closer she got to Ethan.

"I have to know what happened."

"No, you do not," Dottie insisted sternly.

"I do, Mom. How can I fall in love with someone who won't share their past with me?"

"Maybe there's a good reason."

"And I should be aware of that reason."

Dottie narrowed her gaze, holding up a finger. "Samantha Sweeney. Do not go digging."

Sam clenched her jaw.

"Do. Not. Go. Digging."

"I mean..." She sucked in a breath. "I'm not going to dig hard. I just want to know what happened. I can't let myself fall for him until I know it's safe."

"You have to trust him!" Dottie exclaimed. "That is the foundation of a relationship."

"Knowing each other's history is a pretty big part of that foundation, too."

"Don't dig, Sam. You're a digger. You can never leave well enough alone, and it could come back to bite you in this situation. Seriously."

Sam chewed her lip, her mind racing and her heart slipping with uncertainty.

What was she to do?

Well, dig, of course. The question was...how deep?

Chapter Seventeen

Taylor

"You absolutely need to go digging." Taylor eyed her mom sternly as she clumsily dumped her coffee into a travel mug, splashing some on the counter. "Whoops." She glanced at the clock on the oven. "I'm majorly late for work and now I'm spilling things. Great."

Sam absentmindedly yanked a paper towel off the roll and cleaned up Taylor's mess, her brain clearly in a thousand other places.

"But Tay...where do I even begin? I mean, what am I gonna do, Google his name? I'm not going to find anything about his divorce. It's not like those are public records or something."

"Where did he live before Cocoa Beach? He said he moved here after his marriage ended, right?"

"Yeah. Maryland." Sam glanced at Taylor, worry in her blue eyes. "A small town, I think he said Perryville."

"So, start there." Taylor laughed, shuffling around, throwing things into her tote bag. "This is like Lori all over again. Maybe you and Aunt Julie can take a secret road trip and hunt down his ex-wife. And then she can move to Cocoa Beach and start a new life!"

"Not funny."

"Kind of funny." Taylor grinned as she slipped her laptop into her bag. "But in all seriousness, Mom, you need to know what happened before you take one step further with this guy. I cannot even stand the thought of you getting hurt again."

And she couldn't. The very idea that her amazing, sweet, selfless mother could be failed by yet another man she loved made Taylor sick.

From what she could tell so far, Ethan Price was a good guy. She had no reason to believe that wasn't true. But...who knew?

Max Parker had certainly come off as a good guy... and, boy, did he have everyone fooled.

"I'm just worried that there's a reason he's keeping it under wraps." Taylor swung her bag over her shoulder and dug around in the bottom of it for her car keys.

Her mother leaned against the countertop, lost in thought. "When I talked to your grandma about it yesterday, she said I have to trust him."

"Like you trusted Dad?" Taylor shot back, without really thinking, instantly regretting the words. "Sorry. I'm sorry."

"It's okay." Her mom shook her head. "You're right, I did trust your father. Blindly. And look where that got me. I just wonder if maybe I should leave well enough alone and give Ethan the benefit of the doubt."

Finally fishing her car keys out, Taylor brushed her hair over her shoulder, slid her feet into a pair of flats by the front door, and looked at Sam. "If you're going to get serious with him, you need to know everything about his past. Or else there will always be a wall between you two. A disconnect."

Sam thought about this, pressing her lips together as she nodded her head slowly.

"You're right, Tay. I have to figure something out. I can't keep prying and bothering him about it, but...I need to know what happened. And why he's so weird about it."

"He's being sus. And it's not cool."

Sam angled her head. "Sus?"

"Suspect. Suspicious." Taylor took a swig of coffee. "Sus."

"Huh. Sus. Yeah, I suppose he is being sus." She laughed at her new lingo. "Speaking of sus, how was your dinner with Amber?"

"Sus."

They both laughed, and Taylor peeked at the clock once more. "No, seriously, it was cool. She's another one who's very quiet about her past and personal life, though. Can't quite get a read on anything, but we ended up bonding a bit and chatting once the tension wore off. Anyway, I gotta run or Uncle John's going to fire me. I'll fill you in more later."

"Off you go, my little corporate queen." Sam waved her off. "See you tonight."

Taylor swung open the front door of the cottage, instantly flooding the house with morning sunlight and warmth. "Good luck, Momma!"

She hopped in the car and sped down A1A, her mind doing the usual dance as it bounced between work, Kai, Andre, work, family, Andre, the kitties, a few unwanted thoughts about her father...and before she knew it, Taylor was pulling into the parking lot of the office building.

As she headed into the lobby and up the elevator, she thought to herself how much it still bothered her, deep in her soul, whenever she thought about Dad.

Maybe it was talking to Amber about her father, who sounded like a decent dude, but sometimes there were moments—rare, rare moments—that she'd dare say she *missed* him.

With a breezy greeting to the agency's receptionist, she headed into the office, sliding into her cubicle and powering on her monitor.

After her usual morning rundown of email responses and to-do lists, Taylor clicked open a new tab on her web browser and went to Facebook.

Why am I doing this, she thought to herself. *Why am I torturing myself by looking him up, knowing full well it's going to do nothing but put me in a bad mood?*

Unable to resist, Taylor typed the forbidden name into the social media search bar and clicked on his profile page.

Max Parker.

She held her breath as she scrolled down to see his recent updates, which were all photos uploaded by Kayla that she, of course, tagged him in.

Gotta let the world know he's hers for real now, Taylor guessed.

Nausea rose in her stomach as her gaze fell into the first picture, which showed Max and Kayla sitting on the side of the fountain in the middle of Winter Park Village, a location Taylor was all too familiar with.

Surrounded by stores, restaurants, and a movie theater, the village was a common spot for family fun when she and Ben were growing up, back when they could call themselves a family.

But now, there he sat with his new family, his hair slightly dotted with grey that somehow didn't make him look any older. His arm was wrapped tightly around Kayla's bony shoulders and stick arms, and her somehow perfect baby bump actually looked adorable in a tight floral dress.

Taylor stared at the picture, stared at her father and the giant, sincere, joyful smile plastered on his face. How was he so happy? Why was he allowed to be that happy after what he'd done to their family?

All this was, she admitted to herself, was a reminder that a woman needed to choose wisely. And when faced with a decision about a boyfriend, a lover, a husband...it had better be done right.

And all that did was confuse her more.

She clicked off the page and filled the rest of the morning with focus on work, catching up on her projects and answering clients, and when her mind drifted away from her job, she thought about Andre and about how she should be thinking about Kai but was thinking about Andre.

Yikes.

Next thing she knew, it was time for lunch, and Taylor could feel her stomach growling. Before she had the chance to grab her sandwich out of the fridge and send Annie her daily "work lunches aren't the same without you" text, her phone buzzed with a call from Kai.

Taylor pressed it to her ear. "Hello?"

"Hi, Tay. You hungry?"

A smile pulled as she swiveled in her desk chair. "How'd you know?"

"This is when you usually eat lunch, isn't it? Why don't you meet me downstairs and let me take you out?"

He was persistent, she had to give him that.

"I suppose my turkey sandwich can wait. Or get snatched up by my uncle." Taylor grabbed her purse and stood up. "Okay, I'll be down in a sec."

Taylor headed downstairs, quickly fixing her hair and slapping on some lip gloss in the elevator, determined to go into this with an open mind and heart.

Kai was here, coming to her work, making an effort. He wanted her. Maybe it was that simple.

"Hey, gorgeous." Kai stood in the sunny parking lot next to his open-sided Jeep, his arms stretched wide as he reached for her.

"Hey there." Taylor hugged him, closing her eyes for a moment and willing herself to remember the wild, dizzying crush she'd had on him that summer. He felt great, smelled amazing, and just holding him put a smile on her face.

That crush feeling would return eventually, wouldn't it?

"So, where are we headed?" she asked as he helped her into the passenger's side of the Jeep.

"It's a surprise." Kai glanced at her with a smile as he pulled out of the parking lot and headed down the road.

The wind whipped through the open Jeep, but Taylor relished the freeing sensation, extending her arm and letting her hair fly all around her.

She and Kai chatted in the Jeep, mostly about the sponsorship work and a bit about Taylor's job and family. After what felt like a quick drive, Kai pulled into a beach-side building that Taylor had never been to before.

"Where are we?" She hopped out of the car and looked up, holding her hand over her face to block the sun and studying the building.

It was a small, two-story brick building with white shutters and only a few cars in the parking lot.

"Is this a restaurant?"

"No. It's a rooftop garden." Kai reached into the backseat of the Jeep, pulling out a huge wicker basket. "We're going to have a picnic."

"Oh, wow." Taylor held her hands to her chest and smiled. "That's...really nice."

And it was. It was wonderful. He was wonderful. Why did she have to keep reminding herself of that?

"Come on." Kai jutted his chin toward the little building, which was hidden behind sea grapes and shrubs.

They climbed up a spiral staircase around the back side, and ended up on a second-story rooftop covered in greenery. Vines, bushes, and flowers filled the space from top to bottom, and cute picnic tables and benches were scattered around the roof.

A couple of families and groups sat around in various places, but it was relatively quiet, which Taylor was thankful for.

She and Kai set up at a picnic table next to the edge of the roof, overlooking the beautiful ocean view.

"How did you find this spot?" she asked, digging into the assortment of fruit, cheese, crackers and meats that Kai had packed in the basket. "It's such a cool place. I've never even heard about it."

"Honestly? This whole idea was handed to me by my PR manager at Ron Jon. I told her I needed a plan for something sweet and romantic, and she was like, 'Do a picnic on the Eighth Street rooftop.'" He popped a grape into his mouth. "I knew she'd have something brilliant."

A wave of disappointment settled in Taylor's gut as she learned that Kai didn't come up with this on his own. He didn't have this idea to do something for her, he just got someone at his job to help him with it.

She wasn't a prize that could be won, but the last thing she wanted to do was argue with Kai and end up crying again.

A gesture was a gesture, and this one was *very* nice.

"So, you're liking it here?" Taylor asked, eating a cracker with some brie on it. "Is the plan to stay long-term, then?"

"Hopefully." Kai smiled, the sunlight glinting in his eyes. "I'll still have to bounce around a lot for competitions, and now all of this marketing and endorsement stuff, it's a lot. Most of it's local, though, so that's good."

"That is good." Taylor took a sip of the iced tea he'd

packed and studied him. "I'm glad you're enjoying it so much. I wasn't sure if you'd love all the press and attention when you first told me about the gig."

"It was an adjustment, definitely." Kai brushed some hair away from his forehead. "But, I don't know, I've kinda just decided to roll with it, take it as it comes. Besides, it brought me to you, so what more can I ask for?"

Taylor felt herself blush, and she glanced out at the ocean view. "How's your family handling you being gone?"

"They're not thrilled," he said candidly. "But with Kona there taking over the farm, it's really not too bad. She's hired some extra labor and my parents are able to really slow down, which was their goal. I miss them, of course, but...I'm happy I'm here." He locked eyes with Taylor. "I missed you more."

"I missed you, too," she said. And she had...until...

Don't think about Andre, she reminded herself. *Focus on Kai. You're here with Kai.*

As she and Kai chatted, ate, looked at the ocean, and enjoyed each other's company, Taylor couldn't help but notice that nagging voice in the back of her mind that made her feel like something was missing.

He was still charming and funny and completely adored her. But something had shifted, and Taylor wasn't sure it could ever shift back.

After they finished eating, they decided to take a walk on the beach, since Taylor didn't have anything too pressing at the office, and this seemed to be the first real, uninterrupted quality time she'd been able to get with him.

They headed down the spiral stairs and out onto the sand, leaving their shoes in the Jeep as they walked out.

"It's been an adjustment to the waves here, for sure," Kai mused as they talked, the waves splashing up around their ankles. "The waves in Hawaii are so different. I always have to get used to it when I come back to Florida."

"Have you had a lot of time to surf?" Taylor asked. "I haven't seen you in my backyard too much."

"Sadly, no, and when I do, it's only a quick session, so I just go behind my house." He lowered his gaze. "I miss showing up in your backyard."

She smiled.

"Those mornings were wonderful," he added.

"Kai? Kai Leilani?" Suddenly, a young boy's voice caught their attention, and Taylor turned around to follow the high-pitched excitement.

"Mom! That's him, the famous surfer!" Two boys, no older than nine or ten, walked on either side of a woman along the sand, pointing eagerly at Kai.

"Wow, how exciting." The mother grinned, crouching down to her sons, who both broke away from her and tore toward Taylor and Kai.

"Kai! Kai!" One of them jumped excitedly. "Can we get a picture?"

Kai shot Taylor a look that seemed apologetic, but something in his eyes glimmered with satisfaction at the attention.

"Please, go ahead." Taylor smiled graciously and stepped aside.

The mom snapped a picture on her phone of her two sons standing on either side of Kai, all three of them holding up a "hang ten" sign with their hands.

"Awesome! Thanks, bro!"

"Of course!" Kai high-fived the kids and said good-bye, but the peace was short-lived.

A swarm of teenage girls noticed him next, and all wanted him to sign their surfboards and sunhats.

He obliged, of course, and Taylor stepped even further away this time, becoming more and more invisible by the moment.

It wasn't Kai's fault he was famous. And it wasn't like he was self-inflated or egotistical about it. But...he didn't hate the attention, either, that much was clear.

When she met him, all Kai wanted to do was surf. That was all that mattered. But now? It was photo ops and autographs and PR teams and a whole life he came here for. A whole world that didn't involve her.

And, frankly, Taylor wasn't sure she fit in that world at all.

"Sorry about all that." Kai gave her a sheepish smile and shook his head. "They put up those billboards on A1A with my face the size of the moon and now I can't seem to escape it."

"You like it, though," Taylor teased, hoping it didn't come off as a jab.

"I mean, I guess it's more fun than I thought it would

be." His phone rang, and he pulled it out of his pocket. "Sorry, Ron Jon's reps. Gimme a sec."

Taylor couldn't help but remember Andre ignoring multiple work calls just to have a conversation with her. She shouldn't be comparing them. She and Andre were just friends. But...

"Sorry about that, Tay." Kai walked back over, sliding his phone into the pocket of his khaki shorts. "I've got to get back. They're planning this big press event and need me there."

"No worries, I should get back to work anyway. Can you drop me back at the office?"

"I'm sorry, this is really urgent. They're bugging me like crazy and I'm already so close by. Is there any chance you could Uber?"

Taylor's heart sank. Seriously?

"I'm really sorry." Kai gave an apologetic grin.

Taylor knew she had to be understanding about the demands of his high-level sponsorship but...still.

"Of course." She waved a dismissive hand, determined to play it cool despite the uneasiness in her stomach. "No worries at all. I get it."

"You're the best, Tay." He planted a noisy kiss on her lips, and she didn't close her eyes.

The fifteen-minute Uber ride back to Coastal Marketing gave Taylor just enough time to let the dull throb in her heart become a full-on ache as a harsh reality rose to the forefront of her mind.

This wasn't the Kai she remembered.

She squeezed her eyes closed at the very thought,

knowing the insane pedestal she'd had him on as the perfect guy, the man of her dreams, her fantasy.

And yet...nothing about it felt like a fantasy. He was here, ten minutes down the road, planning picnics and making an effort to see her and acting like her boyfriend.

But there was a piece missing. There was an emptiness in the space between them, an emptiness that she certainly never felt for one second when she was with Andre.

Don't compare them, Taylor sternly reminded herself as the driver pulled into the parking lot of her office building. *You're not the Bachelorette.*

For all she knew, her chances with Andre were dead and gone after all of this Kai drama, and the thought stabbed.

He had been classy and graceful to step aside and return to their status as just friends, but what if he wouldn't ever want to be more than that again?

He didn't deserve to feel like someone's second choice, but the more Taylor thought about it, the more she realized that Andre Everett might have been her first choice, the obvious choice, all along.

Chapter Eighteen

Lori

Another wildly successful and beautiful yoga therapy session had Lori floating with joy as she padded along the beach, drinking in the morning light and the whisper of a chill that swirled through the breeze.

Despite her newfound peace and excitement over what this uncertain chapter of her life could bring, Lori couldn't stop the melancholy ache from shifting around in her chest.

She missed Rick. It was hard to accept, but even harder to deny. His voice echoed in her mind, the familiarity of it so engrained, it was as if he was still a part of her.

She supposed he would always be, but never in the same way.

Lori wondered if Sam ever missed Max. It was hard to imagine her having any feelings of even remote fondness or romanticism toward the man who betrayed her so brutally. But still, he'd been her husband. She'd loved him deeply at one point.

Sam was so strong and bold, so courageous in her new beginning. Lori envied that independent spirit, that freedom and determination to walk away from a long marriage with poise, grace, and a whole lot of certainty.

One of the things that nagged at her was the fact that Rick would really like this place. He'd always loved the beach, Lori remembered, her mind wandering back to the yearly family vacations they'd take to the Outer Banks of North Carolina when Amber was young. They'd always been so much fun, filled with quality time and laughter, showering Amber with love and memories and happiness.

Why did they stop taking those trips? When did their yearly Outer Banks tradition fade away? Amber had to have been in middle school when they stopped going for no particular reason, except that...

Lori couldn't get away from work.

She swallowed that harsh lump of guilt that perched in her throat, taking a deep breath as she stepped along the shoreline.

New beginnings. That's what she had to focus on.

Mom also loved the beach, and Lori missed her dear mother in a way that was completely different from how she missed Rick. The grief of her parents' loss was a dull ache, an ache that never fully went away, but remained calm enough for her to go through life and be normal most of the time.

It was the downside of her parents adopting her when they were almost fifty—she didn't have them on Earth with her nearly as long as she should have. But their years together were precious and wonderful, and Lori cherished the memories with her whole heart, thankful every single day that Margaret Edwards and Joseph Sweeney had placed her infant self in the hands of two real-life angels.

Lori longed for her mother. She ached to fall into her sweet, understanding embrace and cry about Rick. Cry about the fact that she'd lost her sense of direction at age fifty-five. Cry about poor Amber and the gross unfairness of what happened to her. Cry about it all to Mom.

As a therapist, Lori knew that many, many people never *truly* stopped needing their mother. And she no longer had one.

"Good morning!" A silhouetted figure several yards away walked toward Lori on the beach, arm waving.

Lori immediately recognized Dottie, taking her morning walk on the beach and heading back to the cottage, probably to have coffee with Sam and Julie.

She noticed the same uncertainty that played in the back of her mind whenever it came to Dottie. They had an odd relationship, with the only thing connecting them a man who Lori had never met, and Dottie had loved greatly for fifty years.

"Morning, Dottie." Lori waved back and smiled as they got closer to each other. "How are you?"

"I'm very well." Dottie took in a deep breath and basked in the morning peace of the beach, the breeze fluttering her dress. "What an absolutely glorious day."

"Isn't it?" Lori smiled, looking up at the sky. "I still can't get over the fact that it's almost December."

"Well, winters are sunshine-filled in Cocoa Beach," Dottie said. "Did you have a yoga class this morning?"

"I did, and it was amazing. I'm loving being an instructor, and it seems like the women who attend my classes really respond well to the interactive style I've been using." She shrugged. "I hope business continues to pick up."

"I'm sure it will. You have a natural calmness, a wisdom that follows you around." Dottie angled her head.

Lori reflected on the compliment, her gaze flickering to the other woman's. "Would you like to walk with me? For a little?"

Dottie hesitated, glancing down the beach and back toward the cottage, then smiling. "I'd love to."

Lori had never felt a strong urge to know much about her biological parents, aside from a bit of youthful curiosity in her teenage years. She felt content with not knowing. She'd always preferred it that way.

And yet, in this quiet early morning moment with Dottie, as they walked along the ocean, Lori suddenly felt a burning desire to know everything about Jay. She was suddenly curious about this man who was so highly revered and deeply beloved and responsible for creating such a tight-knit family.

"Can I ask you something?" Lori asked, glancing at Dottie to see her white curls billowing in the breeze, a look of contentment on her face.

"Of course. Anything at all."

"What was Joseph like? Jay, I mean." She laughed softly, knowing how massive the answer to such a question must feel to Dottie. "I've heard a couple stories and I know he was a wonderful man, I just...I don't know. Recently, I've been curious, especially while getting to know all of the Sweeneys, who are such amazing people. Obviously, a lot of that is due to you and your husband."

Dottie gave a bittersweet smile. "Oh, credit to Jay. He was quite a man, but not perfect." She leaned in, chuckling. "He was opinionated and loud, first and foremost."

Lori snorted softly. "Is that so?"

"Oh, yes. You couldn't get that man to shut up for love or money. But you'd never want him to, because his opinions were hilarious, and always correct, as he was happy to tell you. And he could spin a tale that held anyone listening rapt."

"Really." An image of a tall, talkative raconteur formed in her head, with more blank spots than clarity. "Tell me more."

"Well, he was brilliant. Smartest person I've ever met. He'd tell stories about his time in the Air Force, or the summer he worked on a farm in Idaho when he was fourteen, or the early days of our marriage, when we built Sweeney House from the ground up. And no matter how many times I'd heard the same stories, I'd listen. Mesmerized. Completely captivated by his animation and wit." She sighed lovingly. "The kids, too. He'd bounce little Sam or Erica on his knee, and they'd say, 'Daddy, tell us the story about milking the cows on the farm again!' And Jay would tell it again. And they'd giggle wildly."

Lori felt a warmth in her heart, a small bit of relief rippling through her, reassured to hear she came from such a loving gene pool.

"He sounds incredible." Lori placed a gentle hand on Dottie's arm, whose eyes were misty.

"He had such a command over every room," Dottie continued. "The charisma, the charm...Jay was one in a million. We loved each other in a way that doesn't even seem possible." She shook her head. "We were soulmates. Two halves of a whole."

Lori thought about how she and Rick used to feel that way. It always seemed like Rick was her missing puzzle piece, her other half. They'd been so deeply in love, Lori had always pictured their future like the life Dottie and Jay had, not a mess of divorce papers and sadness.

Her heart ached again, but she focused back on Dottie, wanting to keep her mind on the topic of her birth father.

"He was fiercely loyal to his family. Every single day of his life, no one ever wondered what his priorities were. His family was number one. Always."

Lori felt her eyes shutter closed, an unexpected sadness rocking her for a second.

This man was clearly a deeply devoted husband and father, anyone could figure that out just from spending five minutes with the Sweeneys. But it had been so seemingly easy for him to give her up all those years ago. He never tried to make contact, he never wanted to know her. The adoption was sealed.

Granted, she never reached out, either. But for someone who was obviously such a fervent believer in family, Lori was surprised that love was never extended to her. It was like she didn't exist to her birth parents.

"Wow," Lori said on a soft breath. "That's incredible."

"I didn't mean to make you feel like he didn't care for you, Lori," Dottie added gently, as if she could read her mind.

"Oh, of course," Lori said quickly, flicking her fingers. "I know that. It was a closed adoption, and I was raised by the most amazing parents. It was a different situation with me completely. I hold no grudges or judgments."

Dottie smiled, slowing her walking pace as she turned to Lori, placing a hand on her arm and leveling her sweet, blue gaze. "Then neither do I. And, I'm sorry, I know nothing about your mother. Your biological mother, I mean."

"I understand," Lori said, looking down at the petite woman, feeling a great weight lifting off her shoulders and a new connection with this kind woman. "Thank you for telling me about him and sharing your beautiful family with me, Dottie. I don't know where else I would have turned."

"You can always turn to us." Dottie faced forward again, and they continued walking down the beach as the sun lifted higher in the clear blue sky. "Me," she added with a nod of certainty. "You can always turn to me. I'm, what? Your birth-stepmother? Is that even a thing?"

Lori chuckled, nudging Dottie. "You're a saint, is what you are. Thank you."

"Now, I must ask..." Dottie turned to Lori with a curiously arched eyebrow. "How do you feel about becoming a grandmother in several months?"

"Oh my gosh." Lori groaned and shook her head. "I mean, there are things about it that I'm really looking forward to. I absolutely loved being a new mom, and I hope that it's the same way for Amber. I'm going to help in any way I can, and I'm definitely excited for all of the sweet baby moments and the 'firsts,' you know?"

"Of course I do."

"But it's definitely bittersweet, with Amber's...situation." Lori let her voice trail off, careful not to imply anything or go into any level of detail about Amber's past. No matter how close she got with Dottie or any of the Sweeneys, she would keep Amber's secret.

"Well, she needn't be embarrassed around us," Dottie asserted. "My kids have done worse things than a one-night stand. Stuff happens, and we will embrace both her and her baby with open arms."

Lori sucked in a breath, hating a lie, but knowing it was the only way. "Thank you, Dottie. You're a fantastic birth-stepmom."

Dottie laughed, and wrapped an arm around Lori as they walked.

Chapter Nineteen

Annie

Annie sat flipping through her computer, perched at her favorite sun-washed high-top table in the bakery, looking through her files of recipes, decorating techniques, and coming one step closer to finalizing her menu for opening day.

Which, hopefully, would be happening relatively soon.

Another batch of lemon-blueberry cupcakes were currently in the oven, and Annie was ready to test out the flavor with a hazelnut cream frosting she'd whipped up.

Decorating the place was just about finished and, she had to admit, the store was just darling. She'd also signed contracts with suppliers and delivery companies, and it seemed everything was really starting to come together. All that was left was to hire some staff and finish the menu, and Annie had already posted some help-wanted signs in the window and stuck fliers on some local bulletin boards.

She took a deep breath in an attempt to ease her jittery nerves about the whole undertaking, but as soon as she inhaled, her nose was filled with the bitter, harsh smell of...

Burning.

"Crap!" Annie shot up out of her seat and sprinted to the back kitchen, where there was a small stream of smoke coming from her giant oven.

"No, no, no!" she whined frantically, yanking the heavy duty plug out of the outlet and waving the smoke away as quickly as she could. "Not the lemon-blueberries!"

Cringing, she slowly opened the glass oven doors, which let out an awful smell and a good bit more smoke.

"You have got to be kidding me!" Annie grunted in exasperation as she slid on an oven mitt and pulled out the baking tray.

Lemon-blueberry cinderblocks is what they were. Coal black and hard as rocks. But they'd only been in there for seven minutes! How was it possible they'd gotten torched like that?

Annie hadn't burned a cupcake in years, she had her cook time down to absolute perfection.

Evidently not, she thought as she set down the depressing tray of black rocks and sighed with frustration.

"This darn oven," she whispered, walking over to it to try and understand what had gone so horribly wrong. It wasn't the first time this oven had gone wacky on her, or the second, or the third.

And Annie was starting to get concerned. She'd had an electrician in here, but he thought everything looked fine. She had the temperature set at 350, and this oven was way, way hotter than that. On a brand-new oven!

She cleaned up her burnt mess and decided to redo

her lemon-blueberry batch in her oven at home, which followed instructions and didn't have a mind of its own.

Vaguely aware of the back door opening as Annie scraped off the last bits of charred batter from her tray, she called over her shoulder. "Hey, Wiley Riley. I've got some majorly bad news for you, but I promise I'll make it up to you tomorrow."

"Actually, it's me." Trevor's voice surprised Annie, and she turned from the sink. She quickly wiped the ashy marks from her wrists and tried to scrape the scorched batter out from underneath her nails.

Heaven only knew what her hair looked like.

"Oh, hi!" She smiled, brushing her hands on her apron and walking over to the back doorway where Trevor stood, Riley next to him, holding his hand. "Sorry, I just assumed it was Riley coming in for her daily fix, which, sadly will not be available today."

"I thought I smelled something burning." Trevor glanced around, frowning. "Everything okay?"

"It's stinky!" Riley asserted, crossing her arms. "No cupcakes today, Miss Annie?"

Annie crouched down and gave her an apologetic look, trying not to laugh at the mismatched pink and orange sparkly outfit she had on, complete with glittery neon green Crocs and socks with unicorns on them. "I'm so sorry, sweetie. Something is seriously wrong with my oven, and I completely burned this batch."

"What do you think is going on with it?" Trevor asked. "Just a learning curve?"

"No clue." Annie stood back up, her gaze flickering to his, which was happy and warm and as friendly as always. "I never burn cupcakes, and they were only in there for seven minutes, but man. That thing just went wild. I ended up unplugging it and praying the fire alarm didn't go off again."

"Dang, I'm sorry about that." Trevor scratched the back of his neck, the bend in his arm accentuating a ridiculous biceps.

Annie forced herself to look away, turning back to face the aggravating oven in the kitchen behind them. "I'm going to have to call that electrician again, I think."

"I wish there was something I could do to help you out, but I'm really not much of a kitchen guy."

"It's twue," Riley added, standing up straight. "Daddy usually just makes me chicken nuggets or mac and cheese."

"Riley," Trevor said sternly, looking down at his daughter. "That's not true."

"Mostly," Riley insisted, crossing her arms.

Annie laughed, and Trevor turned his attention back to her.

"It's not true," he said. "She has a very balanced diet."

"Hey." Annie held up her hands defensively. "I'm not judging."

"Do you want to come bowling, Miss Annie?" Riley asked suddenly, a huge grin on her sweet little face as she jumped forward and bounced on her toes. "We're going bowling."

"Oh!" Annie drew back, surprised, and quickly assumed that she wasn't originally supposed to be invited. "That's very kind of you, Riley, but I'm sure your daddy wants to spend some quality time with just the two of you."

"Actually, I'd like you to come." Trevor smiled with just enough charm to give Annie a soft shiver. "That's sort of why we stopped over in the first place."

"Really?" Annie couldn't hide her shock. "Sure, I'd love to. I could seriously use a break from this maddening oven, anyway."

"Yay!" Riley leapt for joy, dancing around the room and rushing over to hug Annie's leg.

"You ready now?" Trevor asked, jutting his chin toward the door. "My last client of the day cancelled, so I figured we could get an early start."

Annie's mind raced with the hundred things she wanted to get done today, but the burnt batch of cupcakes had really ruined her spark. Plus, who could say no to the pair of faces in front of her?

"What the heck—let's do it."

The ride to Beachside Lanes was filled with Riley chattering on about the different places they passed, her new teacher at school, who she loved, and the latest toys that everyone simply *had* to have this Christmas. Which was only forty-four days away, Riley informed them.

Annie made a mental note that roller skates were back in, and that Riley couldn't stop talking about how much she wanted a pair.

"Riley, have you ever been bowling before?" Annie

asked in a rare moment of silence as Trevor drove, his gaze fixed straight ahead but a barely detectable smile inching across his face.

"Oh, yes! My fwiend Elise had her biwthday at the bowling place and I was the best one in the whole group."

"Why am I not surprised?" Annie turned around to give Riley a wink in the back seat.

"It's true," Trevor said. "She's an assassin with the four-pound ball."

Annie laughed, her heart feeling light as they pulled into the bowling alley, walked in and got assigned their lane, and set up at the end of the row.

"Daddy, do I have to wear these shoes?" Riley whined. "They're ugly."

Annie couldn't agree more, she thought, as she slid on the hideous and most unflattering bowling shoes.

"Yes, honey." Trevor, who could quite possibly be the first person ever to look hot in rental bowling shoes, gave her a fatherly stare. "Safety first. You don't want to slip."

"I just wanna wear my Cwocs." Riley sat on one of the plastic benches, wiggling her feet around in their neon green rubber slip-ons. "They're my favowite."

"They are very cute, Wiley, I have to say." Annie smiled at her. "I was pretty jealous when I first saw them. I kinda want a pair of my own."

"See, Daddy?" Riley asked excitedly, her big blue eyes wide with childish joy and bubbling enthusiasm. "Miss Annie knows that Cwocs are the best."

"Is that right, Miss Annie." Trevor glanced over his

shoulder, his brow flickering. "You'd rock a pair of neon green Crocs?"

"Heck, yeah, I would," Annie said, in solidarity with Riley. "Actually, they're supposed to be the best for standing on your feet for long periods of time, which I certainly do."

Riley's eyes lit up, and she ran over to her dad, cupping her hand around his ear and leaning super close to whisper something, her gaze locked on Annie.

Annie heard the words Christmas, crocs, and Miss Annie, and her heart nearly crumbled.

"I think that's an awesome idea." Trevor turned to his daughter with a smile, and Annie couldn't help but adore the two of them.

After they finally got a reluctant Riley into her bowling shoes and set up the lanes, the game began.

As she watched Riley shriek with laughter when she plunged the ball down the lane, and Trevor rush over when it looked, for a split second, like she was about to slip and fall, Annie felt a melancholy sadness settle in her gut.

She thought of the memorial bench. Of Alexandra. Ace, as he'd called her. She couldn't help but feel a little bit like she was living in someone else's life.

Alexandra should be here, watching her daughter giggle and her husband gently guide her arm and help her release the ball. She should be the one laughing and sipping Diet Coke and bowling gutter balls on purpose so Riley didn't feel so bad.

She snuck a glance at Trevor and wondered if he was thinking the same thing.

If he was, he sure didn't look like it. He seemed happy. He seemed lighthearted. Maybe he'd truly healed and was ready to find love again.

Maybe he could let go of the past, but...could she? Could she ever feel like there could be romance between them when he'd loved and lost someone else?

As Riley bowled a spare, with an assist from her daddy, Annie cheered and smiled and pondered this.

He glanced over his shoulder, his deep blue gaze lingering on her like she was seriously worth looking at for a long time. Like she was beautiful.

The extended eye contact made Annie blush.

Maybe Sam and Taylor were right. Maybe, against all odds and apparent rules of the universe, he was into her. Why else would he have brought her along today?

Shaking off her doubts and fears and hesitations, it was Annie's turn to bowl. She stepped up to the lane, clutched the heavy ball between her fingertips and took a deep breath.

Give me a sign, she thought to herself. *If I bowl a strike, this is the real deal.*

With her eyes still firmly closed, Annie swung her arm forward, sending the ball flying down the lane.

A couple of seconds later, the crash and clatter of bowling pins echoed back to her.

"Stwike!" Riley shrieked. "Miss Annie you got a stwike!"

Annie finally opened her eyes, turning to see Trevor and Riley were on their feet, cheering joyfully.

"Wow, I got one!" Annie pumped a victorious fist in the air, her heart floating.

"Beautiful throw." Trevor cocked his head, raising his brows as his eyes danced. "See? You're a natural."

"Thank you, thank you." Annie gave a dramatic curtsy and Riley continued clapping.

She sat back down on the bench and sipped her Diet Coke, watching the two of them like they were the adorable main characters of an aspirational sitcom.

Strike.

"She's out cold." Annie turned around to peek into the backseat, where Riley was slumped against the window, clutching Funny Bunny against her sweet little face.

"Extreme sports will do that to you," Trevor joked. "The way she bowls?"

"Very extreme," Annie agreed with a laugh.

The air in the car was peaceful and calm, but seemed to buzz with electricity every time Annie looked at Trevor.

"Annie, I've been thinking..." He turned the steering wheel and pulled into the parking lot of the shopping center where her bakery and his gym were. "I really want to take another look at the wiring in your bakery."

She smiled, warmed by his concern and kind willingness to help. "I appreciate it. Please, feel free, but the landlord said he'll send an electrical supervisor out here next week."

Trevor pressed his lips together as he pulled his truck into a parking spot, gently and softly, so as not to wake Sleeping Beauty in the back. "I know, it's just bugging me. Can I take a look?"

"Yes, you can, if you really think you might find something. I am fine leaving it up to the landlord, though. It's his domain." Annie glanced back at Riley again. "Plus, I don't want to wake her."

"I know, right?" He unclipped his seatbelt and shifted his body to face her, admiring his adorable daughter. "She sleeps so peacefully. Waking her up is the hardest thing ever."

Annie pressed a hand to her heart, watching little Riley's chest rise and fall with each deep breath, and wondered what she was dreaming about. "She's so darling. And she just adores you."

He lifted a shoulder. "Well, she and I have always had each other's backs. She doesn't adore what I do for a living, that's for sure."

Annie laughed. "Hey, you never know. Maybe you've got a future Olympic weightlifter on your hands."

Trevor looked back at Riley, her skinny little body all curled up in the corner of the seat. "She could be anything she wants to be. Her latest dream is to be a vet."

"She does have a heart for animals."

"But before that it was to be a duck."

Annie cracked up, giving him a quizzical look. "A duck?"

"Yes, she told me she wanted to be a duck when she grew up. I asked why and she told me, 'They just get to swim around and hang out all day, Daddy. That's what I want to do.'"

"Can you blame her?" Annie whispered with a soft laugh, looking back at Riley. "She is a little duck."

"So, of course, when I told her that becoming a duck wasn't really an option, she landed on either zookeeper or veterinarian."

"To be near ducks, I'm guessing."

He chuckled. "You know her all too well. Let's give her a few minutes," Trevor whispered. "Naps this long and peaceful are hard to come by these days."

"Okay." Annie smiled, not at all opposed to the idea of a few quiet moments with him.

He ran a hand through his hair, his dark eyes studying her. "So, Cupcake Queen. I feel like I don't know anything about you. Besides, you know, that you like cupcakes and are weirdly good at bowling."

Annie laughed softly. "Well, I was an accountant up until about a month ago, when I took on this crazy endeavor."

"Wow. Big switch-up."

"Oh, yeah." She brushed some hair out of her face. "I was always a numbers person. Very logical, very math-oriented. Baking became sort of an outlet for me. It was the only thing I've ever done where I felt truly...creative."

"What made you finally walk away from the desk job and pursue your passion?"

"Honestly?" Annie chuckled, lifting a shoulder. "I felt like something was really missing in my life. Of course, I was convinced it was a man that was missing. Love, I guess." Her voice trailed off as she felt her cheeks warm.

Trevor just kept his gaze fixed on her, listening.

"But I didn't find love. My best friend's daughter, Taylor, set me up on one of those dating apps, and—"

"Oh, no." He laughed sympathetically.

"Yeah. It was...bad." Annie rolled her eyes, cringing at the memories of her multiple dumpster-fire first dates. "So, long story short, I stumbled upon the vacant property, and realized that maybe a man wasn't what I was missing, but the career of my dreams was. So, I took a shot."

Trevor nodded slowly. "I get the vibe that you're very independent, Annie."

She shrugged. "I've been alone for a long time, so... you adapt."

"Yes." He swallowed. "You do."

Anne felt a pang of sympathy, knowing that Trevor had to adapt in a far more heartbreaking and awful way than she ever did. She reached out and placed her hand on his arm, giving it a gentle squeeze.

"You never married, then?" he asked.

"I almost did. Like, really *almost*."

He angled his head, clearly interested.

"Like...I had my dress on and was minutes away from walking down the aisle."

"Are you serious?" He drew back, his eyes wide.

Annie nodded. "Yup. You're looking at a woman who got literally left at the altar. It does happen in real life. I'm proof."

The memory seemed so distant. Like a hundred years ago in some other lifetime to some other version of herself. The very thing that broke her, crushed her, sent her into a spiral of loneliness and mistrust now seemed... silly. Humorous, almost.

"Holy cow, Annie." Trevor shook his head. "That's terrible. What a jerk."

She waved a dismissive hand. "It was fifteen years ago, and definitely for the best. But I never did find anyone else."

Until now.

The words echoed through her head, but she refused to even entertain them. She and Trevor were just friends. Neighbors. Weren't they?

"I can't believe that happened to you. I'm so sorry."

"Please," she said softly, meeting his gaze. "It was just a crappy breakup. I can't imagine going through..." She shut her eyes. "Losing someone."

Trevor clenched his jaw, but never looked away from her, never broke eye contact.

Annie didn't know if it was okay to broach the subject of his late wife, but she could feel his energy was very open and honest, and he didn't seem like the type of person to shut down or push away even the heaviest topics.

"It was hard," Trevor said softly, his eyes glancing back at Riley as he spoke about what had to have been the darkest time of his life. "That's an understatement, of course. It was miserable. She had been sick for about two years, and when it got close to the end, I knew it was coming. But, somehow, that didn't make it any easier. Some days I could hardly get out of bed. Some days I didn't. My mom was a huge help, and she really stepped up and took care of Riley when I couldn't even take care of myself."

"Oh." Annie's heart hurt, but she couldn't help but admire his raw honesty and candidness. Was he just that open of a person, or did he feel particularly comfortable with her?

Did he feel...close to her?

"But I didn't let that go on for too long." He jutted his chin toward his daughter. "She needed a dad. She deserved that, and I had to pull it together and figure it out, for her."

"You did an incredible job," Annie said, meaning it. "After what you went through, that level of grief...you have a beautiful little family. And I'm sure your wife is smiling in heaven, knowing that you two are doing so well."

Trevor smiled, his eyes glimmering. "I think so, too. When I lost Alexandra, the only thing that brought me solace was working out. Movement was like therapy to me. It was that one hour of the day where my mind was quiet and everything didn't hurt. That's when I got really into training and eventually decided to open a private gym."

"And you named it after her," Annie said gently. "I saw the bench."

"I did."

"That's beautiful."

He smiled. "I did a lot of grieving. A lot of self-reflection, growth, healing, and therapy. It was five years ago that she passed, and I feel like I am truly at peace with it. I cherish the years I had with her, and the incredible little girl she gave me. But I want you to know, Annie..." he paused, his lips parted as he thought carefully about what to say next. "I'm...okay. I'm not a broken man anymore, and just because I experienced such a tragic loss doesn't mean I intend to be alone forever. Alex wouldn't have wanted that for me, and...I don't want that, either."

She drew back, realizing what the words meant and what he was insinuating. "I'm glad I know that. It's amazing how far you've come and..." She took a nervous breath before continuing. "I'm glad I met you."

"I'm very glad I met you. Thank you for listening to my story and being so sweet to my daughter and being such an awesome neighbor."

She chuckled, inching closer subconsciously, as if she was being pulled by a magnet. "Of course. I feel like I kinda lucked out in the neighbor department."

"Well..." He angled his head lower, suddenly just inches from her face. "That feeling is mutual."

"Daddy, where awe we?"

Annie and Trevor instantly pulled far apart, whipping around to see Riley rubbing her eyes and stretching dramatically.

"We just got back, sweetheart," Trevor said, keeping his gaze locked on Annie's as a smile pulled at his cheeks. "Let's get you inside."

Annie climbed out of the car and said goodbye to Trevor and Riley, noticing that every time she looked in his eyes, the sparks got a little brighter.

Chapter Twenty

Sam

Sam had resisted every urge to try and figure out what happened in Ethan's marriage, despite the burning curiosity. It was so hard not to let it dominate her thoughts every time she was with him, and she wondered if there was ever going to be a day that she stopped wanting to know.

Yes, she had trust issues. She'd been burned in the past, and that probably colored her outlook on love and led her to sometimes assume the worst, or at least consider it as a possibility.

But, in this situation, how could she not?

The only way not to dwell and wonder and drive herself mad was to stay distracted. Which was an easy task these days, with the never-ending pileup of things to do at the inn.

Today, in particular, Dottie and Sam had agreed to focus entirely on the en suite bathroom in the biggest downstairs suite, the Julianna. It was a complete gut job, and they couldn't seem to find a vision for where they wanted the bathroom to go.

"I'm telling you, we want vintage in here," Dottie insisted, leaning against what remained of the bathroom countertop that had been mostly torn out by the demolition team. "This room screams for vintage."

"I know, I get you." Sam looked up at the top of the wall, where a long, rectangular window flooded the standing shower with sunlight. "But look at the natural light in here. It could be so bright and beachy if we modernize it a little. I'm worried the dark vintage woods will be dreary."

Dottie considered this, letting out a sigh. "I'm just not sure. The suite itself has a lot of black and white, so what if we brought that into the bathroom, too?"

"I like that, Mom!" Sam smiled, visualizing it. "We could do a really cool patterned tile on the floor, something that feels very 1940s but keeps the clean, sleek aesthetic we're going for."

"Yes!" Dottie grinned. "And an all-white marble shower with just black details and trim on the tile."

"Oh, that's awesome." Sam whipped out her iPad to start digging around for inspiration.

"Let me go see if we have any of those tile samples left from the upstairs bathrooms." Dottie headed out of the room and down the hallway with a spring in her step that made Sam smile to herself.

After a few minutes of perusing Pinterest and a couple of her favorite design websites, the vision of the black and white modern vintage bathroom was starting to come to life in Sam's mind.

"Hey, Sam, honey?" Dottie poked her head back in, but she wasn't carrying any tile samples.

"Did we use them all?"

"No, I actually didn't make it to the storage room."

"Huh?"

"Someone is here to see you. He's in the lobby."

The glimmer in Dottie's eye made it seem like the obvious suspect would be Ethan, but why wouldn't Mom have just said that?

"Okay." Sam shrugged, setting her tablet down on the edge of the bathtub and walking out of the room.

When she got to the lobby of Sweeney House, she was very surprised to see Andre Everett sitting in one of the chairs.

"Andre, hi!" Sam walked over, and he instantly stood up to greet her with a hug.

Tall, dark, broad-shouldered, and dripping with effortless chill—Sam completely understood why Taylor had been so smitten with this guy. Plus, he and Tay had a ton in common, and seemed to share a very sparkly connection.

Sam guessed Taylor had that with Kai, too, though, and wasn't entirely sure what the latest update in Taylor's ever-changing love life was.

Well, she figured she was about to find out.

"Do you want a cup of coffee or anything? Sadly, that's all I can offer you for now, but before you know it, we'll have a full-service restaurant up and running."

"I'm good, thank you. Can't wait to see how that restaurant comes out." He glanced around, smiling with a nod of approval and respect. "Serving laidback luxury, right?"

Sam lit up. "You remembered my silly slogan?"

"Silly?" He frowned, giving her a playful smile. "I thought it was brilliant. Who doesn't want laidback luxury?"

She laughed and felt her chest warm, waving off the compliment even though she, too, thought it was brilliant. There was truly nothing on Earth as refreshing as a guy who *listened*. Point for Andre. She made a mental note to mention that to Taylor.

"This place is coming along crazy well, Ms. Sweeney. You're doing an awesome job."

"Please, you can just call me Sam." She laughed and sat down on the sofa across from him. "And thank you. It's been a dream. How are you? Is everything okay?"

"Yeah, yeah." He leaned back, leveling his deep brown eyes on hers. "Everything's cool. I just...I wanted to talk to you about Taylor."

Sam smiled. "I had a feeling this visit had something to do with her."

"Not that I don't love your company," he said with a chuckle. "But yes. I didn't know who else to talk to, and you know Taylor better than anyone on the planet, so I was really hoping to get some insight."

"Well, I did give birth to her, and have hardly spent a moment apart from her since, so I know her pretty well," she teased. "I'm happy to chat with you, Andre. I know— elephant in the room—there's been a lot going on between you two lately, with...you know..."

"Kai," he answered with a soft laugh. "It's okay, you can say his name. I'm not going to freak out or anything. I know that he's here and he's all-in on Taylor."

She lifted a shoulder. "Yes, with Kai coming back. It's a lot."

"He's a good dude, really. I've got nothing against Surfer Boy." Andre sighed, leaning forward and resting his elbows on his knees. His hair was styled in thin braids that fell around his face, the ends brushing his jawline. "The thing is, I think I might have made a critical error early on, and I'm not sure how to fix it."

"What was the error?"

"I'm sure Taylor told you that when I found out Kai was back and completely focused on being with her, I sort of stepped out of the equation. I didn't want to complicate things or stress her out, making her feel like she had to make some sort of decision right away. The last thing I wanted Taylor to feel was the pressure of an ultimatum."

Sam could practically feel her heart singing. Andre was practically radiating sincerity and goodness, and she couldn't imagine what more she would want for her daughter. She knew that had been Andre's attitude, but hearing it directly from him made it feel even more admirable.

"I really love that you took that approach, Andre." Sam smiled.

He shrugged. "I wanted her to figure things out with Kai on her own, and if she wanted to be with me, then she'd be with me. I trust her to make that decision, but I didn't want her juggling two dudes and getting really stressed out about it, so I said we should go back to just being friends so she could have the space to sort everything out."

Sam adored that. "I personally think you handled it with a level of class and maturity that is not to go unnoticed."

"Thank you, Sam." Andre smiled. "That means a lot. But now I'm starting to regret taking that approach. Quite a bit."

Sam frowned. "Why?"

"Because I want to be with her," he said, point blank, so straightforward and certain. "I really, really adore your daughter, Sam. You know better than anyone that she's one in a billion, and I think being passive and removing myself from the equation was a dumb mistake. I'm worried it might cost me the most real and awesome relationship I've ever had. The more time passes, the more I miss her. I don't think I realized just how much I've fallen for her."

Sam considered this, her respect for Andre growing with every passing second of the conversation.

"Well, let's think this through. First of all, I don't think you're out of it, by any means, if that's what you're worried about."

He brightened. "Really?"

"She still gets starry eyed whenever she talks about you."

His smile could hardly be contained as he breathed a sigh of relief. "Okay, wow. Good. That's good."

"Now, *I*—a forty-three-year-old woman with a decent bit of life experience and slightly more wisdom than my darling daughter—happen to love your approach. Not wanting to pressure her or back her into a corner or give her, like you said, an ultimatum is very respectful and mature and, frankly, awesome. But as we know, Taylor is young, and despite her slightly jaded perspective, there's a hopeless romantic living in that girl."

Andre smiled, his eyes lighting up at the thought of Taylor, which warmed Sam's heart.

"I know there is," he said. "Which is why I think I messed up. I'm sure Kai is out here sweeping her off her feet, taking her to do all kinds of exotic, expensive things, and I'm just like the passive friend in the corner who gets forgotten."

"Andre." Sam pressed a hand to her chest and made a face. "You're too sweet."

"I know. That's the problem."

They both laughed.

"Okay, here's my advice. If you're worried about Kai, and you know what you feel for Taylor is strong and genuine—"

"It is," he nodded with certainty,

"Then fight for her. Tell her you're done stepping out of the picture and show her why you're the right man for her."

"Fight for her," he repeated, glancing off to the side as he thought about this. "You're so right. I've got to fight for her. I haven't been fighting, because I've wanted to be the nice, respectful, no-pressure guy. But I have to fight for her."

"Tell her what you want. Show her how much you care."

He stood up, clearly inspired and clearly *crazy* about Taylor. "That's what I'm going to do. She deserves someone who would do anything for her, and I don't want to wait in the wings anymore."

Sam smiled adoringly, her heart filled with joy and hope for Taylor's future and happiness.

Kai was a nice guy, and certainly had Taylor smitten for a good while there. But Andre coming to Sam today... that was next level. This guy was the real deal.

"Thank you so much, Sam." He extended his arms out for a hug. "This is exactly what I needed to hear."

"Of course, Andre." Sam hugged him back. "You can always talk to me. I know Taylor can be...a little all over the place with these kinds of things."

Andre waved a dismissive hand. "I don't hold anything against her. She's just trying to figure it all out."

"Well, go make it easier for her by showing her how serious you are."

He grinned, straightening his back. "That's exactly what I'm going to do. I really appreciate you. And I don't know what your plans are for the restaurant in here at night, you know, if it's going to have a bar, but if you need a beer guy, you know who to call."

Sam laughed, glancing back at the restaurant space. "Actually, I think a little bar might be really nice."

"I'm always here. Thanks again, Sam."

Sam walked him over to the front doors of the inn,

swinging one open and letting warmth and sunshine settle onto her skin. "Andre?"

"Yes?" He turned around on the front porch to look at her.

"It's my job as a mom to support Taylor no matter what, so that's what I'm going to do. And it's not my place to push her in any direction."

"I know," he said quickly. "Any decision she makes, I would want her to come to it on her own. I just need her to know how I feel."

"Good. But... just between us, I'm rooting for you." She gave him a wink.

Andre laughed, pushing his braids out of his face and giving her a grateful smile. "There's no one I'd rather have on my team, Sam."

Chapter Twenty-one

Taylor

"Taylor Parker, you're crushing it." Uncle John had an even bigger smile than usual this morning, giving Taylor two thumbs up after he scanned her monthly report while she sat in his office across the desk from him.

"Really?" She smiled, her heart light. "I've been trying to focus heavily on new business we can bring in early next year, get Q1 rolling strong from the start."

"I see that." John scanned the screen in front of him, nodding with pride and approval before looking back up at Taylor. "You know, when Andre and Brock first told me they wanted you to be their account executive, I was definitely skeptical. Not that I didn't believe in you, it was just a big jump for someone with no experience."

"Totally understandable." Taylor raised her hands and laughed softly. "Believe me, Uncle John, I was skeptical, too. I was downright terrified, actually."

He chuckled and shook his head. "Well, you have surprised everyone, including me, and you've more than proven yourself to be an invaluable asset to Coastal Marketing. I'd like to offer you a fifteen percent raise on your salary for next year. No nepotism, just rewarding hard work and value."

Taylor resisted the urge to leap out of her seat with joy. She'd been saving pretty steadily since she'd started her job at the ad agency, and a bump in pay meant that she could possibly move out and get her own place pretty soon.

She loved living at the cottage, but it was getting crowded there and Taylor had begun to crave independence. Not massive independence. Like, five minutes down the road kind of independence. But still.

"Wow, I don't even know what to say. Thank you, Uncle John." She clasped her hands together and beamed. "I really, really appreciate that."

"It's not a gift, Taylor. You earned it." He pressed his palms onto his desk. "Thank you for all the effort and drive you've brought to my company."

She smiled. She had to admit, she was really darn proud of herself. Despite the distractions and drama and family stuff and crazy love life, she found solace and peace and excitement in this work. "I love it here," Taylor said. "I really do."

"I'm so glad." John raised his brows. "And I hope you love it enough to fill in for me at a pitch meeting next Friday. I'll be out of the office."

"Sure, I can definitely do that. Just forward me the client info." Taylor made a mental note about next Friday. "Where are you off to?"

Uncle John's face lit up with a smile. "Imani and the kids and I are taking a long weekend in the Destin area, up in the Panhandle. This new website she's been working for has her writing a feature on a little town up there called Rosemary Beach. And we take all her work trips as a family now." His joy was palpable, and it was awesome to see.

"Wow, that'll be great," Taylor said, standing up. "Rosemary Beach sounds too adorable to be real."

"It's supposed to be very quaint and relaxing." John pressed his lips together. "We'll see how relaxing it is with three kids, but fun is definitely on the table."

Taylor smiled as she stepped to the door of his glass-walled office. "You'll have a blast."

She was so truly happy that their darling family was whole again. The rift between John and Imani had affected everyone, and if they hadn't worked out, then Taylor might have just given up on love entirely.

But they did work out, and she certainly hadn't given up on love.

She thanked Uncle John again before heading back through the office to her desk, feeling giddy about the raise.

After a few emails, notes, and files, Taylor found herself completely immersed in the solace of work, focusing on things she could understand and quantify and control.

Her phone rang, and she picked it up without bothering to check who was calling.

"Hello, Coastal Marketing. This is Taylor," she said cheerfully.

"Hey, Taylor. It's Brock, from Blackhawk Brewing."

The familiar voice of Andre's close friend and business partner warranted her full attention, so Taylor swiveled away from her computer screen and pressed the phone to her ear.

It was impossible not to wonder why Brock was calling her on matters of Blackhawk as opposed to Andre, but she didn't want to read too much into it yet.

"Brock! So great to hear from you. How are you?"

"I'm doing insanely well, actually. Business is booming up here in Asheville, and we are beyond stoked with the success of the Cocoa Beach location. Andre has been loving it down there, and whatever you guys are doing, don't stop, because it's working."

Wow, this back to back with Uncle John hyping her up and giving her a juicy raise. Taylor's ego was happy today.

"Oh, I'm so glad to hear that," she said warmly. She wasn't entirely sure how much Brock knew or didn't know about what had happened between her and Andre, so she opted to tread lightly. "We've had a blast planning all kinds of events and promos, and the people of Cocoa Beach just love the place. Word of mouth has been our friend."

"I love that," Brock said with enthusiasm. "Andre told me the trivia nights have been a huge hit."

Did he also tell you that we were sort of together but then my sort-of-ex showed up and now we're sort of friends? Did he mention that?

"Oh, yeah, those have been so much fun to plan and everything. They've really taken off with the locals."

"That's our target, Taylor. That's what I'm talking about."

She smiled, having to physically bite her tongue to stop herself from asking what else Andre had said and if it was anything about her, did he still like her and—

"So," Brock continued. "I'm actually calling to ask a favor."

"Anything."

"I'm sure Andre's told you about our new location in Denver that's set to open up in just a few weeks..."

What? Denver? He'd never mentioned that. And, wow, her heart dropped. Andre *had* mentioned Denver as his dream city on more than one occasion, and her mind quickly started to race. Off he'd go, taking her heart with him.

"Um, no, I actually hadn't heard that you guys were opening up a spot out west," she managed to say.

"Oh, yeah, we are!" Brock said. "It's gonna be super dope, and with that clientele? We predict some pretty fat margins."

Taylor laughed, but she could feel how forced it was. "I'm sure it's going to be amazingly successful out there."

"Absolutely. I'm shocked Andre didn't tell you about it! Almost as shocked as I was when he said he didn't want to move out there and manage it."

Taylor almost fell out of her chair. "He what?"

"Well, I'm sure you know by now that Andre has this lifelong dream of living out west, snowboarding all the time, soaking up that culture."

"Yeah, he's..." Her throat was tight. "He's talked about that."

"So you can imagine how floored I was when he said he didn't want to head out there and run that brewery. I thought for sure he'd be packing his bags the moment we signed the lease at that spot in the Mile High City, but he didn't want to leave Florida."

"He...he said that?"

"Yup. Total stunner, right? He said he was really happy in Cocoa Beach and even though he thought that was his dream, he realized he has other dreams now. Mentioned your name more than a few times," Brock added, a teasing playfulness in his voice.

"He did?"

"Not sure what's going on there, but...he seems to really, really care about you. He won't move to Denver, which is pretty astonishing, considering he's literally been talking about it since middle school."

It was astonishing.

He had the chance to move to his dream city and do what he loved and he turned it down. Instantly. Without hesitation. Without thinking about it or considering it or weighing pros and cons. He just said no. To pursue...

Other dreams.

He stayed for me.

The words echoed through her mind like they were being shouted in a microphone. She kept her cool on the phone with Brock, despite the whirlwind going on in her brain.

Brock explained that he was looking for a PR

company in the Denver area for the new spot, and asked Taylor if she could relay that to John and see if there was anyone he knew of, since he was very well connected in the industry.

She happily agreed, scribbling down a note, unable to wipe the smile from her face. Once she got off the phone, minutes ticked by at a snail's pace.

Andre had stayed for her. He'd turned down Denver because she was in Cocoa Beach. As much as she didn't want to entertain that thought, she couldn't help it.

Kai came here for his dream job and being with Taylor was an added bonus. Andre turned down his dream job because he didn't want to leave her.

Suddenly, finally, and without a shadow of a doubt in her mind and heart, Taylor had clarity. She knew exactly what she wanted and needed to do, and she needed to do it tonight.

"Everything okay?" Kai jogged out onto the beach with his hands in the pockets of his board shorts, shiny hair flopping around his face. "Your text sounded pretty serious."

"Yeah, no, everything's fine." She pressed her lips into a smile, even though a weight was pressing hard on her chest.

Taylor had asked Kai to meet her at the beach near the cottage, and, despite her racing heart and uneasy mind, she had to follow her gut and do what she knew was right for herself.

The sun was setting in the west, leaving the whole sky over Cocoa Beach streaked with tangerine and purple highlights. The peaceful ocean was soft and quiet tonight, and the beach was basically deserted.

The November chill whispered through the air, just enough to give Taylor goosebumps as she walked to the young man she once thought she'd love forever.

She took a moment to study him, to remember all of the dreams she'd had about those eyes and that smile, and her consideration only made her more certain that he wasn't her forever.

He was her first massive, serious, soul-melting crush, and he always would be. But it wasn't true, sustainable love. It wasn't like what Grandma and Grandpa had, where they would do literally anything in the world for each other. Best friend kind of love, Grandma called it. And that's what Taylor now knew she wanted.

"How are you?" Kai reached out to hug her and she accepted it, nerves prickling down her spine.

"I'm okay. I wanted to talk to you." She gestured to the sand, where they sat down side by side facing the ocean.

"What's wrong, Taylor?" Kai cocked his head, frowning with concern and confusion as he searched her expression. "What is it?"

She dug her fingers into the cool, powdery sand, letting it slide off of her palms as she took a deep breath and gathered her thoughts.

"Kai, I promised you that I would always be honest with you. About everything."

He angled his head. "Okay..."

"And I need to be honest with you now." She swallowed, looking back at the ocean. She was certain in her choice to go all-in on Andre, but that didn't make this goodbye any easier.

He was still Kai, after all.

"I think you're amazing, and I've loved every minute we've spent together. But ever since you got back to Florida, I've been trying to figure out if I feel the same way as I did before. Things have changed, and your sponsorship is hectic, and..." She turned to him, her heart pounding in her throat. "I have to follow my gut and my heart and I don't think we're right together."

His face fell and his posture slouched, drawing back as if he'd just taken a blow to the stomach.

Taylor winced over the discomfort and pain of hurting someone she truly, deeply cared about. "I'm so sorry, Kai. I—"

"I understand," he said slowly. "I mean, I don't understand, because I thought we were made for each other. But I've picked up on the fact that your heart hasn't been into it ever since I got back to Cocoa Beach."

She leveled her gaze on his and nodded.

"I guess I'd just assumed, when I got the offer from Ron Jon, that we would pick up where we left off, you know? We were crazy about each other last summer."

"We were," Taylor agreed quickly. "I'm not denying that one bit. I was nuts about you, Kai. But what I've realized is that I think it might have been more of a crush, more infatuation, rather than something that could be really real and sustainable and potentially lifelong."

Kai shut his eyes, the corners of his mouth flicking up slightly. "Puppy love."

"Exactly," Taylor said, feeling a whisper of relief that he understood. "Puppy love."

Kai drew in a slow breath, brushing his hair back off of his face, the same gesture that used to make Taylor's knees go weak. It didn't anymore.

He leaned closer. "Can I ask you something?"

She nodded. "Anything."

"It's Andre, isn't it?"

Taylor felt her eyes shutter as she eased away, not ready for the bluntness of the question, but also not wanting to lie.

"I feel really strongly for him. We became friends, as you know, and yes—it developed a bit, before you came back. But this is about more than just choosing who I want to be with. You have so much going for you, Kai. You have this insane future filled with fame and money and autographs and magazine covers." She laughed softly. "You have the journey of a lifetime ahead of you. I just don't think I belong on it with you. It's your journey, and it's incredible. But it isn't mine."

Kai inhaled slowly, and for a few moments they sat quietly staring out at the water.

"It's okay, Taylor," he said after a long pause, standing and offering her a hand to help her up out of the sand.

"You don't hate me, right?" she asked with a sheepish laugh.

"Are you kidding?" He cocked his head. "I could never hate you. When I say I want you to be happy, I really do mean that."

"Thanks." She stood in front of him, meeting his gaze and feeling a sense of peace settle onto her skin and in her heart. "You think you'll stick around Cocoa Beach for a while?"

He shrugged. "I mean, this sponsorship thing is going pretty well, but once competition season starts up, I'll be all over the place. Plus, I want to go back to the islands for a good bit and stay with my family over the holidays, so... I'll be in and out."

She nodded, brushing some hair out of her eyes. "Maybe I'll see you around here and there."

Bittersweet sadness climbed through her, but Taylor didn't doubt that Kai was not her forever man.

"You have to make me one promise, though, okay?" He gave her a playful smile.

"Sure. What is it?"

"You have to get on a surfboard one day." He grinned. "And send me a video."

"Hah," Taylor snorted, grateful for the lightness in the conversation and the easing of all the tension. "You might be waiting a long time for that one, but okay."

He held her gaze for several beats, the soft splash of the waves the only sound in the world.

"All right, Taylor Parker." Kai held his arms out. "One more hug for the road."

"Of course." She embraced him tightly, feeling unbelievably grateful for having known Kai Leilani, for having learned the things he taught her about life and love. These sad moments, these tough goodbyes...they were part of living, part of growing up. As those emotions washed over her, she looked up at him.

"Thank you," she said softly.

"For understanding?"

"Yes, and for everything. You helped me heal after my parents' divorce. You taught me how to open up my heart again."

"Open to another guy," he teased, making her tip her head back with a hearty laugh.

"Yeah, maybe. But I'm so grateful." She got up on her tiptoes and gave him a light kiss on the lips. He snagged her a little closer and deepened the kiss, making it real for a few heartbeats.

"Sorry," he murmured into her lips. "I just needed one to remember you by."

She pulled back with a smile, not wanting to encourage him.

"Don't be a stranger, Tay. I'm always here for you."

"Okay." As she took a few steps back, he let his hand slide down her arm and take her fingers, bringing them to his lips for one last kiss.

"Bye," he whispered, then finally let go. It was, all things considered, a perfect goodbye.

"All right, I'm off." He headed down the beach, backpedaling away from her with a wave.

"You're taking the beach?" she asked.

"Yeah. It's a short walk back to my trainer's place, and I could use some ocean air."

"Got it." Taylor waved her hand, unexpected emotion rising in her throat. "Bye, Kai."

"Bye, Taylor." He flashed one more big smile before turning around and heading on his way.

Feeling drained, relieved, a bit shaky, and pretty proud of herself, Taylor headed back up the sand toward the cottage, when her eyes suddenly fell on the last person she expected to see.

Andre Everett was on the deck of the cottage, carrying a bouquet of flowers in one hand and a six pack of Taylor's favorite Citrus Burst from his brewery in the other.

Excitement zinged through her as she picked up her pace and jogged toward the deck, thrilled by the surprise.

"Hey, you! I'm so glad you're here!" She reached the deck a bit winded, stepped up the wooden stairs and quickly realized that the look on Andre's face was not nearly as joyful as hers. "Why are you...What's wrong?"

Andre lowered the beer and flowers down onto the coffee table. "I came here to surprise you. I wanted to..." He huffed out a breath. "Never mind."

"You did?"

Well, there went her fantasy of showing up at Andre's house later tonight, giddy with excitement and the high of finally having clarity. She'd wanted to jump into his arms and tell him she loved him, she wanted him, and there was nobody else.

But now he was here, with flowers...looking not happy.

"Is everything okay?" she asked, searching his face.

He took a step back. "Yeah. No." He shook his head. "It is what it is and you are..." He glanced past her toward the beach. Toward the boardwalk. Toward the very place she'd been with Kai, hugging, kissing, and laughing.

"I came here to tell you I want to be with you," he said softly. "I came here to fight for you."

"You did?" Her heart jumped right into her throat and took up residence.

"But then I saw you with him." Andre turned to her, sadness darkening his brown eyes. "I saw you two together and I realized I'm...wasting my time."

"No, no, Andre." She reached for him. "You don't understand. That wasn't what it looked like. It was actually the opposite. I—"

"Taylor, I just saw you laughing, hugging, and kissing. It *was* what it looked like. And what it looked like is that I'm a freaking idiot, and I've been over here, trying to be the nice guy by not making things hard or stressful for you, when I should have been fighting for you all along."

"You don't have to fight for me," she said, tears of frustration stinging behind her eyes. "I want you."

"You can't have us both."

"I don't want you both. I want *you*," she insisted, her voice quivering.

"That is not what I just saw down on the beach." He took another step back. "Look Taylor, it's my fault. I should have stepped it up. I should have showed you why we were right together and I should have fought harder to keep you. I made a mistake."

"No, Andre. I love how you handled it." Her voice was thick now, emotions threatening to spill over. "I'm telling you, I just ended things with Kai. When I heard that you weren't going to Denver, I decided—"

"Taylor, I'm sorry. I can't." Andre pinched the bridge of his nose.

"I just broke up with him," she insisted. "It's over. Done. Complete. I want to be with you."

He stared at her for a long moment, his dark eyes shadowed with pain. "It's not over," he said softly. As she opened her mouth to disagree, he held up a hand. "I know you've been confused, Taylor, but I also know that he's a fact of life. He lives here now, and he's obviously nuts about you. Anyone with eyes could see that. I don't want to be in the middle."

"You're not in the middle. Can't you give me a chance to prove that?"

"I...I don't want to get hurt, either," he said softly. "I mean, I'm human. I have to protect myself and I know that you and Kai have something real. I don't want it hanging over us, because watching that? It hurt like hell, I gotta say."

Taylor blinked back tears. "You don't believe me? I was breaking up with him."

"I do believe you," he said. "I just don't want to...feel like your second choice."

"You're not!" She reached for him, but he eased back, protective and defensive.

"I don't want to play games, Taylor. I thought what I needed to do was pursue you and show you how much I want to be with you, but after seeing you and him, I just... I don't want to hurt like this again."

"You won't," Taylor said on a strangled sob as Andre started to walk away. "You're my choice. You're the one I want."

"I'm sorry, Taylor. I can't. I gotta go," he added. "I'm leaving tonight."

"Leaving for where?"

His jaw clenched as he glanced off to the side, not quite able to look her in the eyes when he said the next sentence. "Denver. I can get on a flight tonight and the brewery out there opens in two weeks, so...I'm going."

No.

Suddenly, Taylor could hardly stand up straight, and her vision swam with tears. "You're just leaving? Just like that? Do you even believe me that I choose you?"

"I believe you think that, but..." He rubbed his forehead, his brows drawn into a stressed and hurt frown. "I just saw what I saw and...it made everything clear. I have to go. I think this is better for both of us."

With that, he jogged down the stairs of the back deck, walked around the cottage, and she heard him get into his car in the driveway.

She dropped her face into her palms and let the sobs come. Somehow, in the span of an hour, she'd lost them both. Taylor knew she'd been playing with fire, and now she was badly burned.

Chapter Twenty-two

Sam

Sam's finger hovered over the Enter key, her gaze glued to the words she'd typed into the search bar a hundred times now, but hadn't yet had the courage—or perhaps stupidity—to launch the search.

Ethan Price Teacher Perryville, Maryland

She truly didn't expect to find anything out about Ethan's divorce from a Google search with his old town's name, but if there was something serious he was hiding, maybe she could get a clue?

She knew she shouldn't dig. She knew she shouldn't go searching for answers that she was never meant to find.

But, darn it, it was killing her. She could hardly look Ethan in the eyes these days without her mind spinning a million different possibilities about what had happened and why on Earth he was so sketchy about it. So...*sus.*

Sam drew in a slow, deep breath, staring at the computer screen, unable to move.

The cottage was quiet and empty this evening while the sun set outside. Dottie was out at the grocery store, Julie and Bliss had a rehearsal for their next gig with a local band, and Taylor had slipped out to talk to Kai.

No, a Google search wasn't going to tell Sam if Ethan had cheated on his ex-wife. Obviously, divorce papers were not public records. She knew that. But maybe she'd find something out about him.

She had to at least try and get a clue. She couldn't very well let herself fall in love with someone who had some kind of awful past she knew nothing about, could she?

On that thought, she closed her eyes, lifted her finger over the Enter key, and...

"Mommy." Taylor's voice, thick with emotion and sadness, instantly grabbed Sam's attention, and she turned to face the bedroom doorway.

Taylor stood in the hall, her cheeks wet with tears and her eyes puffy and red.

"Tay." Sam stood up and rushed to her daughter, momentarily forgetting completely about anything else on her mind.

Her baby was hurting, and suddenly nothing else mattered.

"Taylor!" She wrapped Taylor up in a long, tight hug, feeling her skinny body quake with sobs as she held her. "What on Earth happened?"

Taylor wiped her tears and sniffed loudly as she walked into Sam's room and flopped down onto the bed, ignoring the open laptop on the nightstand. "I lost them both."

"What?" Sam rushed to her side, sitting right next to her and pushing a strand of hair out of Taylor's tragically miserable face. "What are you talking about?"

With a deep, shuddering breath, Taylor gathered herself. "I was saying goodbye to Kai, because I realized that I want to be with Andre."

"You did?" Sam tried to hide the happy note that slipped through her tone of voice. "I didn't know you'd reached that kind of clarity yet."

"Well, I did. Andre was offered a position in Denver, which is, like, his dream place. He's always wanted to move there. Blackhawk is opening a Denver location, and he was first in line to go out there and manage it."

"Oh, no, honey." Sam stroked her daughter's hair.

Sam found that shocking after he had come to see her at the inn yesterday, so dead-set on pursuing Taylor and being with her. She never dreamt in a million years that the kid in the lobby of Sweeney House who had stars in his eyes at the mention of Taylor's name would be packing up to move cross-country a day later.

"I know it has to hurt," Sam said. "But he's young, and if it's his dream, I can't fully blame him for wanting to go after it." It bugged her, though.

"No, no." Taylor sat up, her eyes wide. "You don't get it. He turned the job down. Well, he did at first."

"Huh?"

"I heard about it through Brock, who called the office the other day. He told me about the new Colorado location and that he was so shocked when Andre didn't want to go out there, but he stayed for me."

Sam's heart folded. "He did?"

"That's what Brock said. He sacrificed that because he wanted to be with me. And when I heard that, I knew. I knew without a shadow of a doubt that he's my person and he's become my best friend and he's all I want."

Sam smiled sadly at Taylor. "Well, that all sounds wonderful, sweetie." Not to mention the part where Andre had come to Sam and said how badly he wanted to fight for her daughter. But Sam would keep that to herself. "So what happened?"

"I had to break up with Kai," Taylor said. "Which was fine. Kind of sad and bittersweet, but it was on really good terms, no hard feelings, all of that. What I didn't know was that while I was saying goodbye to Kai, we hugged and kissed, and Andre had come to the cottage to surprise me."

"Oh. Oh, *God*." Sam cringed at the mental image. That could not have been good. "He saw you with Kai?"

"Yes." Taylor rolled her eyes. "At the worst possible moment. And he was so hurt, so heartbroken."

"But you and Kai were just saying goodbye, right?"

"Well, yeah, but...you know. We were hugging for a long time, laughing a little, and he kissed me goodbye and...it probably didn't look like a breakup from fifty feet away."

"But you explained that it was?" Sam asked.

"I did but he just said Kai would always be around and he didn't want to get hurt." Taylor let out a little moan. "Oh, Mom. Why did I think I could juggle feelings for both of them? I've been awful."

"You have not been awful, Tay. You've been a little indecisive." She stroked her hair again. "It'll be okay.

You'll talk it out with Andre once the emotions die down."

"I can't. He's on his way to the airport to go to Denver."

"Oh, no." Sam pressed a hand to her chest.

After a bit more consoling, musing, discussing, and sadness in solidarity, Taylor's spirit had lifted ever so slightly, and Sam got her mind off things by telling her what she was about to do.

"I'm not happy you just went through that, Tay, but I could use a second brain on this whole Googling my boyfriend undertaking."

"I don't know, Mom." Taylor sat up on the bed, her knees tucked in against her chest. "Do you really think there's going to be anything about his divorce on the internet?"

"I don't know." Sam shrugged, staring at the Google home screen again. "But I don't know where else to look."

"It's worth trying, I guess."

"You really think I should?" Sam asked, uneasiness rippling through her stomach. "He was pretty serious when he told me he didn't want to talk about his past. Ever."

"Well, he's not talking about it. You're just doing some research." Taylor lifted a shoulder. "Besides, people Google their boyfriends all the time, especially in a new-ish relationship." She sniffled, still stuffy from the water-works of tears. "You're not breaking any rules."

Then why did it feel like she was doing something so wrong? Taylor was right. People Googled their dates, boyfriends, acquaintances, and colleagues all the time. It was not weird. She was just...curious.

"Okay." Sam looked once again across the words she'd typed into the search bar, sliding her finger over the Enter key. "Here goes."

After a quick little countdown in her head, she pressed it.

Taylor scooted forward to the edge of the bed so the two of them could stare at the screen as the search results loaded, filling the page with links, words, pictures, and articles.

"That's him," Taylor said abruptly, pointing to a small thumbnail picture of Ethan next to an article on the first page of results.

"Okay, okay," Sam said, hovering the selection arrow over the link. "You're too fast."

"I found him!"

"Well, I was still looking."

Before she had a chance to bicker back with Taylor, Sam's eyes fell on the headline of the article next to Ethan's face: *"Perryville High calculus teacher forced to resign after alleged romantic relationship with 17-year-old student."*

Sam felt her jaw go slack and the world stop turning. Her gaze was glued to the words in front of her, and her throat was so tight she couldn't breathe.

"Holy cow," Taylor whispered next to her. Her voice sounded like it was miles away. "He dated a student?"

"I don't..." Sam suddenly felt nauseous and light-headed and like everything she'd known about this man—this good, honest, upstanding man—was a lie.

No wonder his wife left him. And no wonder he didn't want to talk about it.

Sam smacked the laptop shut and set it to the side, sitting back on the bed and attempting to formulate something that resembled a thought.

"Mom...is that real?"

"It was his photo," Sam said weakly, her voice quivering. "It was him."

Taylor reached for the computer to open it back up. "We didn't even read it, though. What if it wasn't true? Or there was some kind of explanation?"

"Taylor." Sam turned to her daughter, feeling the color physically draining from her face as she shut her eyes. "He had a relationship with a high school student. He's not who he says he is. That's what he's running from, and...and that's what he's hiding."

"Oh, Mom." Taylor reached out and hugged Sam.

Sam wondered if she was going to start crying, but her eyes didn't sting and her throat didn't thicken. She felt numb. Like ice had been injected into her veins and the world around her was still and silent and shut down.

She wasn't even sure what her biggest fear had been, but this? This was far worse than anything she'd imagined.

Suddenly, Sam's phone vibrated with a call on the bed between the two of them.

Taylor looked down at it, then back up. "It's Annie. Do you want to talk to her?"

Not particularly, but it wasn't in her DNA to turn down a call from her best friend, even in the most shockingly horrifying of moments.

"Hey, Annie," she said coolly as she answered the phone, expecting Annie to instantly read the stunned sadness in her tone and demand to know what was wrong and who hurt her.

"Sam! Sam!" The frantic voice on the other side of the phone call broke Sam right out of her heartbroken fog as she realized that something was seriously wrong.

"Are you okay?" Sam sat up straighter, putting the phone on speaker so Taylor could hear too.

"What's happening?" Taylor asked.

"Sam! Taylor!" Annie shrieked, fear and panic heightening her voice. "The bakery! It's...it's on fire!"

Chapter Twenty-three

Annie

This must be shock. This had to be what "being in shock" meant—her body trembling down to the bone as she clung to Riley, who was shaking just as much.

"Listen for the siren, honey," she said, squeezing her tighter. "They're coming. Any second. Any second."

But where were they? What was taking so long?

The whole thing felt like time had stretched out and it was hours since she'd first noticed the pungent, acrid smell coming from the kitchen while she worked on her laptop in the front with Riley playing on her kiddie tablet right next to her. Her father had run an errand and left her here, as he often did.

Before she'd taken a breath, the alarm screamed, and so did Riley, the first clouds of smoke billowing out from the kitchen.

In a matter of seconds—although it felt like she'd been moving through mud—Annie flung open the front door and got Riley out, ordered her to sit on the bench and not move. As she ran back to the kitchen, shaking fingers already attempting to dial 911 on her phone, she came to a complete stop at the reflection of orange flames swallowing her kitchen.

Her kitchen. Her bakery. Her big, fat, giant dreams...
up in smoke.

Now they waited, calling for help—Trevor didn't
answer but she knew he was in a meeting with the bank.
Sam was on her way, but where was the fire department?

She sat outside on the bench with Riley, holding her,
fighting tears.

"There!" she yelled as she heard the distant sirens.
"There they are! I hear the sirens!" Annie held Riley
close. "They're coming."

"Where's Daddy?" Riley whined, her lower lip
quivering.

"He's coming." The second he sees the text, Annie
presumed, but didn't want to promise the little girl as
they watched the patrons and owners of the strip center
gather in the parking lot to watch with fear and concern.

Just then, the first of the firetrucks rolled up and
pulled into the lot.

Riley smashed her hands over her ears to block out
the deafening sirens and alarms, and Annie kept her close
by her side.

Tears fell down Annie's face as she watched the firefighters move with choreographed grace and breathtaking
speed. Soon, water gushed from fat hoses and dozens of
heavily suited people swarmed around the building.

The front of the bakery looked normal, but she could
still see flames and smoke coming from the back. Bile rose
up and tears poured and her whole body vibrated in
horror.

"Miss Annie!" Riley screamed.

"What is it?"

"I left Funny Bunny inside!" she wailed, already pulling away like she wanted to run back in. "I have to get her!"

"No, no, no, no." Annie clung to her, holding her close.

"She's gonna die! Funny Bunny is gonna die! Just like my mommy did!" She collapsed in Annie's arms, sobbing.

"No, no. She's in the front. Someone will get her, I promise!"

"She's gonna die!"

"Just wait here! Don't move." With a quick squeeze, Annie ran toward the first firefighter she could find, who was on a phone, barking orders.

"Back away, ma'am. Do not come closer to the building! Behind the line!"

"Please, please. There's a stuffed animal in the front at that table right there. By the window. A bunny. And that child right there already lost her mother. Please!"

The man peered through his helmet, and even with the plastic shield separating them, she could see the dark look in his eyes. And then she saw it soften.

"Don't move!" He jogged away to the front door, where two firefighters were pulling a long hose. One disappeared inside and Annie just stood and prayed.

Please get the bunny. Please don't let this child have one more moment of sadness. Please—

A firefighter came hustling out, Funny Bunny in hand. He gave it to the guy, who lifted it to Annie as he walked closer.

"God bless you," she whispered as she took it.

"Get back! Far!"

She followed the order, spinning around to run to where Riley was, with two strangers comforting her.

"Riley!" Trevor's voice, loud and booming and terrified, caught her attention, and Annie saw him sprinting toward his daughter, falling to his knees and pulling her into a hug.

Annie ran to them, unable to say anything as she held the bunny out.

"I'm so sorry, Trevor. It happened so fast. I had no idea a fire started, and before I knew it, there was smoke and there was..." She broke into tears again, her whole body quivering with the dump of adrenaline.

"Funny Bunny!" Riley reached for the toy, grabbing it and kissing the little head over and over. "You saved her! Miss Annie, you saved her! I love you!"

Riley threw herself at Annie, wrapping her little arms around her waist and squeezing, and letting Annie pick her up and hold her.

Trevor stood, too, engulfing them both in a hug.

"I'm so sorry," Annie said. "I'm so—"

"Stop," he insisted. "Everyone's fine. That's all that matters." He drew back, looking over Riley's head into Annie's eyes. "You saved her. You saved her toy and you saved her and you..." He closed his eyes, unable to finish.

"I love you, Miss Annie," Riley said again, snuggling between them.

"I love you, too, Wiley."

Staring at her, Trevor broke into something that fell

between a cry and a smile, and reached his hands out, placing them on Annie's cheeks. "I don't know what I would have done if I lost her. I couldn't...I couldn't have handled it. I can't lose her, too."

"I wouldn't have let anything happen to her."

"I know, I know, and I...that...I..." He leaned in closer and for one crazy, wild, breathtaking second, she thought he was going to kiss her. "Annie....I—"

"Annie! Annie!"

They broke apart, turning to see Sam, Taylor, Dottie, Ben, Julie and Bliss all spilling out of an SUV, with Sam in the lead, running to her.

Was he going to kiss her? She'd never know. But she'd certainly think about that moment when she wanted to forget the awful ones that came before it.

ANNIE SPENT the next several hours, well into the darkening evening, in the controlled chaos that was post-fire. Unlike the horrifying minutes that started all this, time seemed to speed by, propelling her from one minute to the next.

The good news was that the fire had been contained to the kitchen, with just smoke damage to the front of the bakery. It was not a total loss by any stretch, and the landlord came with his insurance adjuster, and they both assured Annie that, should she want to rebuild, that could happen over the course of the next few months.

Also, Ace Fitness, the business adjacent to hers, only sustained minor smoke damage.

Early that evening, while Annie was talking to the landlord and adjustor, Trevor's parents arrived from Tampa to take Riley to stay with them for a few days. He went with them to pack her things and grab some food, practically insisting that Annie come with, but she just had no appetite at all.

While all that unfolded, the Sweeneys stayed with her, the group growing as hours passed until they were all there in support of her.

It was nearly nine when the last firefighter left, and Annie joined the group that had gathered around a few picnic tables that someone had set up in the parking lot.

"Can you go in?" Sam asked, glancing at the bakery.

She shook her head. "Not for a few days. The fire inspector will be back tomorrow and they will do a complete assessment of how safe it is. They found the wiring that started the fire, though, and it was really, really old and had been patched over. The guy who owns the building is responsible for that, and he's working it out with insurance. The electrician I had in just never found it."

They all commiserated over that, as exhaustion weighed down on Annie. Sipping a bottle of water, she finally looked around the group.

"Thank you for coming, fam," she said softly. "I don't know where I'd be without the Sweeneys."

Next to her, Erica put a loving arm around Annie's

shoulder. "You'll rebuild," she said encouragingly. "And we'll help you."

"Darn right we will," Sam added.

"We *all* will, Annie." Imani leaned forward, reaching Annie with a reassuring touch.

"We're family." John wrapped an arm around his wife and smiled at Annie.

Dottie nodded. "Sam and I now know more contractors, builders, and construction companies than we know what to do with. We will get you on a shortlist for repair."

Annie took a long moment to appreciate the cast of characters. Sassy, bold Julie; fun, confident Sam; graceful, kind Imani; practical, logical John; and brilliant, selfless Erica.

And, of course, Dottie, the elegant matriarch who kept them all together. Lori and Amber, the new additions, who had clearly fallen as deeply in love with this crew as Annie had.

The kids, each more beautiful and spectacular than the last. Damien, Liam, and Ellen, talking peacefully with Jada, giggling as they wandered around the parking lot and peeked into the other businesses. Bliss was glowing and gorgeous, laughing with her mom. Ben had blossomed into a young man, and Annie could tell he was thriving in high school and growing up way too fast for Sam's liking.

This was her family. They weren't blood-related, but it didn't matter. Annie had made one phone call, and the Sweeney family showed up in numbers. Massive numbers, actually.

She'd do the same for them. And that was family. For someone who felt like she had nothing several months ago...she had a whole heck of a lot.

And then...her eyes fell on Taylor. Taylor looked blue —seriously blue. Broken, even.

As John gathered his troops to take off and a few others chatted and made ready to leave the scene, Annie got up and walked to Taylor, who was sitting on the edge of a bench, staring off into space.

"Hey, girl." Annie plopped down next to her. "You look worse than I feel."

"Oh, Annie. Work Momma." Taylor sighed, dropping her head on Annie's shoulder. "This was a fitting end to the dumpster fire that is my life." She lifted her head. "Too soon for fire jokes?"

"A little. But what happened?"

Taylor shook her head. "I am not about to burden you with my problems right now. Sadly, you have enough of your own."

"Please tell me, Taylor," Annie said softly, putting a gentle hand on Taylor's leg. "I want to know."

With a long sigh, Taylor filled her in on the heart-breaking conclusion to her love triangle, her voice thick with emotion and hurt as she recounted the double-barreled breakups.

"Oh, Tay." Annie closed her eyes and shook her head. "You were certain, huh? You were a hundred percent on Andre?"

"A million percent," Taylor replied without hesitation. "I was so sure, Annie. I literally broke it off with Kai because I was ready to go all-in with Andre. I knew without a doubt that he's my guy. I still know. But now he's gone."

"Already?"

Taylor nodded. "He's getting on a red-eye to Denver tonight."

"Well...what the heck are you still doing here?"

Taylor angled her head, her brow furrowing in confusion. "What do you mean?"

Sam walked up. "Hey, having FOMO here. What are my bestie and my daughter talking about?"

Annie pointed to Sam. "Ask your mother, Taylor."

"Ask me what?"

Annie answered for Taylor. "Don't you think this lady needs to get her booty to the airport and stop Andre from leaving her?"

Sam's eyes popped. "Oh, a grand gesture. A staple in every fabulous rom-com."

Taylor made a face. "This isn't a movie, mom. His mind is made up and he's taking the job managing a new brewery. I don't think he's going to stay, especially not after I hurt him so much."

"Taylor." Sam looked at Annie, then back at her daughter. "Do you love him?"

"So much."

"Would you move to Denver to be with him?" Annie asked, knowing for a fact that she wouldn't move to Hawaii for Kai—she'd already turned him down once on that score.

"Yes," Taylor said quickly, looking like the answer

shocked her as much as it did Sam and Annie. "Yes...I would."

Annie and Sam exchanged a glance, both mutually, wistfully proud of and excited for the beautiful, brilliant young woman they both loved so much.

"Tay." Sam put her hand on Taylor's shoulder and squeezed it, flipping her the keys to her SUV. "Go. It's your moment."

"My...my..."

"Go!" Annie nudged her hard. "Save this day for one of us, please."

Taylor stood slowly, pressing her fingers to her lips. "You're right. I'm going. Grand gesture. One last chance. Oh my gosh, I'm doing this!" With that, she blew them a kiss and took off.

Annie and Sam looked at each other and just started laughing. And crying. And then they hugged for a long, long time.

It was nearly eleven when Annie reached the driveway of her townhouse, blind and numb from the events of the day. As she pulled up the driveway, she frowned at the shadow of a vehicle parked there.

Then the frown disappeared.

That was no ordinary vehicle. She pulled in behind it and watched the driver's side door open.

And that was no ordinary man.

"I thought you'd never come home," Trevor said as he walked to her car and she opened her window. He leaned in and held up a white paper bag. "Brought you dinner."

"Trevor." She looked up at him, her heart bouncing

around her chest as she got a little lost in his eyes. "Thank you."

"You doing better?"

She was now. Nodding, she unlatched her seatbelt and closed her eyes, taking a second to catch her breath.

"Annie?" He inched in. "Are you all right?"

"I am...a little overwhelmed," she admitted.

"It's not every day your business burns down, thank God." He opened the door slowly and reached for her. "C'mere."

She took his hand and let him guide her to her feet, pulling her right into his arms.

"Trevor." She sounded breathless but there was no way to hide how she felt in that moment.

He put the bag on top of her car and wrapped both arms around her. "Annie," he whispered.

She melted into him, letting her eyes shutter as the wretched day faded into a distant memory. He held her so close she couldn't tell whose heartbeat she felt, but it was strong.

He finally drew back, looking at her. "I know I said it again and again, but thank you."

"For having your daughter in a fire? Please don't—"

"For caring about her. For being there. For...being Annie. She loves you."

Okay, this was about Riley. She had to remember this was a father thanking her for what he perceived to be a heroic act. But he—

"I'm kind of crazy about you, too."

"Oh...you...really?" she asked on a laugh.

"Annie! Are you blind?"

"Just...uncertain."

He searched her face, still keeping her tight in his arms. "Of...me?" he asked.

She tried to swallow but her mouth was an absolute desert. "Of...this."

Sliding his hands up, he cupped her cheeks, holding her tenderly as he looked into her eyes. "Don't be."

Then he brought her face to his and pressed his lips against hers and everything—the fire, the smoke, the panic, the pain and disappointment and lifetime of hurt... yes, even the old ache from being left at the altar—all of it disappeared.

The tender beginnings bloomed into heat as both of them leaned into the kiss and the moment and the attraction that they'd both been fighting.

When they finally broke apart, Annie's head was buzzing and her whole body felt boneless and light and happy.

"I've wanted to do that for a while now," he admitted with a half-smile, his eyes glinting. "I'm crazy about you, Annie. I think...I think you're gorgeous and funny and perfect."

A slight whimper escaped her lips, making him laugh.

"And I'm not the only one."

"I know, Riley likes me."

"She loves you, as she said. And she announced to my parents that you are my girlfriend."

She choked. "Excuse me?"

"Well, 'she's a *giwl* and a *fwiend*,'" He imitated Riley's pitch and nailed her sweet speech. "And I...I..."

"Set your parents straight, I hope."

He lifted a brow. "If by straight, you mean I told them I'm crazy about you, then yes."

She stared at him, speechless.

"You want to go inside and eat your dinner and talk about how we're going to make this work? 'Cause I do."

"I want to..." She bit her lip and looked up at him. "Kiss you again."

"You never have to ask twice, Annie."

Chapter Twenty-four

Taylor

Taylor had no idea what was in her suitcase. She'd sped back to the cottage in Mom's car, her mind a total blur as her heart raced a thousand miles an hour. Fueled by adrenaline, love, and a decent bit of lunacy, Taylor had thrown together a mess of a suitcase and promised the cats she'd come back for them in a week or so and their grandma and great-grandma would take care of them in the meantime.

Right now, her focus was on one thing and one thing only.

As she pressed her foot on the gas pedal and flew down the Bee Line toward Orlando, it occurred to Taylor that she hadn't even thought twice about her majorly impulsive "yes" when Annie had asked if she'd move to Denver.

If it meant being with Andre, she'd move anywhere. And it was impossible to ignore the fact that when Kai begged her to pack up and fly off to Hawaii with him... she couldn't do it.

The realization only pushed her foot harder onto the gas pedal, her hands gripping the steering wheel as she finally reached the exit for the Orlando International Airport, and zipped through the entrance to the terminals.

Through the haze of emotions and the electric zings blasting through her all the way to her fingertips, Taylor managed to find the long-term parking and decided she hadn't really thought through the whole car situation if she was, in fact, moving to Denver right now.

Whoops. Mom would come and get the car. There were far more important things at stake tonight than car parking logistics.

Swinging her luggage full of God knows what out of the trunk, she rolled it behind her as she ran as fast as she could toward the terminal. It bounced around on the uneven pavement, flying all over the place as she nearly sprinted through the entrance.

This was her big moment. This was her grand gesture, happy ending, romantic comedy "dashing through the airport to chase after the man she loves" scene.

Taylor could envision it clearly—jetting through the terminal, blindly ignoring security agents, screaming, "I love you, Andre Everett!" as she leapt over a barricade and into his arms.

She didn't know what airline Andre would be on, or even if his plane was still at the gate, but she wasn't giving up. She'd come this far, darn it.

On a whim, she ran up to the Delta help desk. "Hi! Can you tell me when the next red-eye to Denver is? On any airline?" she asked breathlessly, pressing her palms into the countertop as she caught her breath.

"Um, yes, I can check for you..." The woman behind the desk pushed her glasses up onto the bridge of her nose and started typing rapidly onto the computer.

Taylor shut her eyes, listening to her pounding pulse in her eardrums.

She had to pull this off.

"There's a direct flight to Denver on JetBlue that leaves in twelve minutes from Gate B32, and then another one about two hours later on American at A18. That's the last flight out to Denver tonight."

Twelve minutes.

"Would you like me to check if the later flight has any availability?" The woman asked brightly.

"Uh, I don't know yet..." Taylor pressed her palms into her head. She should probably check the gate for the flight that boarded in twelve minutes, but she couldn't get through security without a plane ticket and she'd probably miss Andre if he was already on board.

If he was on the later flight, she had a better shot. But she'd better get started on her dramatic romantic comedy airport moment soon, because—

"Taylor?"

She whipped around, staring through what felt like a sea of people. Taylor could have sworn she was hallucinating when her eyes landed on Andre Everett.

She stepped shakily away from the help counter, walking toward him as everything and everyone else in the hectic airport faded away to silence.

"What are you doing here?" He rushed over, dumb-founded as he studied her and his eyes fell onto the giant suitcase. "Where are you going?"

Taylor sucked in a breath, looking at him. He had a carryon-size roller in one hand, and in the other a rolling cat carrier with his three cats in it. In any other moment, she would have laughed, but she couldn't even think.

"I'm...I'm..." She shook her head. "I was trying to chase after you. Shouldn't you be at the gate already?"

He cocked his head. "My flight isn't for two hours. I haven't even gone through security yet."

"Oh. Well..." She stepped closer to him, locking her gaze with his and resisting the urge to drop the handle of her suitcase and jump into his arms. "This isn't how I envisioned it. I had a whole plan. I was going to run through the airport...I ...I'm supposed to be leaping over security checks and dashing through metal detectors and being chased down by TSA agents."

"You are?"

"Yes!" she insisted. "This was my big, dramatic moment, my rom-com finale, my chance to catch you right before you get on the plane and tell you that I love you and I want to be with you and you can't go to Denver..." She rolled her bag upright next to her. "Without me."

His jaw went slack as he stared at her, his eyes widening with emotion. "Taylor...are you serious?"

"Yes." She inched closer. "I'm serious. I know that the way I've handled everything wasn't fair to you, and I was confused and immature and overwhelmed. But I'm not confused anymore, Andre. I'm a thousand percent certain that you have somehow become my best friend, and I love you as so much more than that. I'll go anywhere with you. And I came here to tell you that and to stop you from getting on the plane unless I'm getting on it with you."

A few beats of stunned silence echoed between them, and Taylor held her breath, feeling like she had just literally dumped her heart out onto the shiny linoleum floor of Orlando International Airport.

"Taylor Parker..." Andre shook his head, a smile pulling at his cheeks as he drew closer to her. "You are something else, you know that?"

"Is that a yes? Can I come with you?"

Andre took a deep breath and reached out, holding her cheek in his hand. "No, you can't come to Denver with me."

Oh.

She...didn't expect that. So much for her rom-com ending.

Taylor's heart plummeted into her stomach and she suddenly felt like she couldn't stand up straight. "I thought that..."

"You can't come to Denver with me, because I don't want to go," he said, smiling bigger and running his thumb along her cheek, which felt flushed.

Taylor focused on his dancing brown eyes as she processed the words. "What do you mean?" She looked around. "We're at the airport. You even packed your cats."

Andre laughed, the sweet sound making her heart skip. "Seeing you here...the suitcase, the determination, the fact that you were ready and willing to give up everything? No one has ever loved me like that, Taylor."

"*I* love you like that."

"I love you like that, too. And I don't want to take you away from your family and your beach town and your life. I would never ask you to do that. If we're going to be together, I want to stay here, with you. And all the Sweeneys."

Taylor felt so much joy and relief she wasn't sure if she wanted to melt into the ground or leap out of her skin. "So, you're saying that we're going to be together?"

He slid his hands down her waist, drawing her in close to him and smiling wide. "That's all I want in the world, girl. You."

She shut her eyes and let the happiness wash over her like a wave, falling into him and savoring every second of this incomprehensible joy.

He kissed her, and the kiss felt like the space between the thrill of excitement and the comfort of home.

"One promise, though." He pulled back and arched a brow.

"Anything."

"No more ex-boyfriends showing up and messing with things."

Taylor gave him the most serious look she could muster. "Please get that out of your head. It's over and I'm yours and you're all I want, and I've never been so sure of anything."

He jutted his chin at her giant suitcase. "You're committed, I'll give you that."

She laughed freely, tilting her head back. "I had total clarity. I tried explaining it to you at the cottage earlier, but...I understand why you felt so hurt."

He pressed his lips together. "I should have given you a chance. I should have listened better. I reacted emotionally, and I'm sorry."

She waved a dismissive hand. "You're sure you aren't bummed about not going to Denver, though?"

He curled a lip and shrugged. "Everything I want is right here in Florida." He pulled her in for another kiss, this one giving her butterflies that spread through her body all the way down to her toes.

Taylor glanced around, vaguely aware that they were still in a public airport, although it was pretty empty this time of night and she didn't care what people thought, anyway.

"Just to be clear." He took her chin in his fingers and tilted it up so her eyes met his. "We're doing this thing, like, for real now. No games, no casual dating. Serious relationship happening here."

"This is the real deal, Andre Everett." She locked her fingers together behind his neck and stood on her tiptoes. "You're stuck with me."

As they left the airport with her suitcase full of craziness and his rolling cat carrier, Taylor decided that she truly had never been this happy in her life.

This was the kind of happiness that people in movies

felt, that song lyrics described. The kind of happiness that seemed so dramatic and overexaggerated and not real.

And yet, somehow, it was the most real thing she'd ever known.

Chapter Twenty-five

Sam

I t had been a couple of days since the fire, and Sam had done her best to stay busy and distracted. She hadn't yet confronted Ethan, but she really hadn't had the chance to.

Taylor had come back to the cottage late that night, announcing that she and Andre were together for real, and they were both staying in Cocoa Beach. Sam had felt like it was a gift from God, and was certain that Andre was deeply good, and wonderfully worthy of Taylor.

Annie was in high spirits, too, all things considered. She'd already contacted some of Sam's construction connections and begun the trudge toward rebuilding, except that woman was so happy with her new romance that she wasn't trudging toward anything but her own happy ending.

All around Sam, life returned to normal, while she was left with the shock and horror of the *Perryville Times* headline burned into her mind forever.

She realized she must not have ever truly known Ethan at all, because the fact that he would get involved with a *teenager* was so astonishing and vile and heartbreaking that Sam couldn't think about it without getting sick to her stomach.

She hadn't seen him, but all that would change tonight when she met up with him for a late-night drink at his place. He might have thought it was a romantic rendezvous; she knew it was the end of their secret relationship.

She pulled into his driveway, noticing that her hands quivered on the steering wheel, and her breathing was shallow and shaky. This felt like a nightmare—like some worst-case scenario she'd dreamed up and awoken with that familiar rush of relief and said out loud to herself, "Thank God that wasn't real."

But it was real. The man she'd been falling for harder and faster every day since she'd arrived in Cocoa Beach was not who she thought he was—he was something far worse, and she had to accept that, end it with him, and never look back.

Men, Sam decided, were officially no longer welcome in her life in any capacity whatsoever. Except the ones she was related to.

She stepped out of her car on an uncharacteristically chilly night, even for December. The night sky was clear and full of stars, and Sam looked up at them, begging for strength and comfort as she walked toward Ethan's front door.

She knocked twice, swallowing her emotions until they sat in her stomach like a block of cement.

He would probably try to explain himself, and maybe she'd give him the chance to do so. But maybe when she saw his face, she'd be so horrified that she wouldn't want to hear another word from him again. She didn't know yet.

"Hey, you." Ethan smiled as soon as he opened the door. But that smile faded pretty quickly the second he laid eyes on her expression.

"I have to talk to you," Sam said weakly, stepping past him and walking into the house, her knees shaky.

She wasn't even sure what she felt. Anger, sadness, pain, disgust? All of the above, she supposed.

"What is it?" Ethan asked, concern laced through his tone as he shut the front door and stepped around to look at her. "What's wrong?"

Without a word, Sam walked over to the table in the breakfast nook next to his kitchen. A bay window over-looked the dock and the canal in the backyard, but at this hour of night the view that was usually bright and blue and beautiful was just dark.

She stared straight down at the handcrafted wooden table that Ethan had made himself, her eyes glued to the intricate seams of wood and the different shades of mahogany.

"Samantha." Ethan sat down on the stool across from her, his eyes shadowed. "What is it? What happened? Please, talk to me."

She slowly willed herself to look up, her heart hammering.

I should hear him out, she thought. *I should give him a chance to explain what really happened.*

Or maybe she shouldn't. Maybe she had given men

the benefit of the doubt far too many times in her life, and she should have learned by now that it didn't end well. Maybe he truly wasn't who she thought he was, and she should just end it now.

"I..." She drew in a shuddering breath, bracing hard for the discomfort of this conversation. "I found out what happened in Perryville."

Ethan's expression went flat, and his shoulders sunk visibly. His eyes shut, and Sam watched as he processed the words. He went cold. Silent. Numb.

"And...I just want to talk to you about it. I want to understand. I just can't believe that—"

"Let me guess: Google told you?" He drew back, his eyes icy and his lips pressed together.

"I had to know," Sam insisted, emotion heightening her voice. "I had to."

"No, Sam, you didn't have to. You could have just trusted me. You could have just believed me when I said that I wanted to leave the past in the past and focus on the future with you. Why was that so hard?"

"How can I fall in love with someone who I don't even know?"

"You feel like you don't know me?" He shook his head, disappointment shadowing his gaze.

"I..." She ran her hand through her hair. "I don't know anymore."

Silence fell between them, the air thick with tension.

"Is it true?" Sam asked softly, her voice, barely above a whisper, echoing through the quiet kitchen.

Ethan drew in a breath, leveled his gaze with her, stone-cold serious. "No, Samantha. It's not true."

Despite the overwhelming anxiety and fear of all of this, a trickle of relief wormed through her chest.

Maybe he had an explanation. Maybe it wasn't what it sounded like. Maybe he was a good guy after all, and they could get past this and be together.

"It said that you..." She cleared her throat, the words making it tight and uncomfortable. "Had a relationship with a student. A senior."

"And you believe that?" Ethan frowned, his blue eyes darkened with hurt. "You just believed it right away, without even thinking that I would never do something like that?"

"I only saw a couple of headlines, I..." She stammered. "I didn't want to look too far into it without talking to you first."

"But you took the internet's word for it. You believed it."

"It was right there in front of me," Sam said defensively. "If there is a real explanation, and you didn't actually do what those articles said you did, then why didn't you just tell me the truth? Why did you keep it hidden and say you didn't want to talk about anything that happened in Maryland?"

"You want to know the truth, Sam?" His tone was harsh, cold, and distant. He wasn't yelling, but he didn't have to. His frustration, hurt, and sadness was palpable, and it made Sam's heart ache.

"Yes," she said softly. "Please, Ethan."

He swallowed and looked down. "There was a student in my calculus class in Perryville. She was very bright, and excelled academically. I told her that she could have a future in math or engineering, because she was a total brainiac and a really fast learner. She didn't have a lot of friends at school, sort of the lone-wolf type. But you know how high schoolers can be. She was picked on for eating lunch by herself and made to feel like an outcast all the time. Seriously bullied, a lot. So, she'd come hang out in my classroom during lunch. I'd give her advanced, college-level calc problems and she'd figure out how to solve them. That's all that happened."

Sam's breaths were shallow as she listened closely to every word, and pictured Ethan Price extending a friendly hand to a lonely, bullied student. It fit everything she knew about him.

"But I guess..." He scratched the back of his neck. "I guess somewhere in there she developed a crush on me, and got the wrong idea. I was oblivious to it. I thought she was just a nerdy senior who had an affinity for math and needed a friend. I was happy to help her out, as I would any other student. But then one day, she tried to kiss me."

Sam froze, gasping softly.

"She didn't succeed," Ethan glanced up, raising a brow. "I instantly put a stop to it, but I couldn't put a stop to the rumors that she spread within an hour. My first plan of action was to contact her parents and tell them about the inappropriate behavior, but it was too late. She had told every single person with ears that we kissed, and that I was her boyfriend. By the end of the school day, what I said didn't matter, because the rumors had made their way to the principal and school board, and despite me begging everyone to believe me, I was fired the following week."

Sam felt her eyes shudder closed as she pulled her hands up to her mouth in shock. "Oh, Ethan."

All of the anger and rage she'd felt upon reading the article melted away completely, and her heart broke for him. She believed his every word. He was genuine. She knew it.

"No one believed me. No one. It was her word against mine, and she was an underage girl, so her word was truth." He shrugged. "Not even my ex-wife could get past the rumors, no matter how many times I told her what had really happened. Hence, the divorce. Perryville is a small town, and I don't think she could stand the sideways glances she was getting from neighbors or in the grocery line."

"She didn't know you well enough to realize that it was a lie?"

"She didn't care. All that mattered was what people thought, and they thought she should leave me, so she did."

"That's so unimaginably awful." Sam shook her head, her mind spinning from the horrendous story. "I can't even fathom what you must have gone through, the things people said. No wonder you had to move away."

"Far away," he said. "And I now have a strict 'no lunch with students' policy, regardless of age or gender. I guess I should have sensed that she had a crush but..." He shrugged. "I was clueless, so part of this is on me for being an idiot."

Sam thought about what it would be like to be a seventeen-year-old social outcast, and to have a teacher as good-looking and cool as Ethan be nice to you. She understood how it might have been easy for the girl to let it go to her head, despite Ethan's pure intentions.

But still, spreading the lie was unbelievably wrong, and it darn near ruined this man's life.

Selfishly? Sam was beyond relieved. Her boyfriend had *not* had an affair with a student, nor did he cheat on his ex-wife or do anything terrible to cause the divorce.

Now they could move on. Now they could be happy.

"Well..." Sam reached out and pushed a smile onto her lips as she grabbed his hand. "I know that probably wasn't easy to talk about, and I'm so sorry you went through all of that. It's unthinkable. But at least now it's all out there, and we don't have to worry about the past or keep secrets anymore."

Ethan looked at her for a long time, but he didn't crack a smile. His didn't look relieved or refreshed or ready to move on.

Instead, he slowly pulled his hand out of Sam's touch and drew back.

Worry tightened her chest.

"I don't know, Samantha."

"What? What do you not know? I have the truth now, and we can focus on us. Focus on the future and our life together, like you said. Now it can all be put to bed."

"It was all put to bed." His voice sounded far away. "I

put it to bed when I moved here five years ago. I decided that was going to be the last I ever spoke of the incident. I didn't want people finding out, I didn't want this to follow me. I left a world, a town, a marriage where I wasn't trusted. I wasn't believed."

"I believe you," she said quickly.

He shot his brows up. "Not at first. Not when you read the article. The truth is, you didn't trust me. I asked you to leave it alone. I asked you to understand that there are things that I don't want to carry with me into the future, and you couldn't respect that."

"I...I do respect it, Ethan, but..." For the first time that night, Sam felt tears stinging in her eyes.

"No, you didn't." He frowned, his mouth turned down with hurt and sadness. "I needed you to believe that I would never hurt you and never lie to you. I needed you to trust that I am who I say I am. I needed you to understand my wishes and accept them and move forward with me. And you couldn't do that, Samantha. You had to go digging for information and confronting me with it."

Sam knew she had trust issues, but he had a point. Why didn't she just respect his wishes? Why couldn't she ever just let well enough alone?

"I didn't want to talk about my divorce," he continued. "I was so clear about that. But you had to know."

"I felt like...I felt like I needed to know. Like you were hiding something from me."

"I would have told you eventually, but I didn't want to."

"Were you testing me?" she countered. "To see how I would act if I found out?"

"I don't know. Maybe. But I can't fake it. I feel like you went behind my back and researched me and...it feels a bit like a betrayal, Sam."

The word twisted a knife in her gut, and she actually winced. "It's not like that—"

"You couldn't trust me. You couldn't respect me."

"I do respect you," she insisted.

Ethan sighed, shaking his head as he pinched the bridge of his nose. "I think you should go."

"What?"

"I think...this isn't going to work." He stood up.

Sam suddenly felt like she could fall into a heap onto the floor at any moment. "Are you breaking up with me?"

"I..." He groaned, clearly hurting and confused. "I think so. I don't know."

"Ethan." Sam stood up to level her gaze with his, a tear slipping down her cheek as sadness gripped her. "Don't do this."

"I'm sorry, Sam." He shook his head and swallowed. "I need to be trusted. I need to be believed. Of all the things in the world I need, that's at the top of the list."

"I do believe you!"

"Please."

"I believe you, Ethan! I just...I couldn't fall in love with you until I knew the truth about what happened."

"Well...now you know the truth. And you don't have to worry about that anymore."

Sam walked out of his house as the sky started to

sprinkle rain. It poured onto her face, swirling around and mixing with her tears.

Now what? Now what was she going to do? Start over...again?

She drove home battling tears and pulled up to the cottage, spotting Lori sitting on the front steps with Amber. As much as she usually wanted to talk to them, she was so not in the mood. All she wanted to do was climb into bed and cry.

They were deep in conversation, so she parked by the inn and sat in her car for a long, long time, waiting for the waves of regret and pain to pass. Finally, after half an hour or so, she climbed out and walked through the darkened yard to the cottage.

As she approached, she heard their voices and slowed her step, wishing she didn't have to see anyone. Could she go around the back and slip into Taylor's room? Could she—

"Mom, I'm not going to do that!"

Amber's voice carried across the path, the pain in every word bringing Sam to a halt.

"I can't apply for any job in my field because they'd want a recommendation. And what will he say?"

"That you were a fantastic junior campaign manager who—"

"Who had an affair with a married congressman?"

Sam's eyes widened. That was not a one-night stand. And...a *congressman*?

"He said his divorce was imminent," Lori replied. "He lied to you, Amber."

Don't they all, Sam thought bitterly. She swallowed, but then she heard Amber sob.

"I just don't know what to do. I don't know if I want this baby or not. I mean, I do, but I don't want *his* baby. And I'm sick of hiding the truth, Mom. I can't get close to anyone because my life is one big lie."

Sam put her hand over her mouth, a wave of sympathy rolling over her...along with a new certainty.

This was what she was going to do now. Love, help, support, share the burden, and do what she did best... keep this family together. Amber needed help. Lori needed a sister. And they all needed her to be the glue holding the Sweeneys together.

Encouraged by the thought, she put her pain away and stepped forward, ready for the next chapter, whatever it might bring.

*Want to know what's next in store for the Sweeney Family? Look out for book five, **Cocoa Beach Cabana!** Sign up for my newsletter to get the latest on new releases and more, at www.ceceliascott.com.*

The Sweeney House Series

The Sweeney House is a landmark inn on the shores of Cocoa Beach, built and owned by the same family for decades. After the unexpected passing of their beloved patriarch, Jay, this family must come together like never before. They may have lost their leader, but the Sweeneys are made of strong stuff. Together on the island paradise where they grew up, this family meets every challenge with hope, humor, and heart, bathed in sunshine and the unconditional love they learned from their father.

About the Author

Cecelia Scott is an author of light, bright women's fiction that explores family dynamics, heartfelt romance, and the emotional challenges that women face at all ages and stages of life. Her debut series, Sweeney House, is set on the shores of Cocoa Beach, where she lived for more than twenty years. Her books capture the salt, sand, and spectacular skies of the area and reflect her firm belief that life deserves a happy ending, with enough drama and surprises to keep it interesting. Cece currently resides in north Florida with her husband and beloved kitty. When she's not writing, you'll find her at the beach, usually with a good book.